*Literary Angel*
*Program*

County of Brant
Public Library

**Donated by**
**Burford District**
**Optimist Club**

# Much Ado About Anne

THE MOTHER-DAUGHTER BOOK CLUB

# Much
# Ado
# About
# Anne

## Heather Vogel Frederick

Simon & Schuster Books for Young Readers

New York  London  Toronto  Sydney

SIMON & SCHUSTER BOOKS FOR YOUNG READERS
An imprint of Simon & Schuster Children's Publishing Division
1230 Avenue of the Americas, New York, New York 10020

Book design by Jeremy Wortsman
The text for this book is set in Chaparral Pro.
Manufactured in the United States of America
2 4 6 8 10 9 7 5 3 1
Library of Congress Cataloging-in-Publication Data
Frederick, Heather Vogel.
Much ado about Anne / Heather Vogel Frederick.—1st ed.
p. cm.—(Mother-Daughter Book Club)
Summary: Entering seventh grade at Walden Middle School, four girls continue their mother-daughter book club, reading Lucy Maud Montgomery's "Anne of Green Gables" while dealing with a mean, troublemaking classmate.
ISBN-13: 978-0-689-85566-5 (hardcover)
ISBN-10: 0-689-85566-4 (hardcover)
[1. Interpersonal relations—Fiction. 2. Books and reading—Fiction. 3. Mothers and daughters—Fiction. 4. Clubs—Fiction. 5. Montgomery, L. M. (Lucy Maud), 1874–1942—Fiction. 6. Concord (Mass.)—Fiction.]
I. Title.
PZ7.F87217Mp 2008
[Fic]—dc22
2008007324

For my niece Madeline, whose mother always
fell for the invisibility potion trick

Much
Ado
About
Anne

# AUTUMN

"It's fun to be almost grown up in some ways, but it's not the kind of fun I expected, Marilla. There's so much to learn and do and think...."

—L. M. Montgomery, *Anne of Green Gables*

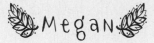

# Megan

*"Well, this is a pretty kettle of fish."*
—*Anne of Green Gables*

"What are you girls up to out there?"

I swear all mothers have radar that doesn't quit.

"Nothing, Mom!" Jess calls back, motioning frantically to Emma and me.

Giggling, the two of us scoop up the evidence—garlic powder, cinnamon, peppermint extract, and blue food coloring—and hastily stuff it back into the spice cupboard.

"Doesn't sound like nothing to me." We hear Mrs. Delaney's chair scrape on the dining room floor as she pushes back from the table and comes to the kitchen to investigate.

Emma and I quickly wipe the grins off our faces. Jess leans back casually against the counter, blocking our concoction from view.

"Hmmm," says Mrs. Delaney, scanning the kitchen suspiciously. She spots the open spice cupboard and lifts an eyebrow.

"Uh, we were thinking of baking cookies," Jess explains, which isn't technically a lie even though we decided not to because the kitchen is sweltering.

Normally, any of our mothers would have seen through this in a flash, but Mrs. Delaney seems kind of distracted today. She shakes her head and sighs. "Please don't bake anything, girls, it's hot enough in here already without turning the oven on. We've got peppermint ice cream—you can have some of that if you want a snack." She opens the freezer and sticks her head inside. "A day like today kind of makes you wish it was winter, doesn't it?"

"Or that we had air conditioning," says Jess mournfully.

Mrs. Delaney pulls her head out again and gives her a sympathetic smile. "Maybe someday, honey. Right now we have other priorities." She looks over at Emma. The smile disappears. "Emma Hawthorne, you must be roasting in that turtleneck! Didn't you offer her a T-shirt, Jess?"

Jess looks uncomfortable. "Uh—"

"I forgot to bring something to change into after school, and nothing of Jess's fits me, Mrs. Delaney," Emma replies matter-of-factly, patting her stomach. Emma is a little on the plump side, and Jess is really petite.

"Well for Pete's sake, you should have said something," Mrs. Delaney tells her. "We have plenty of things around here that will work for you. Hang on a sec."

She trots upstairs. As soon as her mother is out of sight, Jess grabs the jar of blue liquid from the counter behind her and sticks it in her

T-shirt pocket. I glance over at Emma. Emma is one of my best friends, but she's not exactly the fashion queen of Concord, Massachusetts. I mean, I like to dress up for the first day of school too, but a turtleneck on a day like this? You'd think she'd know by now that the beginning of September is pretty much still summer everywhere, except maybe Alaska. At least she picked a good color. Purple goes well with her brown eyes and curly brown hair. And it matches her new lavender glasses, too.

Mrs. Delaney reappears and tosses Emma a white T-shirt with a *HeartBeats* logo on it. "Try this," she says.

*HeartBeats* is the soap opera that Mrs. Delaney was on last year. You'd never guess by looking at her now that she's an actress. When we visited her in New York this past summer, she was all glamorous. Now—well, now she looks the way she always did. Today, for instance, she's wearing jeans and a faded Red Sox T-shirt. She's still pretty and everything—really pretty, just like Jess, with the same sparkly blue eyes, though Mrs. Delaney's hair is dark, not blond like Jess's—but she looks ordinary, too. Like a mom. I wonder if she misses all the makeup and clothes and stuff from her acting job. I sure would. But Mrs. Delaney seems really happy to be back home at Half Moon Farm.

"How's your mom doing, Megan?" she asks me. "We missed her yesterday at yoga class."

"She just got elected to the board of the Concord Riverkeepers," I tell her. "Yesterday was their first meeting." My mother's kind of a nature freak. If something on the planet needs saving or protecting, you can bet Lily Wong is there on the front lines to make sure it gets done.

"Oh, that's right, she told us about that," Mrs. Delaney replies. "I guess I forgot." She spots the pile of mail on the counter where Jess left it. "Bills, bills, nothing but bills," she grumbles, flipping through the envelopes. Shaking her head, she disappears back into the dining room.

Jess gets three bowls from the cupboard and dishes up some ice cream for us. Crossing the kitchen, she beckons Emma and me to follow. One of her chickens—Johnny Cash or Elvis or something, I can't keep their names straight—darts in the minute she opens the screen door. Jess nabs it and it lets out a big squawk.

"You know the rules, Loretta," Jess tells it firmly. "No chickens in the house!"

Sometimes I still can't believe I'm friends with somebody who talks to chickens. Or somebody who even *has* chickens.

Emma and I follow Jess to the barn. Mr. Delaney let us fix up an old storage room in the hayloft for a secret hangout. Not that it's much of a secret, what with Jess's little brothers always sneaking around.

Right now, there's no sign of them. We scared them off after we caught them spying on us in Jess's room when we were changing out of our school clothes. They'll turn up eventually, though—they always turn up—and when they do we'll be ready for them, thanks to the concoction that's safely in Jess's pocket.

"I wish it could stay summer forever," sighs Emma, climbing up the hayloft ladder behind me.

*Heather Vogel Frederick*

"Me too," echoes Jess.

*Not me,* I think, but I don't say anything. I've always liked the first day of school. Mostly because I get to wear one of the new outfits that I spend all summer picking out. I can't help it—I like clothes. I want to be a fashion designer when I grow up.

"Hey, did you guys see Zach Norton at assembly this morning?" I ask them. "He's so tall! He must have grown about a foot over the summer." I take a bite of ice cream and give Emma a sidelong glance. "He's cuter than ever too."

Emma shrugs, but her cheeks turn as pink as her ice cream. Lately she's been telling us that she doesn't have a crush on Zach anymore. Jess and Cassidy and I are pretty sure she still does, though. Not that I'd mind if she didn't—the way I see it, the fewer girls lined up hoping Zach Norton will notice them, the better my chances are.

The fact that we both like Zach is one of the only things Emma and I have in common, when you come right down to it. Well, that and the mother-daughter book club our moms cooked up last year. We look different, for starters. I'm Asian American—Emma's not. She's a bookworm—I'm not. I love fashion and clothes—she couldn't care less. And although she's not off-the-charts smart like Jess, she's a good student. Me, I just scrape by, which drives my parents nuts. Somehow, despite our differences we're still good friends.

Emma sticks out her lower lip and puffs at her bangs, which are sticking to her forehead. It's even hotter out here in the barn than it was in the Delaneys' kitchen. Jess turns on the table fan and aims it straight at the old sofa where the three of us are sitting.

"Can you believe we're in seventh grade now?" she says. "Just think—two more years and we'll be in high school."

We eat our ice cream for a while as we think this over.

"We're going to be *teenagers* this year," Emma adds. "We're practically grown-ups!"

Sometimes I feel like I've been looking forward to being a teenager forever. I can't wait until I'm old enough to drive. And have a summer job. And I especially can't wait until I'm old enough to date.

"So do either of you have any classes with Zach this year?" I ask, trying to sound casual.

"Zach! Zach! Ooooo, Zach Norton!" squeal a pair of voices behind us.

We whirl around to see Dylan and Ryan, Jess's twin brothers, emerge from under a pile of old horse blankets in the corner.

"I TOLD YOU TO QUIT SPYING ON US!" hollers Jess.

She launches off the sofa toward them, but they're too fast for her. Shrieking in alarm, they duck past her out the door. The three of us are close on their heels. The boys fling themselves over the edge of the loft and tumble into the pile of hay below. Jess dives after them. So does Emma. I hesitate. My friends all love doing this, but it always seems like a long way down to me.

I close my eyes and force myself to jump.

"Ouch!" I cry when I land, wishing I were wearing jeans and not shorts. The hay is stiff and prickly, and it jabs into my bare legs. I

*Heather Vogel Frederick*

scramble off of it as quickly as I can and run after Emma and Jess.

We corner her brothers by the chicken coop.

"Pest Control 101," Jess whispers to Emma and me, taking the small jar from her T-shirt pocket. "Watch and learn." She holds it up. The blue liquid inside shimmers in the September sunlight. "Gee," she says, "too bad you guys are such little weasels—I was going to share some of this with you."

"What is it?" one of them asks cautiously. Like the chickens, I can't tell Dylan and Ryan apart.

Jess glances around, like maybe somebody is listening, and her voice drops to a whisper. "It's an *invisibility potion*."

Her brothers' eyes widen.

"Really?" says one of them.

Jess nods. "If you drink it, you'll disappear just like that." She snaps her fingers and looks over at Emma and me. "Isn't that right?"

Emma nods. "Yup. You'll vanish right into thin air."

"Vaporize," I tell them.

"Dematerialize," adds Jess for good measure.

The three of us are smothering grins. Emma's family invented this thing called the synonym game. I used to think it was dumb—actually, I still do—but it's kind of addictive.

"Please, can't we try it?" one of the twins begs.

"C'mon, Jess!" says the other.

Jess shakes her head. "No way. You broke your promise. You said you wouldn't spy on us anymore."

The boys exchange a glance. With their blond curls and brown puppy-dog eyes, they look like angels, but there's hardly anything angelic about them. "Double trouble," Jess calls them. "Pests with a capital *P*," and she's right. I still think they're kind of cute, though. I wish I had a brother or sister, but my parents decided on just one child. Me. My mother tried to explain it to me once—something about zero population growth. Another one of her schemes to save the world, as usual.

"We're sorry, Jess. Right, Dylan?"

"Yeah, really sorry," says Dylan. "We promise never to do it again."

"Cross your hearts and hope to die?" Jess demands.

They both nod.

"Well, I guess in that case . . ." Slowly, tantalizingly, she unscrews the lid and passes the jar to Dylan.

He sniffs it cautiously. "P-U!" he cries, and hands it to his brother. "You first."

Ryan takes a sip and makes a face.

"You have to drink more than that or it won't work," Jess tells him.

Grimacing, her brother gulps down half the liquid, then passes the jar to his brother, coughing.

"Yuck! That is *gross!*" Dylan sputters after he finishes off the rest.

I have to bite my lip to keep from laughing. Beside me, Emma is doing the same. The twins crowd around us. "Is it working?" they demand.

We pretend to examine them.

*Heather Vogel Frederick*

"You're fading at the edges," Emma says.

"It probably takes a minute or two," I explain.

Suddenly, Jess jumps back, her eyes wide in mock disbelief. "Wow, guys, look! It worked! They're gone!"

Emma shades her eyes with her hand and scans the backyard. "Where are they? Where did Dylan and Ryan go? Do you see them anywhere, Megan?"

I shake my head, still trying not to burst out laughing. Was I this gullible when I was seven?

Dancing around us, Dylan and Ryan chant, "Nyah, nyah! We're invisible!"

They stop and stare at each other.

"Hey, how come I can see Ryan?" says Dylan.

"Yeah, and how come I can see Dylan?" says Ryan.

"It's because you're *both* invisible," Jess explains, making it sound perfectly logical. "Invisible people can always see each other. It's the people who *aren't* invisible who can't see you."

Just then there's a crunch of gravel behind us. We turn around to see Cassidy Sloane flying up the driveway on her bike. She skids to a stop right in front of us.

"Hi guys," she says.

Dylan and Ryan poke their heads out from behind Jess. Dylan sticks out his tongue.

"Hey dude," says Cassidy. "What's up?"

His eyes narrow. "How come Cassidy can see me? She's not invisible."

"Uh, it's because she has special powers," Jess replies. "Right, Cassidy?"

"I guess so," mutters Cassidy, not really paying attention. She must have ridden over straight from baseball, because she's still wearing her practice jersey. It's the same one she had on at school today. No back-to-school outfits for Cassidy Sloane. She cares even less about fashion than Emma does. Cassidy is a jock and proud of the fact that she's the only girl at Walden Middle School good enough to make the boys' fall baseball team. I notice that her face is streaked with dirt and sweat.

"You tricked us!" shrieks Ryan. "I'm going to tell Mom!"

The boys head for the house, howling for Mrs. Delaney. A minute later Jess's mother sticks her head out the dining room window. "Jessica Delaney! You are too old to be teasing your brothers!"

"But they've been spying on us again!" Jess protests.

"I don't care what they've been doing! You quit it this instant, do you hear?"

"Yes, Mom," Jess calls back meekly.

Beside me, Emma is staring at Cassidy. "Are you okay?"

Cassidy wipes her nose on the sleeve of her jersey. I look at her face more closely. What I thought were streaks of sweat in the dirt are actually tears. I stare at her, dumbfounded. Cassidy Sloane is *crying*.

"Emergency session of the Mother-Daughter Book Club," Emma announces crisply. "Well, the daughter half." She tugs Cassidy toward the barn.

"Hurry, before my brothers spot us," Jess urges.

We pick up our pace to a trot. Once safely inside and out of sight,

*Heather Vogel Frederick*

# CASSIDY

> *"We can't have things perfect in this*
> *imperfect world, as Mrs. Lynde says."*
> —*Anne of Green Gables*

I slam my locker door shut, startling Kevin Mullins, who le[ts out a] terrified squeak.

"Sorry," I say gruffly. I hadn't even noticed him standing ther[e.] hardly taller than Jess's little brothers. Kevin's kind of a twerp, b[ut] okay, even though he's only, like, nine or something. Emma say[s he] skipped a lot of grades. He and Jess are total brainiacs. Emma's pr[etty] smart too—well, except for math—but Kevin and Jess are light-ye[ars] beyond all the other kids at Walden Middle School, including th[e] eighth graders.

"There you are!" Jess flies up behind us and grabs Kevin by one of his toothpick arms. "Hurry up, we're going to miss the bus! Hey, Cassidy!" she calls back over her shoulder as she drags Kevin down the hall behind her, her long blond braid bouncing against her backpack.

I jerk my chin in greeting and head down the hall toward math

Jess leads the way back to the hayloft, then pulls the ladder up behind us so the boys can't follow this time.

"What's going on?" Emma asks, as Cassidy flings herself face-first into the pile of blankets.

"Nothing." Cassidy's voice is muffled.

"Doesn't sound like nothing," says Emma.

She and Jess sit down beside her. Jess reaches out and pats Cassidy on the back, the way I've seen her do with Sugar and Spice, he Delaneys' Shetland sheepdogs. "C'mon, Cassidy," she coaxes. "You ll us."

sit down to . The blankets smell good. In fact, the whole barn smells —like hay and horses and leather and old wood and other stuff all ed together. *Eau de Barn*. I make a mental note to jot it down in my tchbook later. It might make an interesting men's cologne.

"It's my mom," Cassidy says finally in a low voice.

Emma and Jess and I exchange a worried glance. Cassidy's dad died couple of years ago. What if something's wrong with her mother?

"Is she okay?" asks Emma gently. "She's not sick or anything, is she?"

Cassidy sits up. "No, it's not that," she says. She draws her legs n close to her chest and rests her chin on her knees. "She's not sick," she repeats, plucking at the blankets. "It's just that she . . she . . ." Her sentence trails off.

"She what?" I prod.

Cassidy looks up, and tears start to spill from her eyes again. She swipes at them angrily. "My mother's started dating again."

class. Kevin and Jess take the bus to Alcott High every morning for math—geometry for geniuses or something like that. Me? I stink at math. I don't care, though. Hockey players don't have to be math whizzes. And I plan on playing pro hockey when I grow up.

I see Third heading toward me and I jerk my chin again. Third isn't his real name, of course. His real name is Cranfield Bartlett III, but who'd want to be known as that? As he walks past, he hipchecks me. Or tries to. Third is on the short side, and I'm pretty tall. Even taller, these days. I grew a bunch over the summer.

"Eight more weeks, Sloane!" he crows.

I slap him a high five. "Counting the days, dude!" Like Third, I live for hockey season. I like baseball, too, but hockey is my life.

But right now I could care less about hockey, or baseball, or anything else. Right now all I can think about is my mother's new boyfriend, Stanley Kinkaid. Stan the man. The man who doesn't belong in our life.

My mother met him at the Coffee Connection a few weeks ago when she stopped for a latte after yoga class. They got to talking and he asked her out and she said okay. At least that's the way she explained it to my older sister Courtney and me. I couldn't believe my eyes when he showed up at the door to pick her up. He's shorter than my mom, for one thing. Of course, most people are—my mother is six feet tall, and used to be a model—but besides being short, he's also bald except for about a two-inch fringe of dark hair. I mean *bald* bald, too, not peach-fuzz bald. The top of his head is as shiny as a bowling ball. Plus, he's kind of soft around the middle. I could tell just by looking at him that he'd probably never played a sport in his life. And my mother was going to go out with him?

Courtney said he has nice eyes, but I didn't notice. She said we couldn't expect Mom to stay a widow forever, and I said it hadn't even been two years yet and I couldn't believe she was being so disloyal to Dad. We got into a big fight about it, and now she's not talking to me.

I'm still ticked off about Stan the man when I get to pre-algebra class.

"Hey, Cassidy."

"Hey, Emma," I reply, sliding into the seat beside her. Emma stinks at math too. Jess tutors us both, which helps Emma, but I'm pretty much a lost cause.

"Guess what?" says Emma. Her brown eyes are shining behind her glasses. She's excited about something. I sigh. That makes one of us. It's hard for me to feel excited about anything at the moment.

"What?"

"I just saw Ms. Nielson in the hallway, and she told me they're going to start a school newspaper, and she wants me to be on it!"

"Cool," I reply, without enthusiasm.

Emma shoots me a look. "What's the matter?"

I shrug.

"Are you still bugged about that Stanley guy?"

"What do you think?" I snap.

Emma's face turns red, and I instantly regret barking at her. Emma Hawthorne is one of my closest friends in the whole world. Before I can apologize, though, the Fab Three flounce in. The Fab Three are Becca Chadwick, Jen Webster, and Ashley Sanborn. They used to be the Fab Four, before Megan Wong wised up and ditched them for us. They're the three most popular girls in the seventh grade, although why anybody besides them thinks so is beyond me.

They head for desks on the far side of the classroom, carefully avoiding us. Well, avoiding me. They know better than to mess with me. Emma's another story. One of these days, though, she'll grow a backbone and tell that snooty Becca to go jump in the lake.

As soon as they're seated, they immediately start whispering. I can tell they're talking about Emma and me, because they keep looking over at us and laughing. I ignore them. Emma's face flames again.

I give her a nudge with my elbow and pass her a stick of gum as an apology for being crabby a minute ago. "Buzz buzz buzz," I remind her. Emma's the one who explained to me about queen bees. They're the girls who think they're better than everyone else, and who like to boss everybody else around. Queen bees are nothing new. They've always been around. They even had them over a hundred years ago. I know this because we read *Little Women* last year in our mother-daughter book club. The author, Louisa May Alcott, lived right here in Concord when she wrote it in the 1800s, and she put a queen bee in the story— Jenny Snow. Jenny was stuck-up and mean to Amy March, just like Becca Chadwick is to all of us.

"Did you hear they're starting a school newspaper?" Becca says to Jen and Ashley, talking extra loud so that Emma and I and everybody else can hear. "Ms. Nielson wants me to be in charge of the social calendar. She says she's asking all the school's best writers to help out." Becca looks over at Emma and smirks. I notice she's careful to keep her lips together. Becca got braces over the summer, and she's still a little sensitive about them.

I can see the excitement drain out of Emma, like air leaking out of a soccer ball. I don't blame her. Who'd want to work on the newspaper with Becca Chadwick?

"Don't worry," I whisper to her. "Nobody cares about the stupid social calendar. That's not real writing."

Emma musters a smile, but I can tell she's not convinced.

Math class is endless. I struggle my way through a fraction-review worksheet and make a complete mess of two word problems. Then, while Ms. Santiago blathers on about the joys of the metric system, I draw a cartoon of Becca, giving her hairy legs and enormous buck teeth with braces. I pass the picture to Emma, which makes her giggle. Out in the hall afterward we say good-bye. Emma's in higher groups for all of our other classes. Jess is in a different league altogether, but my mother would turn cartwheels if I got Emma's grades. Or even Megan's.

"See you at lunch," I tell her. "Don't let Becca spoil your day. The newspaper's gonna be great, you'll see."

It's funny how your own problems kind of fade when you have a friend who's in trouble. I suddenly realize that I've been so busy cheering Emma up, I've hardly thought about Stanley Kinkaid for the past hour.

*Heather Vogel Frederick*

I start thinking about him again now, though, and by the time I get to English I'm all bent out of shape again. The class period limps by with me slumped in the back row biting my nails and worrying about Stan the man. Fortunately, we're not doing much yet since it's just the second day of school, and Ms. Nielson only yells at me once for not paying attention.

Science class is pretty much the same, except a little more fun. Ethan and Third are in the same lab group with me, and the three of us goof off when the teacher's not looking. I actually like science okay. The experiments can be fun, and sometimes we get to do stuff outdoors.

Mr. Doolittle dismisses class a little early, and since I get to the cafeteria ahead of everybody else I save seats for Emma and Megan and Jess. Our table is a weird mix of Mother-Daughter Book Club members and jocks. And Kevin Mullins, who Emma says defies classification. It's so stupid how middle school cafeterias work. Every group has its own table. There are the drama kids, the band kids, the brainiacs, the popular kids, the nerds, the jocks, the artists—the list is endless. Jess calls our table "the hybrid." I don't care what anybody wants to call it, I just like sitting with my friends.

Emma is the first to arrive, followed by Zach Norton and Third. Emma slides in beside me and smiles shyly at Zach, who sets his tray down across from us. Zach is playing fall ball this year with me, and even though Emma has been telling Jess and Megan and me for weeks now that she doesn't have a crush on him anymore, that he's "so yesterday," as the Fab Three would put it, I'm not completely blind. I can tell by the way she gets all quiet and tongue-tied when he's around that she still likes him.

I take a bite of burger and give Zach a sideways look. I still don't see what the big deal is. Light brown hair with blondish streaks, blue eyes, big deal. So he got a lot taller this summer, so what? I did too, and nobody's falling all over themselves to have a crush on me. Not that I'd want them to. I don't like all this boy/girl stuff.

Ethan MacDonald slouches over and plops down beside Zach, emptying his lunch bag onto the table. He makes a face. "Peanut butter and jelly, as usual." He looks over at Emma's tray. "Can I have your French fries? It's not like you need them or anything."

Emma's face flames again.

"Shut up, Ethan," I tell him, kicking him under the table. "Last time I checked, you were still shopping in the husky section." I hate it when people make fun of Emma. It's not like she's fat, anyway, only a little chubby.

"Yeah, lay off, Tater," adds Zach.

Third starts to laugh. So does Emma.

I look at them, mystified. "Who's Tater?"

Zach grins at Ethan, who scowls and punches him in the arm. "Too bad you weren't here in first grade," he tells me. "Every time they'd serve Tater Tots for lunch, we'd find Ethan under the table, hunting for the ones that kids dropped."

"Why?"

"Why do you think?" says Third. "To eat them, of course."

*Heather Vogel Frederick*

"Off the *floor*?"

"Yup."

"Dude, that is gross," I say to Ethan. I flick him a French fry. "Here. Out of pity."

This makes him laugh in spite of himself, and then we all laugh and start throwing French fries at one another until the lunch monitor comes over and tells us to cut it out.

Megan and Jess and Kevin show up with their trays, and Emma and I squish together to make room for them.

"Hey, Beauty," says Zach.

Jess flashes him a smile. "Hey, Beast."

The two of them were the leads in last year's school musical. They've called each other "Beauty" and "Beast" ever since.

"Awwwww," says Ethan. "Isn't that adorable!"

Zach wings another French fry at him, then turns back to Jess. "How's high school math?"

She shrugs, glancing quickly around the table at the other boys and then down at her tray. Jess is still a bit shy. Not as bad as when I first met her, though, and only around people she doesn't know all that well. I thought maybe she was a mute or something when we first moved here from California. "It's okay, I guess. Hard. Right, Kevin?"

Kevin doesn't reply. He rarely does. Not because he's shy, but because every time he opens his mouth somebody calls him "twerp" or stuffs him in a locker. When you're Kevin Mullins, it's safer just to keep quiet.

"So, Emma, did Ms. Nielson talk to you?" Zach asks.

Emma nods.

"Yeah, me too. Sounds like fun."

A little smile hovers on Emma's lips. Her cheeks get pink—not embarrassed pink this time but happy pink. I look over at Jess and mouth the words *I told you so.*

"What sounds like fun?" says Third.

"They're starting a school newspaper," Zach explains. "Ms. Nielson asked a few of us if we'd like to work on it. She wants me to cover sports."

First Becca, now Zach—for half a second I'm offended that Ms. Nielson didn't ask me. Then I remember that I don't like to write.

"She's still looking for a couple of photographers," Zach continues. "Any of you guys interested?"

Ethan and Third both shake their heads. So do Megan and Jess and Kevin.

"Yeah, maybe," I say, the words popping out before I can even think about them.

"Since when do you know how to use a camera?" asks Third.

Since my dad taught me, I think, but aloud I just say, "Since California."

"Cool," says Zach. "I'll tell Ms. Nielson."

As he and Ethan and Third start trying to gross everybody else out by sticking French fries up their noses, I think back to the last time I took a picture. Dad and I used to go shooting together around

Laguna Beach, just the two of us. He taught me about light, and composition, and all that stuff. A couple of weeks before the car accident, he gave me a new digital camera for my birthday. That afternoon we went down to Crystal Cove, right before what he used to call "magic hour"—that time toward the end of the day when the light goes all golden. We took pictures for a while, and then he said he wanted a shot of the two of us. He put his arm around me and pulled me close, and I held my new camera out as far as I could from our faces and snapped. The picture turned out perfectly. The wind is blowing my hair across my face, and the setting sun is sparkling on the ocean behind us, and we're both laughing. I still remember how happy I was.

Thinking about it now just makes me sad, though. I push the memory away, just like I pushed my camera away after the accident. I shoved it into my bottom drawer under the jeans I'd gotten too tall for. I take it out and look at that picture once in a while, but I've never printed it and I've never shown it to anyone. Not even to Mom or Courtney. Some things are just meant to be private.

Beside me, I feel Emma stiffen. I don't even have to look up to see who's coming.

When the Fab Three reach our table, Becca stops and puts her hand on her hip. She's always striking poses, like maybe the paparazzi are lurking nearby ready to spring out and snap her picture for *Seventeen* or something. Becca doesn't look too pleased to see us sitting with Zach Norton. For some reason she thinks he's her private property.

"So, Megan," she says, "my mother told me you're going to be in some new teen fashion magazine."

Megan wants to be a fashion designer someday, and she's already really good at sewing clothes and stuff. Our book club went to New York last summer, and one of the editors my mom knows at *Flash*, from back when she used to model for the magazine, spotted Megan's sketchbook. Now he's planning to feature her in this new spin-off magazine called *Flashlite*.

Megan shrugs and tries to look modest, but she can't keep the smile off her face, and it's easy to tell she's pretty thrilled. "Um, yeah, that's right."

"Awesome," says Becca, giving it her stamp of approval. As if Megan needed that. Jen and Ashley immediately start gushing about it too. I swear the two of them are like robots or something. Becca probably keeps a remote control for them in her purse. "Maybe we can hang out at the mall sometime and check out the new clothes and get ideas for you," she adds.

Megan looks like she's not sure what to say. "Uh, yeah, maybe."

Emma and Jess are both looking like they wish the cafeteria floor would open up and swallow the Fab Three.

"Why don't you go polish your braces or something," I tell Becca.

Kevin lets out a little snicker at this. Big mistake.

Becca swivels around and glares at him. "Shut up, dwarf," she snaps. "Shouldn't you be off playing with Sleepy or Sneezy or something?"

Ethan and Third both laugh at this, which is mean of them, and

Kevin shrinks down in his chair. Jess gives him a sympathetic glance. "Why don't you pick on someone your own size, Grumpy?" she fires back at Becca.

"Oooooo, score one for Delaney," I crow.

Ignoring me, Becca pulls out her lip gloss and makes a great show of smearing it on her mouth. She glances over the top of her mirror at Zach, who is too busy throwing French fries again at Ethan—make that Tater—to notice. Becca thinks she knows everything about boys, but she is so clueless. If she really wanted them to notice her, she'd put down the lip gloss and pick up a hockey stick or a baseball glove or something.

The bell rings and we all gather up our trays and start to scatter.

"See you tonight!" Emma says.

Tonight is our first book club meeting of seventh grade. It's at the Wongs'. It was supposed to be at our house, but my mother is swamped right now taping the first few episodes of her new TV show, *Cooking with Clementine*. Our house has been a complete wreck for weeks, with camera crews and set designers and all sorts of people from the Cooking Channel underfoot. I had no idea a TV show took so much work. But it does have its benefits. The food, mostly. I can hardly wait to get home from school every day to see what they've been whipping up in the kitchen.

Unfortunately, I don't feel that way about tonight. Mrs. Wong is a terrible cook. She doesn't believe in sugar, for one thing, which I personally think should be one of the four major food groups. Snacks are an important part of book club. At least for me.

Megan and Jess and I all trade "good-byes" and "see you laters" and head off to our afternoon classes. I spend the rest of the day worrying about Stan the man—and about the horrible vegan zucchini cookies or brown rice muffins or some equally awful snacks that are probably being baked right now in the Wongs' kitchen. Plus, I have something new to worry about too. Why did I ever tell Zach Norton that I might be interested in being a photographer for the school newspaper?

I'm still regretting that particular slip-up several hours later when Mom and I head up Strawberry Hill and pull into the Wongs' driveway.

"Wait, honey, take this in with you," says my mother as I start to climb out of the car. She reaches into the backseat and produces a plastic container. "Leftovers from today's taping," she says, winking at me. "Just in case."

I lift up a corner of the lid and peek inside. Brownies! I inhale their deliciousness and smile, filled with a sudden rush of love for my mother. Her brownies are the best. They're so good, in fact, that I am almost ready to forgive her for dating Stanley Kinkaid. Almost.

"For heaven's sake, Cassidy, you'd think I never feed you!" my mother protests as I snatch one and cram it in my mouth.

I give her a chocolate-coated grin and she shakes her head and laughs. "Just try and leave a few for everyone else, okay?"

Inside, I deposit the container on the glass coffee table in the living room and head down the hall to Megan's room. Jess and Emma are already there, and the four of us hang out, talking, while our mothers get everything set up.

*Heather Vogel Frederick*

A few minutes later the intercom on the wall crackles. The Wongs' house is so big they need an intercom system to talk to each other. Megan's dad invented some computer gadget, and they're really rich.

"Girls, we're about ready to start," Mrs. Wong announces.

Megan presses the button under the speaker. "Okay."

"Race you," I call, charging out her door. You could practically run a marathon in the hallways in this place. Megan and Jess and Emma chase me back to the living room, and we burst in, breathless and giggling, to find our moms all discussing something in low voices. They look up, startled.

"That eager to get started, are you?" says Mrs. Hawthorne, and she and the other moms all smile.

Mrs. Delaney's smile looks a little strained, but maybe it's just my imagination. Or maybe she's just tired. My mother says Mrs. Delaney deserves some kind of medal for raising twin boys.

"My goodness, Cassidy," says Mrs. Wong, whose T-shirt has a big picture of planet Earth on it with LOVE YOUR MOTHER printed underneath. "I swear you've grown another inch or two since I saw you last week!"

"A chip off the old block, eh, Clementine?" adds Mrs. Hawthorne. "Cassidy will be sashaying down the catwalk one of these days in your footsteps if she keeps this up."

My mother reaches out to give me an affectionate pat. I twist away and slump into a white armchair. I don't care if I get to be seven feet tall, no way am I ever going to be a model.

"So how's school?" asks Mrs. Delaney.

I grunt in reply. My mother gives me her Queen Clementine look, the one that says she means business and I'd better shape up. I think of Stanley Kinkaid and start to scowl at her, then I think about the brownies she saved for us for tonight, and I sigh and sit up a little straighter. "Oh, you know, school is—school," I reply politely.

Mrs. Delaney laughs. "Things haven't changed much, I guess. I always felt the same way come September."

It's really nice to have Jess's mom here at book club with us. Last year she was away working in New York as an actress. She sent letters and presents and stuff sometimes, but it wasn't the same as her being here in person. I can tell Jess is glad too. She's snuggled up next to her on the sofa, which is white just like my chair. Everything in the Wongs' living room is white, or chrome, or glass. I call it the "winter room."

Emma settles onto the floor below me—which is covered with a white rug, of course—and Megan perches on the arm of her mother's chair. Mrs. Wong gestures at the coffee table. On it are a vegetable tray—carrot sticks, red pepper strips, celery, that kind of stuff—along with a bowl of gross-looking greenish dip, my mother's brownies, and a platter with a round, lumpy thing on it.

"Help yourselves, everyone," she says. "This is organic spinach dip, and that"—she points to the platter—"is a new recipe I've been wanting to try. I have to confess that you're my guinea pigs tonight. I thought it might work for your show, Clementine. It's a vegan cheesecake."

*Heather Vogel Frederick*

I glance over at Megan. It can't be easy, having a health nut like Mrs. Wong for your mother.

We all stare at the round, lumpy thing.

"Why, Lily, how interesting," says my mother finally. "What did you substitute for cream cheese?" Like her brownies, my mother's cheesecake is amazing. My mouth starts watering just thinking about it.

"Whipped tofu," Mrs. Wong replies. "You'll never notice the difference."

There's a brief silence as we eye her creation. Somehow I'm pretty sure we'll notice the difference. My mom takes a notebook out of her purse and jots something down. "I'll talk to Fred," she tells Mrs. Wong brightly. Fred is Fred Goldberg, the producer of *Cooking with Clementine*. "Maybe we can squeeze in a vegan episode."

Mrs. Wong smiles happily.

Mrs. Hawthorne clears her throat. "So, tonight is our official kick-off meeting for the Mother-Daughter Book Club, year two," she announces. "And girls, we have a surprise for you. We got to talking after yoga class the other day—"

Emma groans—she says something bad always comes from yoga class, which must be true because it was right after yoga class that my mother met Stanley Kinkaid—but her mother ignores her and continues. "And although we realize we probably should have discussed this with you all first, we thought it might be a good idea to broaden the scope of our group, as it were. Build a few bridges."

I poke Emma with my toe. She shrugs. Neither of us has a clue what her mother is talking about. By the looks on their faces, Megan and Jess don't either.

There's a knock at the front door.

"Ah," says Mrs. Hawthorne. "Right on time."

"Girls, we're expecting you to be gracious," warns my mother.

Mrs. Wong nods in agreement as she gets up to answer the door. There's a brief murmur of voices in the front hall, and then Mrs. Chadwick and Becca walk in.

The room goes dead quiet. Emma looks stunned. I shoot my mother a desperate glance, and she gives me the Queen Clementine *don't you dare* narrowed eyes in response. Megan has a funny look on her face, and I can't tell if she's sad or glad to see Becca. Becca, on the other hand, looks as unhappy to see us as the rest of us are to see her. Mrs. Chadwick looks like she just single-handedly won the Stanley Cup.

"Girls, please extend a warm welcome to the newest members of our book club," says Mrs. Hawthorne in her best official librarian voice. "Calliope recently started taking yoga, and after class one day—"

Emma groans softly under her breath again and her mother raises an eyebrow in warning, then continues, "—she asked if she and Becca might join us this year. Now that you girls are all in seventh grade, we know you'll want to expand your circle of friendship."

Expand our circle of friendship? Is Mrs. Hawthorne completely *nuts*? I glare at my mother. I can't believe she and the other mothers would do something like this behind our backs! Don't they know how we feel about the Fab Three? And especially about Becca Chadwick?

Mrs. Wong pats the far end of the sofa. "Calliope, why don't you sit here. And Becca, you can have that armchair beside her."

The Chadwicks sit down and we all stare stiffly at one another for a moment.

"I made vegan cheesecake," Mrs. Wong announces, like that's going to break the ice. She cuts a piece and puts it on a plate and hands it to Mrs. Chadwick.

Mrs. Chadwick looks like she's just been given a plate of dead possum. Her lips purse tightly, but she manages to squeeze out a thank-you. Apparently she's on her best behavior tonight too. Megan's dad calls Mrs. Chadwick "the snapping turtle," and Mr. Delaney calls her "the old battleax." She's famous around Concord for her sharp temper and critical eye. I watch her closely, trying not to smile. No way is Mrs. Chadwick going to be able to hold her tongue once she takes a bite of Mrs. Wong's cheesecake.

She forks up a little nibble and wedges it in her mouth. "Yum," she croaks.

Mrs. Wong looks pleased. "It's made with tofu."

I can't resist. "Free-range tofu?"

My mother looks over at me sharply.

Mrs. Wong takes the bait. "Now, Cassidy, tofu isn't an animal," she chides. "It's soy bean curd. Soy bean curd doesn't need to roam free."

On the floor below me, Emma lets out a little snort. I nudge her again with my foot. We're both grinning at the thought of a corral somewhere with little cubes of tofu wandering around. "*Home, home on the range,*" I sing to her under my breath. "*Where the deer and the tofu roam free . . .*"

Mrs. Wong doesn't hear me, fortunately. She's too busy explaining the recipe to Mrs. Chadwick. "And all the other ingredients are organic, of course."

"Of course," echoes Mrs. Chadwick politely.

"Tonight is our first official meeting of the year," says Mrs. Hawthorne, steering the conversation away from Mrs. Wong's pet subject. "We should start by deciding which book we want to read first."

"How about *The Diary of Anne Frank*?" says Emma.

Her mother shakes her head. "You'll be reading that in English class this year."

"*To Kill a Mockingbird*?" suggests my mother.

"Eighth-grade reading list," says Mrs. Hawthorne. "I checked with the school librarian."

"I know—*Gone with the Wind*," says Mrs. Delaney. "That would be a fun one to read together."

Mrs. Chadwick's mouth goes all pruney again. "Inappropriate material for my Becca."

Her Becca squirms at this.

Mrs. Wong holds up a couple of books. "These are two of my all-time favorites," she says. I squint at the titles: *A Little Princess* and *The Secret Garden*.

"Oh, mine too!" says my mother. "I loved those books when I was a girl."

"My daughter is far too advanced for Frances Hodgson Burnett," Mrs. Chadwick decrees. "I was under the impression that your club's selections would be challenging the girls."

There's an uncomfortable pause, then Emma says, "Actually, I agree with Mrs. Chadwick. I love those books, but I read them back in fifth grade. We're seventh graders. Can't we read something more grown-up?"

Jess and Megan both nod.

"But not too grown-up," warns Mrs. Chadwick, and Becca squirms again.

"That's kind of a tall order," says Mrs. Hawthorne, chewing her lip. She looks around the room at us. "Hmm. Perhaps it's time for Jane Austen." Mrs. Hawthorne is a huge Jane Austen fan. Emma and her brother Darcy are even named after characters in Jane Austen books. "Shall we try and tackle *Pride and Prejudice*?"

My mother shakes her head. "Probably still a bit beyond Cassidy, I'm afraid. Maybe another year."

Now it's my turn to squirm. Sometimes my mother still treats me like a baby. "How do you know it's beyond me?" I grumble.

My mother pats my knee. "Trust me, sweetheart, I know."

I yank my leg away.

"How about a different Jane, then," suggests Mrs. Delaney. "How about *Jane Eyre*?"

"Shannon, really! That's much too advanced thematically for these girls!" huffs Mrs. Chadwick.

"I've already read it," says Emma smugly.

Mrs. Chadwick turns to Mrs. Hawthorne. "Phoebe, when we discussed this you promised me you'd be making appropriate choices for the girls."

Emma's mother looks like she swallowed a tack. I think Mrs. Chadwick is starting to get on her nerves.

"Perhaps we should save the Janes for another year," says my mother. "I have an idea that might meet with everyone's approval. How about *Anne of Green Gables*?"

All our mothers sigh happily. Even Mrs. Chadwick's lips unpurse a little.

"Perfect!" says Mrs. Wong.

"Absolutely," agrees Mrs. Delaney.

"Now that's a splendid idea," says Mrs. Hawthorne.

"But I've already read it!" Emma protests.

"You've already read everything," Jess tells her.

"Not everyone in our group has read as widely as you have, sweetie," Mrs. Hawthorne says to Emma. "Maybe you can give the others a chance to catch up. And somehow I don't think you'd mind spending a little more time with Anne Shirley."

"I guess not," Emma concedes.

Mrs. Wong has a dreamy expression on her face. "*Anne of Green Gables* was another of my favorite books when I was growing up," she

*Heather Vogel Frederick*

says. "I used to call Jerry 'Gilbert' when we were first dating."

The mothers all laugh.

"Who's Gilbert?" I ask.

"You'll find out," says my mother, as Mrs. Wong disappears down the hall to the library—this house even has its own *library*, believe it or not—to dig up her old copy of the book.

"It's settled, then," says Mrs. Hawthorne. "*Anne of Green Gables* it is. And if we decide we like Lucy Maud Montgomery, we can read more in the series. *Anne of Avonlea* comes next and then *Anne of the Island*—I can't remember all the other titles, but I think there are a total of eight."

Mrs. Wong returns and passes her well-worn copy of the book around our circle. When it gets to me, I inspect it, wrinkling my nose. It must be at least a hundred years old. The cover is practically falling off, and the pages are all dog-eared and faded.

"Another musty, dusty old book," I mutter to Emma.

"Another well-loved book," corrects my mother.

Mrs. Hawthorne looks over at me and smiles. "I seem to recall that you liked the last 'musty, dusty old book' we read, Cassidy."

I shrug. She's right, though. I never thought I'd like *Little Women*, but it turned out to be an awesome story. Maybe *Anne of Green Gables* won't be so bad. "I guess," I admit grudgingly. "But couldn't we read some sports biographies one of these days?"

"I'll make a note of it," says Mrs. Hawthorne, grabbing her pen. "Even if we don't end up reading one of them for book club, I'll scout around the shelves at the library and see what we have that might interest you, okay?"

I really like Emma's mother.

Mrs. Wong offers to go to the bookstore and round up copies of *Anne of Green Gables* for all of us. Then she points to the snacks. "Dig in!"

"Before we all enjoy these wonderful, uh, healthy treats, perhaps you'd like to watch this," says my mother, pulling a DVD out of her purse.

"Is it the *Anne of Green Gables* movie?" Emma asks, bouncing up and down with excitement. "I love that movie!"

Becca rolls her eyes.

"No, honey, it's not *Anne of Green Gables*," my mother tells Emma. "Nothing that thrilling. It's just the first episode of my new TV show."

Everybody squeals—everyone except Becca, of course. And me. I've seen it already. It's okay, but now I'm really wishing I never agreed to be in it. I look like a dork. Especially since I let my mother and Courtney talk me into wearing a dress.

My mother hands the DVD to Megan, who picks up the remote from the coffee table and pushes a button. A huge oil painting—of white flowers, naturally—over the fireplace suddenly slides into the wall, revealing a widescreen TV. Mrs. Chadwick's mouth drops open, which makes her look like a tuna, or maybe an orca whale. Mrs. Chadwick is pretty hefty. She'd make a good linebacker.

*Heather Vogel Frederick*

I'm guessing Mrs. Chadwick hasn't seen the Wongs' entertainment setup before. It's impressive, there's no doubt about it. She watches, fascinated, as Megan pops in the DVD and pushes another button. The theme music to my mother's show swells, filling the room. Mr. Wong installed state-of-the-art speakers, of course, and even I have to admit the tune is pretty catchy in surround sound.

The title sequence appears, and the camera zooms in on my mother, who's standing at the front door of our house waving to the viewers. Emma and Jess wave back, giggling. Becca pulls out her cell phone and starts texting like mad. Probably reporting in to Ashley and Jen, her two wanna-bees. I feel like reaching over and snatching the stupid thing away from her, but my mother gives me another of her Queen Clementine looks, so I just make a face at Becca instead.

After the *Cooking with Clementine* logo fades, the camera swoops up and pans Concord from the air. The moms all *ooh* and *aah*, and even I have to admit our town looks good, what with all the white steeples and cool old houses and trees and rivers and ponds. Then the actual episode starts and suddenly we're at Half Moon Farm, where Mom is picking fall raspberries and talking with Mr. and Mrs. Delaney.

"Oh, look, there are the twins!" cries Mrs. Wong. "Don't they look adorable!"

Adorable is not exactly the word I'd use to describe Dylan and Ryan. Seek and Destroy is more like it. The boys make faces at the camera, then run off through the berry patch laughing like maniacs while their parents and my mother continue to pick berries.

After their baskets are full, my mother looks at the camera and says, "Let's go back to my house and make raspberry jam!"

Becca throws me a pitying look. I glare back—sure it's corny, but who is she to criticize? She makes a big show of taking her phone out of her purse and texting again. I grab a carrot stick and lob it at her. It lands in her lap and she looks up, startled. I stare innocently at the TV.

My mother looks really pretty on-screen. Watching her, I can't help but think about Stanley Kinkaid. I can understand why he'd want my mother for his girlfriend. What I can't understand is why she'd be interested in him.

The camera follows the Delaneys' truck past some of Concord's famous sites. The producers faked a route from Half Moon Farm to our house for this episode to show off more of the town. Emma squeals again when the truck passes her house.

Becca sends another text message.

The camera continues on its crazy path, past the Old North Bridge, through Monument Square, then on to Orchard House where the Alcott family lived and finally to Walden Pond. Eventually it winds up on the doorstep of our old Victorian on Hubbard Street. Inside, my mother leads the way to the kitchen, where she walks viewers through the jam-making process. Looking like a slightly shorter version of my mother, Courtney appears at this point to assist her, and when they're finished I show up to help test the finished product.

"Woo-hoo!" calls Megan, and I wad up my napkin and throw it at her. Onscreen, I'm wearing this ridiculous sundress my mother bought me, and the stylists from the Cooking Channel poufed up my hair and even put makeup on me.

"Cassidy, you look beautiful!" says Mrs. Delaney.

I cringe. "I look like an idiot."

"Big time," whispers Becca.

"Shut up," I whisper back.

"That was absolutely delightful, Clementine," says Mrs. Hawthorne, as the credits roll. "I predict it will be a big hit."

"Hmmph," says Mrs. Chadwick sourly. "It's all well and good, I'm sure, but it'll only bring a lot more tourists to Concord. As if it wasn't crowded enough here already. You can hardly find a parking spot downtown anymore."

"Now, Calliope, we have a beautiful, historic town," says Mrs. Wong. "Naturally people are going to want to visit."

"I have some more news," says my mother. "I've been going over the line-up of potential episodes with Fred Goldberg, and he and the other producers are very eager to schedule that mother-daughter tea we talked about earlier this summer."

"Do we get to be in it?" asks Becca, shoving her cell phone back in her pocket and sitting up straight. It's the first time she's showed any interest all evening.

"You bet," says my mother cheerfully.

My mother is such a traitor.

"I'll get more details to you all soon," she continues, "but it looks like we'll be filming in a few weeks."

Great. Just what I've always wanted, to be stuffed back into a dress and stuck in front of a camera with Becca Chadwick. My teammates will never let me live this down.

"Becca and I should be going," says Mrs. Chadwick, glancing at her watch. "It is a school night, after all."

"But you haven't finished your cheesecake," Mrs. Wong replies, disappointed.

"I need to go soon too," says my mother. "Phoebe, can you drive Cassidy home?"

I look over at her in surprise.

"Let me guess—prep work for tomorrow's show?" asks Mrs. Hawthorne.

My mother blushes slightly. "Um, no. Actually I, uh, have a date."

Becca's mother frowns. She opens her mouth to say something disapproving, but before she can, Mrs. Delaney leans over and pops a brownie into it.

"You really must try one of Clementine's brownies," she says sweetly. "They'll be featured on the show next week."

"Mmmph mmph," says Mrs. Chadwick.

I put my plate down. First Becca, and now this. What a way to spoil a perfectly good evening! I wish my mother could see that our family is just fine the way it is. We don't need anybody—especially not Stanley Kinkaid—butting in where they don't belong.

She just doesn't get it.

Final score: Clementine—1. Cassidy—0.

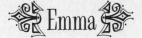

# Emma

*"'Josie is a Pye,' said Marilla sharply, 'so she can't help being disagreeable. I suppose people of that kind serve some useful purpose in society, but I must say I don't know what it is any more than I know the use of thistles.'"*
—*Anne of Green Gables*

"Mom, do you think I'm fat?"

My mother sets her hairbrush down on the sink. "Emma Jane Hawthorne! Where on earth did you get that idea?"

The two of us are upstairs in her bathroom, getting ready to go over to Cassidy's. We're filming the Mother-Daughter Book Club tea party this afternoon, and my mother insisted on fussing with my hair. Not that there's much a person can do with hair as curly as mine.

She pulls me close to her for a hug, leaning her chin on top of my head and smiling at me in the mirror. "Don't you know I think you're perfect just the way you are?"

I give her a rueful smile. We're dressed in matching skirts and holiday sweaters—the producers decided to put a festive spin on the tea party—and I can already imagine what Becca Chadwick will have to say about this. I don't bring it up, though. Becca Chadwick is still a sore spot for my mother and me. I know she meant well and everything, inviting the Chadwicks to join our book club, but it still hurts that she didn't discuss it with me first. Especially since she knows how mean Becca has been to me. How mean Becca still is to me.

My mother hasn't answered my question. "I know you think I'm perfect, but you're my mother," I tell her. "It's your job to think I'm perfect."

She laughs. "Oh, it is, is it? Well, please be informed that I am highly aware of the areas where you need improvement." Kissing the top of my head she adds in a more serious tone, "Come on now, honey, where did you get that ridiculous notion?"

I pull away. "I don't know."

She waits, watching me in the mirror.

I sigh. "Well, for one thing, I was over at Jess's last month, right after school started, and I couldn't fit into any of her T-shirts. It was really embarrassing."

"For Pete's sake, Emma, Jess is just a wisp of a thing! You have a completely different body type, honey."

I know she's trying to be encouraging, but somehow this doesn't make me feel any better. "I wish I was a wisp of a thing," I mutter.

My mother picks up the hairbrush and pulls it through my curls again. "Emma, this world is a bit like a garden," she says. "Each flower is

*Heather Vogel Frederick*

unique, just like each person is unique. There are daisies, and lilacs, and roses, and peonies—all sorts of lovely flowers. Now, wouldn't it be silly for a tulip to mope around wishing it were an iris?"

"I guess it would depend on how fat the tulip was."

She pokes me with the hairbrush. "Be serious. You get my point, right?"

I lift a shoulder.

"You're beautiful, Emma, and so are Jess, and Megan, and Cassidy! You need to try and appreciate your own uniqueness, instead of worrying so much about comparing yourself to others."

*That would be a lot easier if my own uniqueness wasn't quite so round*, I think, eyeing myself in the mirror. But I keep this thought to myself.

My mother is quiet for a moment, then asks, "So, is there any other reason you're bringing this up now?"

"Oh, you know," I tell her. "People say stuff."

"What people?"

"Kids at school."

"What kids?"

I fidget with the cuff of my sweater. "Becca Chadwick," I admit reluctantly.

My mother sets the hairbrush down again and sighs. "I might have known."

"I still can't believe that you guys invited Becca and Mrs. Chadwick to join our book club!"

"Sweetheart, we've been over this before," my mother replies. "It seemed like the right thing to do at the time. And besides, being around the four of you girls can only be good for Becca. You'll help set an example for her."

"But I don't want to set an example!" I protest. "Especially not at book club!"

Our mother-daughter book club is special. It's one of the few places where I can completely be myself, and not worry that anybody's going to tease me about writing poetry or about the way I look or make fun of my clothes, which sometimes are hand-me-downs. Now that Becca's there, everything's changed. "It's like I can't get away from her," I moan. "She's in half of my classes, plus now we're working on the school newspaper together. I can't go anywhere or do anything without having stupid Becca Chadwick in my face."

And on my case as well. Like on Thursday, after school, when we had our first meeting for the newspaper. Becca's older brother Stewart is a volunteer editor. He's a freshman in high school, like my brother Darcy, but he gets some sort of community service credit for helping us out. The regular editor is an eighth grader named Katie Malone, and there are two other reporters besides me, plus Zach, who is covering sports, and Becca. Becca's been going around telling everyone she's a "columnist," but really she'll just be writing up the social calendar. She's supposed to report on what's happening around school, what the team schedules are and when the clubs meet and when the band concerts and dances and plays will be and stuff like that.

Becca spent most of the meeting sucking up to Katie. Her voice got all high and chirpy, and she kept saying things like, "Oh, your haircut is soooo cute, Katie!" and "That nail polish is soooo pretty, Katie!" and "Where did you get those adorable shoes, Katie?" I was about ready to throw up, listening to her. I could tell that her brother was annoyed too, and even Ms. Nielson looked like she wanted to tell her to be quiet. Finally, Zach and the other reporters left to go home. Ms. Nielson went to the office for a minute to check with the principal about something, and the minute she left the classroom Becca turned to me and said, right in front of Katie and Stewart, who I hardly know at all, "Emma, I just thought of the perfect byline for you: Porky the Poet!"

I could feel my face flame. Katie looked shocked for about half a second, but when Becca started to laugh, she joined in.

"Sheesh, Becca!" Stewart looked embarrassed and disgusted and kind of angry. He's a dork and a Chadwick to boot, but still, it made me feel a teeny bit better that somebody stuck up for me, even if it was only Stewart.

Cassidy would have laughed it off and dished it right back, calling Becca "Metalmouth" or something, but I'm not Cassidy, plus Becca caught me off guard so I just sat there like a lump not knowing what to say. Becca likes to needle me about my weight and my poetry. Last year, she stole my journal and read this poem I wrote about Zach out loud right in front of him and his friends. I thought I was going to die of embarrassment. What's worse is that now she knows I want to be a writer. I don't like her knowing that about me. It makes me feel like I'm standing in the middle of Monument Square in my underpants.

Ms. Nielson came back before Becca could say anything else, thank goodness. When she caught sight of Becca and Katie snickering, Stewart glowering, and me with my face the color of a stop sign, she must have known instantly that something was going on because she asked, "Is everything okay?"

Katie wiped the smile off her face and started shuffling papers. "Yes, Ms. Nielson."

"Absolutely, Ms. Nielson," Becca chimed in, the picture of innocence.

Ms. Nielson looked over at me but I didn't say a word. I just sat there feeling foolish. And porky.

"Emma," my mother says, interrupting my remorseful daydream, "unfortunately you're going to find as you go through life that you will occasionally run into people like Becca. There have always been the Becca Chadwicks of the world, and I suppose there always will be. Last year when we read *Little Women* it was Jenny Snow, remember her? And now in *Anne of Green Gables* it's Gertie and Josie Pye."

She's right, of course. My mother usually is. She's a librarian.

"You can't listen to the Pyes of the world," she tells me.

We're both quiet for a moment, contemplating the Pyes of the world.

"Maybe I should talk to Becca's mother at the tea party this afternoon," my mother says finally.

*Heather Vogel Frederick*

I spin around. "No!" I beg her, horrified. "Please don't! Promise me you won't!"

She holds up her hands in mock surrender. "Okay, okay, I promise! But only if you promise you'll try not to let her bug you."

Anything is better than my mother making a scene with Mrs. Chadwick. Becca would never let me hear the end of that. "I'll try," I mutter.

"Good," says my mother. "Now let's get a move on here and finish up." She leans closer to the mirror and starts putting on her mascara. My mother doesn't wear much makeup. Just lipstick, usually, and maybe a little blush. Eye makeup is too big a deal and takes too much time, she always says. But she's making an exception for the TV taping today. She says she wants to do Mrs. Sloane proud. She fixed her hair different too. It's loose, instead of in its usual ponytail, and she fluffed up her bangs a bit. I like it.

"Cassidy says I just need to get more exercise," I tell her.

My mother's mascara wand halts in midair. "Excuse me?"

"What we were talking about earlier. You know, the weight thing. Cassidy says more exercise would help."

My mother frowns. "Oh she does, does she?"

"She says I spend too much time sitting around reading."

"Well, from what Clementine tells me about Cassidy's grades, it sounds as if she could do with a little *more* sitting around reading." My mother slants me a glance. "So what do you think about her advice?"

I shrug.

"Do you want to take up a sport? You love to swim—you could join the swim team, maybe, or play water polo."

I make a face. I've never liked team sports.

"Well, maybe you could ride your bike a little more often. Heaven knows we could all do with a little more exercise, myself included." She pats her tummy. My mom's not as slender as Mrs. Delaney and Mrs. Sloane, and definitely not as thin as Mrs. Wong, who my dad says practically disappears when she turns sideways, but she's still in pretty good shape. My mom and my dad like to go for long walks. They call it "clearing the cobwebs." Sometimes they loop over the Old North Bridge and around back through town, and other times they go farther away, like to the trails around Walden Pond and through Estabrook Woods.

"Could we get a dog?" I ask. Instantly feeling disloyal, I reach down and pat Melville, our cat, who's wandered in to join us and is twining himself around my ankles.

"I doubt I could sell your father on that idea," my mother replies, dabbing on her lipstick. "He says two children and one cat are plenty."

"Cassidy says I should try skating."

"Hockey? Really?" My mother's brow furrows.

"Not hockey—figure skating. Cassidy thinks I'd really like it. She says it's kind of like swimming."

"Hmmm," says my mother.

"Well, not exactly like swimming," I reply, trying to explain. "Just the same feeling. She says it's sort of like flying, too."

My mother laughs. "Swimming and flying. I see. Sounds pretty

*Heather Vogel Frederick*

good." She puts her makeup away and turns around. "I can certainly give Eva Bergson a call and check into figure-skating lessons if you want me to, Emma."

Eva Bergson is about eighty. She was an Olympic skater ages ago, and now she runs a skating school in Concord. "But I thought skating lessons were really expensive," I say. My family is on kind of a tight budget. My dad works at home. He's a freelance writer and what my mother calls "an aspiring novelist," and he doesn't make a whole lot of money.

"Well, I get a small consulting fee from Clementine's show"—Mrs. Sloane hired my mom as a research assistant—"and it's looking like the tax levy will pass too. If it does, there's a raise budgeted for yours truly at the library, and I can think of nothing I'd rather spend it on than my darling daughter." My mother plants another kiss on top of my head, and I smile up at her.

The doorbell rings.

"That's probably Shannon and Jess," says my mother. The four of us are going to drive over to the Sloanes' together.

"Look what Shannon brought us!" crows my dad as my mother and I come downstairs to the front hall. He waves an apple pie under our noses. "She says the Macouns are finally ripe."

Jess's mother thinks Macouns are the perfect kind of apple for making pies. She should know—she makes a ton of them for their farm stand. Jess and I help her bake sometimes. We gather eggs and pick fruit for her too—whatever's in season—and vegetables from the garden, and herbs from the greenhouse. Plus, I learned how to milk a goat last year when Jess got Sundance, and Mr. Delaney says we're such a help to him that he's going to make us official apprentice cheesemakers next summer.

"Wow, Shannon, thank you!" says my mother. "What a treat! Heaven knows baking is not my strong suit."

Jess looks at me and smiles. She's sampled plenty of my mom's fiascos. In our house, my dad does all the cooking.

The front door swings open and Darcy bursts in, all sweaty from football practice. Like Cassidy, my older brother is a jock. "Hi, guys!"

Jess smiles shyly at him. She kind of has a crush on my brother. Not that I've told Darcy about it. I would never betray my best friend's secret.

"Phew, Darcy, go get in the shower!" says my mother, waving her hand in front of her nose. "And leave those grubby cleats outside, would you?"

Darcy dutifully unties his shoes and tosses them out back onto the front steps. "Yum," he says, spotting the pie. "Can I have a piece?"

"After you're odor-free," my dad tells him, and Darcy peels off his dirty socks and waves them around his head.

Jess and I shriek, and my dad grabs an umbrella from the coat stand and raises it in front of him like a fencing sword.

"Be off, you scurvy dog!" he cries, advancing across the front hall. Darcy grins and thunders upstairs, whistling.

"Boys are so gross!" I say in disgust.

"You won't think that way forever," says my mother lightly. She whisks the pie away from my father and heads for the kitchen. We follow her. "I'll leave this here for Darcy," she tells my dad, cutting a piece of pie and putting it on a plate. "But I think you'd better hide the rest of it in your office, where it'll be safe from marauding football players. Otherwise none of the rest of us will ever get a bite."

Mrs. Delaney smiles ruefully. "I can only imagine what our food bill will be like when the twins get to be teenagers."

"No kidding!" says my father. "I keep telling Phoebe we're going to have to take out a second mortgage just to feed Darcy."

Jess's mother grows quiet. My father gets a funny look on his face, and he and my mother exchange a worried glance.

"Well, I, uh, guess I'll head back to work here," my dad says. "I, uh, have a review to finish up before quitting time. Thanks again for the pie, Shannon."

He disappears down the hall with it, and my mother turns to Mrs. Delaney.

"So any more word on, um, things?" she asks.

Mrs. Delaney shakes her head. My mother takes the kettle from the stove and starts to fill it with water. "We don't have to be over to Clementine's for half an hour," she says. "Why don't you sit down and I'll make us a nice cup of tea." She turns to Jess and me. "You girls go on up to Emma's room now and play until I call you."

"Mom!" I protest, exasperated. "We're in seventh grade! We don't 'play' anymore!"

"Then go hang out, or whatever it is you call it."

I can tell she's trying to get rid of us. I can also tell something's up with the Delaneys. I want to stay and listen and find out what it is, but my mother makes shooing motions at us. Reluctantly, Jess and I trudge out of the kitchen. Melville is right behind us.

"What's going on?" I ask Jess a minute later, closing my bedroom door.

She shrugs. "I'm not sure. My parents have been whispering a lot lately."

"Your mother's not going to leave again, is she?"

A panicked look appears on Jess's face and I instantly regret my words.

"I don't know," she says unhappily. "I hope not."

"I'm sure that's not it," I tell her, wishing I felt more certain. It wouldn't make sense, though—her mom's been really happy since she came home from New York. At least up until recently.

About twenty minutes later my mom calls us back downstairs again and the four of us pile into our car for the short drive to Cassidy's. The Sloanes' house is bustling with activity. Mr. Goldberg, the producer, is there, along with a couple of cameramen and crew. Everybody's shouting directions and rushing back and forth, trying not to trip over the cables that snake through the hallway and the downstairs rooms. Mrs. Sloane appears, looking frazzled but gorgeous.

"Nice outfits," she says to my mother and me, casting an eye over our matching skirts and sweaters. "Very pretty."

Her compliment makes me feel a teeny bit better. Even if Becca

*Heather Vogel Frederick*

thinks I look stupid—which I have absolutely no doubt she will—what does her opinion matter compared to former supermodel Clementine's?

"Cassidy's in her room with Megan," Mrs. Sloane tells us. "Why don't you girls go on up and wait there, while we finish getting everything ready on the set. Phoebe, Shannon, come with me. I'm going to put you to work icing the cupcakes with Lily. The Chadwicks should be here any time and then we'll be good to go."

As our mothers disappear down the hall toward the kitchen, Jess and I head upstairs. I peek into the dining room as we go past. There are spotlights facing the table, which is set for our tea party. The windows are draped with panels of gold and silver fabric, and there are gold and silver candlesticks everywhere. It looks like a palace. We're not supposed to be having a Christmas party, exactly—Mrs. Sloane and the producers wanted it to be a bit more general than that, something viewers could picture doing for Thanksgiving or Christmas or New Year's or even Hanukkah. It's a bit weird, though, since it's not even Halloween yet. Cassidy says the filming schedule takes some getting used to. She's never sure from week to week what time of year it will be inside her house.

"Hi, guys!" I say, flinging myself onto Cassidy's bed and startling Murphy, the Sloanes' dog, who was sound asleep on the pillow. He gives me a reproachful glance.

"Sorry, pal." I scratch him behind his ears, and, somewhat mollified, he rolls over on his back so I can scratch his tummy, too.

Cassidy's older sister Courtney pokes her head in the door. "Mom says I'm supposed to inspect you all." She looks us over and spots Cassidy's high tops. "Come on, Cassidy! What's the matter with you? Take those sneakers off and put on your nice shoes like Mom asked. You don't want to embarrass her. And could you maybe brush your hair?"

Muttering to herself, Cassidy unlaces her sneakers. Courtney turns to Megan and Jess and me. "You three look great," she says. "Fun sweater, Emma. That color is perfect on you."

I'm beginning to suspect that my mother called the Sloanes ahead of time and asked them to work on boosting my confidence. But Courtney sounds completely sincere. I wish I had an older sister. I love Darcy and everything; he's great most of the time as far as big brothers go, but compliments are not his strong point.

"Thanks, Courtney, you look nice too," I tell her. Courtney always looks pretty. She's like a little photocopy of Mrs. Sloane. She's not dressed up today, because she's not part of our book club, so she's just wearing jeans and a turquoise hoodie. Somehow she still manages to look grown-up and sophisticated, though, and she makes me feel about ten years old in my red sweater with the little snowmen on it.

"How's Lois Lane?" Cassidy asks after Courtney heads back downstairs.

I make a face. "Not so great." I explain what happened at the newspaper meeting after school on Thursday.

"Man," Cassidy says when I'm done. "The queen bee sure has her stinger out for you."

*Heather Vogel Frederick*

"You can't let her get to you, Emma," Jess adds.

Megan doesn't say anything. She's sitting on the other side of Murphy and seems very interested in the bedspread. Her dark, shoulder-length hair has swung forward, obscuring her face.

"Becca tried that 'Goat Girl' stuff on me the first day of school and I let her have it," Jess continues. "I called her a 'cretinous troglodyte' right in front of Zach Norton. That shut her up fast."

"A what-inous troglo-who?" sputters Cassidy.

Jess grins. "*Cretinous troglodyte.* I've been saving it up all summer. My dad helped me pick it out as ammunition, just in case. It means stupid cave-dweller, but it sounds much worse, doesn't it?"

We all laugh, and Cassidy gets Jess to write the insult down for her so she can memorize it. "This'll come in handy at the rink," she tells us, sticking the note in her desk drawer. "Some of those hockey players can be real trash-talkers."

"You know, Emma," Megan says softly, "Becca doesn't really mean it. She only says those things because she knows they bug you. It's just a bad habit."

We all stare at her. Since when did Megan start sticking up for Becca Chadwick again?

"That's easy for you to say," I tell her indignantly. "You've never been Becca's punching bag the way I have."

Jess quickly changes the subject. But I can't stop thinking about Megan and Becca. Katie Malone's not the only one Becca's been sucking up to lately. Now that she's in our book club, and now that she knows Megan's fashion designs are going to be featured in *Flashlite* magazine, Becca's been acting really friendly again toward Megan. And Megan hasn't exactly been fending her off.

"So, how are your designs coming?" Cassidy asks.

Megan flops backward onto the bed and heaves a dramatic sigh. "Don't ask."

"Anything we can do to help?" says Jess.

Megan shakes her head. "The launch issue is scheduled for next summer. It seems like a long ways off, but they said they'd need my designs by the middle of March. I'm already getting nervous about it. Plus, everything I've drawn so far just looks stupid."

"Let's take a look," says Cassidy, rooting in Megan's shoulder bag for her ever-present sketchbook.

Megan sits up and lets out a screech of protest. "No!" she cries, grabbing it away from her.

Cassidy snatches it back, laughing. "C'mon, Megs, we're your friends." She flips it open. We crowd around to inspect the pages. The outfits look fine to me, but when I look more closely at the models, I realize they're all Becca.

"Girls! The Chadwicks are here! We're ready to get started!" Mrs. Sloane calls up the stairs.

None of us says a word as Megan stuffs the sketchbook back in her bag. We file downstairs to the dining room in silence and wait outside the door while Mr. Goldberg, who is overseeing the crew, makes sure the candles are all lit and the cameras are in position.

*Heather Vogel Frederick*

Becca and her mother are waiting outside the door too.

"Nice snowmen, Emma," whispers Becca, quietly enough that nobody else can hear. "I had a sweater like that once, too—back in *preschool.*"

Despite the promise I made to my mother earlier, and all the nice things Mrs. Sloane and Courtney said, I feel my eyes fill up with tears of rage and humiliation. How can Megan possibly like someone as mean as Becca?

"You're awfully quiet," Mrs. Wong says to us as we take our seats around the table.

I don't answer. I'm afraid if I say anything the tears might spill over.

"We're just excited, that's all," Jess tells her.

Willing the tears away, I concentrate on how beautiful everything looks instead. There are gold and silver ribbons twined around the chandelier, and the candles in the candlesticks are glowing all down the center of the table, their reflections shining in the centerpiece—a big glass bowl filled with gold and silver ornaments. I don't remember seeing these plates and teacups before—they're gold-rimmed and very fancy—and I wonder if they belong to Cassidy's mom or if they're just part of the stage set.

Two crew members come in carrying three-tiered trays laden with fancy finger food—tiny sandwiches and mini cupcakes and things like that. They set them on the table, alongside a silver teapot. Cassidy reaches out for a truffle and her mother swats her hand away.

"We're going to film the tea party first, and then later we'll all go into the kitchen and do some baking for what will eventually be the first part of the episode," Mrs. Sloane explains. "And we'll take the decorations down and put them up again as well."

Filming a TV show is complicated, I decide. But Mrs. Sloane's cheeks are pink and her eyes are sparkling, and it's obvious she's really enjoying herself. I muster a smile and decide I'm going to try and enjoy myself too. Like my mother, I want to do Cassidy's mom proud.

I glance over at Becca. She's smiling too. Not at me, though. She's smiling straight at the camera. With her lips together, of course.

"It's not on yet," says Cassidy in a stage whisper.

Jess snickers; Becca blushes; and Mrs. Sloane shoots Cassidy a warning glance.

"What I thought we'd do for this first segment is combine the tea party with our usual book club meeting," she says. "That way, we can help give other book clubs ideas for fun things they can do too."

"Quiet on the set," says Mr. Goldberg as Mrs. Sloane takes her seat. My mother, who is sitting next to me, squeezes my hand. I take a deep breath. I'm not really nervous, just a little jittery. Cassidy told us there's nothing to be scared of, since it's not like live TV. They'll tape a whole bunch, she says, then afterward the editors will look everything over, and keep the good stuff and toss the rest.

Maybe they'll toss Becca, I think, and my smile broadens at this prospect. I can feel myself relax a little.

"Action!" calls Mr. Goldberg.

*Heather Vogel Frederick*

"Welcome to today's episode of *Cooking with Clementine*," says Mrs. Sloane, flashing the smile that made her famous. "We have a special treat for all of you today, a festive mother-daughter book club holiday tea party!"

She goes around the table introducing each of us, and then starts pouring tea as our meeting gets underway. Mrs. Delaney, who is sitting on the other side of me, passes one of the towers of treats, and I take a cucumber sandwich, a chicken salad sandwich, a truffle, and three mini cupcakes. Then I glance over at Becca and remember her "Porky the Poet" comment, and I put one of the cupcakes back, hoping they don't catch this on film.

"Here's your first official handout of the year, girls," says my mother cheerfully, passing out sheets of paper. "L. M. Montgomery— Lucy Maud, or just Maud to her friends—was a fascinating woman. I think you're going to enjoy getting to know her just as much as you enjoyed getting to know Louisa May Alcott last year when we read *Little Women*."

"Hey!" says Cassidy. "They had the same first two initials."

"Well, what do you know about that," my mother replies. "I hadn't noticed. A good omen for a smooth transition, I'd say."

We all laugh politely and sip our tea and nibble at our food. Across the table, Cassidy is chomping on an egg salad sandwich, and I remind myself to chew with my mouth closed as I see her mother elbow her discreetly.

"Let me explain a little about how our book club works," says

Mrs. Sloane brightly, launching into a conversation with the camera. While she's describing our reading schedule and how we try and learn a little about the author at each of our meetings, and sometimes bake food or do crafts from the books, I scan my handout.

## Fun Facts About Maud

1. Lucy Maud Montgomery was born on November 30, 1874, on Prince Edward Island in Canada.

2. Her mother died when she was two, and her father moved to Western Canada seeking a better life, leaving Maud in the care of Lucy and Alexander Macneil, her mother's parents. Maud would later base the characters of Matthew and Marilla Cuthbert partly on these grandparents.

3. Maud always knew she wanted to be a writer. She started keeping a journal at age nine, received her first rejection letter at twelve, and published her first poem in a Charlottetown newspaper a few days before she turned sixteen. She later wrote, "It was the first sweet bubble on the cup of success."

4. Her literary career would go on to span some fifty years, until her death on April 24, 1942. Overall, Lucy Maud Montgomery wrote twenty-four books, 530 short stories, and more than five hundred poems.

Heather Vogel Frederick

I glance down at my teacup and wonder if I'll ever be lucky enough to taste that sweet bubble of success. I haven't had the courage to try and publish any of my poems or stories yet. They're too private. Especially the poems. *Well, except for the one about Zach Norton that Becca read aloud to everybody last year, that is,* I think bitterly. That one certainly wasn't private anymore.

"So," says my mother briskly, as Mrs. Sloane winds up her explanations and gives her a nod. "Let's get this discussion started. You've all read up through chapter fifteen, right? Are you enjoying the book so far?"

Everyone raises her hand except Becca.

"Rebecca Louise," barks Mrs. Chadwick.

Becca halfheartedly raises her hand.

"Cut!" says Mr. Goldberg. He sighs. "It's Mrs. Chadwick, isn't it?"

She fixes him with a cold stare. "That's right, young man."

Mr. Goldberg looks a little flustered at this. He's got grayish hair and is at least as old as Mrs. Chadwick. "Uh, you do recall that you're on camera here, don't you? You might want to watch the tone of your voice."

"Don't tell me how to raise my children, and I won't tell you how to film a TV show," snaps Mrs. Chadwick.

Mr. Goldberg shoots Cassidy's mother a look.

"What Fred means, Calliope," Mrs. Sloane says smoothly, "is that we wouldn't want to give viewers the wrong impression. You're such a devoted mother to Becca, and that's what we want to convey here on film."

Mrs. Chadwick preens at this. "Well," she says, a tad less waspishly, "I'll try and keep that in mind. But watch your manners, Becca."

For a moment I almost feel sorry for Becca. It can't be easy, having a snapping turtle like Mrs. Chadwick for your mother. But then I remember "Porky the Poet" and I don't feel so sorry for her anymore.

"Roll 'em!" says Mr. Goldberg.

"Let's talk about the characters," my mother suggests, and we go around the table telling who our favorite and least favorite characters are.

Almost all of us like Anne Shirley best, except my mother, who is particularly fond of Marilla.

"She's so steely and stern on the outside, but she's really a cream puff underneath," she says, plucking a tiny cream puff from the top tier of the nearest tea tray and holding it up for emphasis.

The other mothers all laugh. Becca looks over at me, shaking her head in pity. I stretch out my leg under the table, wondering if it's long enough to give her a good swift kick. It's not, unfortunately.

When it's my turn, I look Becca right in the eye. I don't care if the cameras are rolling or not. "My least favorite character is Josie Pye," I say.

Becca doesn't even blink. I'll bet she hasn't even read the book.

"Mine is Mrs. Rachel Lynde," says Mrs. Wong. "At least in the beginning. She turns out okay in the end. But what a busybody! I can't imagine anybody in real life being that nosy and outspoken, can you?"

There's an awkward pause. Actually, that description fits someone

*Heather Vogel Frederick*

in this room to a T. I try not to look at Mrs. Chadwick, who's furtively removing the last two truffles from the tea tray and isn't paying the rest of us the least bit of attention.

"How about you, Shannon?" my mother says hastily to Mrs. Delaney. "Do you have a favorite or least favorite?"

"You know, this may sound odd, but my favorite character is Green Gables itself," Jess's mother replies. "Lucy Maud Montgomery describes that old farmhouse so vividly it almost seems alive."

"I know what you mean," agrees Mrs. Wong.

Mrs. Chadwick gives an ungracious snort. I hope the film editor will be able to cut it out or erase it or something, because like Mrs. Wong, I know exactly what Mrs. Delaney means.

"When I first read this book as a girl, I desperately wanted to move to Green Gables," Jess's mother continues. "It seemed so beautiful to me, like heaven on earth!"

"And then you grew up and married Dad and moved to Half Moon Farm instead," says Jess happily. "Which is even more beautiful than Green Gables."

Her mother puts her arm around her shoulders and draws her close. "That's right, honey." There's a hint of sadness in her voice, and I see my mother and Mrs. Sloane exchange a glance across the table. I sure wish I knew what was going on with the Delaneys. I just hope it isn't anything bad. Last year was really hard on Jess.

"How about you, Becca, do you have a favorite character?" my mother coaxes.

Becca gives me a sly glance. "Gilbert Blythe."

I turn bright red. I know as well as she does that she's not talking about Gilbert Blythe. She's talking about Zach Norton. The girls at Walden Middle School are just as crazy about Zach as the girls in Avonlea were about Gilbert Blythe. Becca knows I have a crush on Zach because of the poem I wrote last year. She has a crush on him too, just like Josie Pye did on Gilbert. She must have read the book after all.

"I don't get what the big deal between Gilbert and Anne was in that last chapter we read," says Cassidy. "All he did was call her 'Carrots' and she turned around and whapped him over the head with her slate."

"She was sensitive about her red hair," I explain, spearing another glance at Becca. "It's like somebody teasing you about the one thing you don't want to be teased about."

Becca mouths the word *Porky* silently at me. Then she says aloud, "Maybe we should start calling you 'Carrots,' Cassidy."

"Maybe you should think twice before you do, Metalmouth," Cassidy shoots back.

"Cassidy Ann!" says her mother, shocked.

"Cut!" shouts Mr. Goldberg. "Ladies, please! This is supposed to be a friendly tea party!"

"Becca started it," says Cassidy.

"Nonsense!" barks Mrs. Chadwick.

"I'll handle this, Calliope," Mrs. Sloane tells her stiffly.

My mother holds up her hand. "How about we all just take a deep breath and forge ahead here? I'm sure Mr. Goldberg and the crew

*Heather Vogel Frederick*

want to wrap things up this afternoon as speedily as possible."

Across the room, Mr. Goldberg nods vigorously. The camera starts rolling again, and my mother pulls out her cheeriest Mrs. Hawthorne-the-librarian tone of voice. "Continuing our lively discussion here, let's turn to the concept of kindred spirits," she says. "I've always loved that concept, haven't you, Lily?"

"Absolutely," Mrs. Wong replies. "It's the very best kind of friendship."

"I always wished I had a friend like Diana Barry when I was growing up," says Mrs. Delaney wistfully. "You girls are all so lucky to have each other."

I look over at Becca Chadwick. She is so not a kindred spirit. Whatever the opposite of a kindred spirit is, that's Becca. She sees me watching her and crosses her eyes. My mother catches her doing it and frowns, shaking her head slightly. Becca has the grace to look embarrassed. She shifts her gaze and takes a sip of tea.

"You know what I don't get?" says Cassidy. "The way Anne keeps naming things. 'The White Way of Delight,' and the 'Lake of Shining Waters.' And that dumb tree, the 'Snow Queen.' That is so lame! Who names a tree?"

I hide a smile behind my napkin, careful not to look in Jess's direction. I wouldn't admit it on camera—and certainly not in front of Becca—but Jess and I have been naming things at Half Moon Farm. *Anne of Green Gables* inspired us. The Delaney's duck pond is now officially "The Mirror of the Sky," and the row of birches that line the driveway are "The Silent Guardians."

"Actually," says my mother, flipping through her notebook, "I was reading a biography of Lucy Maud Montgomery in preparation for our meeting today, and it turns out that was something she used to do. Here it is—she said she used to name 'all the pretty nooks and crannies about the old farm.'"

"I still think it's dumb," Cassidy continues, popping an entire cucumber sandwich into her mouth. "And what's with that invisible friend of hers in the bookcase with the glass doors?"

"Don't talk with your mouth full," her mother whispers.

Across from me, I see Becca's cell phone peeking up over the tabletop. She snaps a picture of Cassidy chewing. She sees me watching her and gives me a triumphant little smile. I look away.

"You mean Katie Maurice?" my mother says. "Well, in the story Anne was just lonely, that's all. But lots of children have imaginary friends. Maud Montgomery herself did. And so did Emma."

I gape at her, horrified. I can't believe she just said that! And on camera, too! I feel my face getting warm. I can only imagine the hay Becca Chadwick will make with this juicy little factoid. Not that she'll have to—the whole world will know about it once the show airs. Unless the editor snips it out.

Mrs. Wong laughs. "Wasn't his name Waldo?"

She and my mother both start giggling.

"Remember that time we decided to take the kids over to Ipswich to Crane's Beach for the day?" my mother continues. "And we had to turn back because Emma forgot Waldo?"

*Heather Vogel Frederick*

Megan's lips are twitching now too. Cassidy is grinning at me, and so are Mr. Goldberg and even the cameraman. Only Jess isn't smiling. She gives me a sympathetic look.

"I was five!" I protest.

But my mother is caught up in telling the story, and doesn't hear the panic in my voice. "Emma shrieked for ten minutes straight, until Nick finally relented and turned the car around."

It's stupid, I know, but I can still remember that horrible feeling in the pit of my stomach, and how relieved I was when my dad brought me back home to get Waldo. He was very real to me.

Becca looks over at me and smirks. I close my eyes. I am never going to live this down.

"I'm sure this is all very entertaining to those of you who were there, but I suggest that we confine our conversation to *Anne of Green Gables*," Mrs. Chadwick says sourly.

"Cut!" cries Mr. Goldberg. He looks weary. "On that note, I think we'll wrap things up here. We should have enough footage at this point for the tea party scene."

The rest of the afternoon passes quickly. Mrs. Sloane organizes us in the kitchen where they film us making tea treats and decorations. I stay as far away as possible from Becca, who is teamed up with Megan. As I watch the two of them together, I begin to wonder if Megan is a kindred spirit after all. She's not exactly acting like one.

The phone rings just as we finish filming. Courtney answers it, then passes the receiver to her mother.

"Uh-huh," says Mrs. Sloane. "Really? Wow! That would be great." She hangs up and looks over at us. "You'll never guess who that was."

"Waldo?" whispers Becca from behind me.

Cassidy steps on her foot.

"Channel 5 heard about the mother-daughter tea party episode, and they want to do a promotional spot about it on their morning show the day it runs," her mother tells us.

"You mean we're going to be on *Hello Boston!*?" squeals Becca.

Mrs. Sloane nods, beaming.

I have the same horrible feeling in the pit of my stomach that I did when we drove off years ago without my imaginary friend Waldo. Taping an episode of *Cooking with Clementine* is one thing. But live TV with Becca Chadwick?

It's going to be a disaster.

## ❦ Jess ❦

*"What do you do when you meet with
an irresistible temptation?"*
—*Anne of Green Gables*

Shivering, I kneel in front of my bedroom window and peer out at the darkness. The sky is beginning to lighten over the back pasture, and I can just make out the fringe of trees at its far edge. A brisk wind whips through their tops, then gallops across the pasture and rattles my windowpanes. I pull my quilt closer around me, glad to be indoors on this chilly November morning. Usually I'd be out in the barn by now, milking the goats and feeding the chickens. But since this is a special day, my father said he'd do my chores for me.

I press my face close to the glass, trying not to fog up the windowpane with my breath. There it is! To the southeast, over the duck pond, just like the Almanac promised. I smile in satisfaction at the pale crescent moon, and slightly above it, bright Venus. I let my thoughts drift for a while, pretending that I'm Anne Shirley, upstairs in her bedroom at Green Gables swooning over nature's stark beauty.

"'*Don't you feel as if you just loved the world on a morning like this?*'" I whisper to myself, quoting Anne.

I know I'm too old for make-believe—I'm nearly thirteen—but sometimes, when nobody's around, I still like to pretend things. Since we started reading the Anne books this fall, I've been daydreaming about Green Gables a lot—which is kind of surprising because reading is not my favorite thing in the whole world. Now, Emma, she'd rather sit around with a book than do just about anything else. I'd rather be outdoors. But I liked reading *Little Women* last year, so I was looking forward to book club again this year. Still, I didn't have a clue how much I would absolutely love *Anne of Green Gables*. There are parts of it that I read over and over again. Anne Shirley feels the same way I do about everything, especially nature. She *notices* things—sunsets, trees, flowers, all of it. Just like I do. If she were real, the two of us would definitely be kindred spirits.

"Jess!" my mother calls, startling me out of my little fantasy. "Are you ready?"

"Almost, Mom!" I call back. Feeling guilty for dawdling—and nervous all of a sudden—I scramble up off the floor, toss the quilt back on my bed, and get dressed as fast as I can. Mom says it's not that big a deal, and that an old pro like me doesn't need to worry so much, but how can I help it? This is a lot different than a middle school play. We're going to be on *Hello Boston!* Everybody in the world watches *Hello Boston!* Well, okay, not *everybody*, but enough people to make me worry about doing something stupid, especially on live TV, like

*Heather Vogel Frederick*

having hay stuck in my hair or something. Everybody thinks I'm weird enough as it is.

There's a tap on my bedroom door and my mother pokes her head in. "We should get going, honey," she says. She smiles at me. "You look really pretty."

"Thanks." I'm wearing the same outfit I wore when we filmed the tea party a few weeks ago. It's a light blue velvet dress with a white lace collar that my dad says makes me look like Alice in Wonderland. He means it as a compliment, but I think of it as my Anne of Green Gables dress, because it has puffed sleeves and Anne Shirley always wanted a dress with puffed sleeves. It's kind of old-fashioned, but that's what I like about it. My mom picked it out for me, and her taste in clothes is every bit as good as Mrs. Sloane's and Megan's. Not that you'd know it to look at her. Living on our farm, she doesn't get to dress up much. At least not the way she did when she played Larissa LaRue on *HeartBeats* last year. When she quit the show she traded in her glamorous soap opera wardrobe for jeans and T-shirts, and instead of fancy hairdos, she mostly just pulls her hair back into a ponytail and sticks it through the back of one of her baseball caps. And who's going to bother with makeup when there's nobody to see you but chickens and goats?

Today she looks as glamorous as she ever did on *HeartBeats*, though. She's wearing slim black velvet pants, high heels, and a white satin blouse. Her dark hair is twisted up into a French braid, and she's got these really gorgeous pearl earrings on and lipstick and everything.

I wonder if I'll be as pretty as my mom when I grow up. I squint at myself in the mirror, trying to imagine myself ten years from now. It doesn't work. All I see is Jess, but blurry because I'm squinting.

"We'd better get a move on—we're supposed to be at Clementine's soon," my mother reminds me. As if I could forget. She sees the look on my face and laughs. "Relax, honey, it's going to be fine. You'll hardly notice the cameras. Just try and think of it as a fun party."

Is she kidding me? I'm going to be on live TV with Becca Chadwick! That hardly qualifies as a party. Filming the *Cooking with Clementine* episode was bad enough. Cassidy says by the time the editors cut out all of Mrs. Chadwick's snarky comments and Becca's shenanigans, there was hardly any tea party left at all. Plus, since Becca kept calling Emma "Waldo" and "Porky" under her breath, she made Emma so miserable that in the final cut Emma looks like she's at a funeral instead of a festive holiday party. It was too late to film it over again, though, Mr. Goldberg said, so they had to go with it. Cassidy says it's not that noticeable, but I suspect she just doesn't want to hurt Emma's feelings.

"I'll meet you downstairs," my mother says.

After she leaves I open my top dresser drawer, take out something I put there last night, and slip it into my pocket. I look at myself in the mirror and smile. Miss Queen Bee Becca is in for a surprise this morning.

"Ta-da!" cries my father from the foot of the stairs. "My beautiful girls!"

*Heather Vogel Frederick*

My mother twirls around the front hall, showing off her outfit. Sugar and Spice do their best to twirl too, running in circles chasing their tails and barking in excitement. My mom and dad both laugh. It's good to see my parents happy. They've been looking so serious lately.

My father sweeps his arm toward the front door. "Ladies," he announces in a fake British accent, "your chariot awaits."

Our "chariot" turns out to be the farm truck. While I'm waiting for my brothers to pile into the narrow backseat, I look up at the dawn sky again. There's a Leonid meteor shower predicted for next week, and my father has promised to get up with me to watch it. He likes astronomy too. When it's my turn to climb up into the cab, I settle in between my parents in the front seat. My father turns on the heater.

"Winter is just around the corner," he says cheerfully, and starts to sing "Over the river and through the woods..."

We all join in. I gaze at Half Moon Farm as he backs out of the driveway. I forgot to turn the light off in my bedroom, and its warm glow lights up my window like a beacon, making our house look like something you'd see on a postcard. Sometimes I love our home so much it almost hurts. If I never had to leave it again I'd be perfectly happy. It's the place I feel safest and most content in all the world—especially now that our family is together again.

It's only a short drive to the Sloanes', and we barely finish the song before we're pulling up in front of their house. There are a lot of cars parked on both sides of the street, and the Channel 5 van is already in the driveway. My heart starts thumping wildly in my chest, like a caged animal trying to escape. *This is really happening. I'm going to be on* Hello Boston!

"Give me a shout when you're done, and I'll come get you," my dad calls to us as my mom and I climb out of the truck. He and the twins are heading home to watch the show. My mother said absolutely no way was she going to risk having the boys underfoot during a live TV taping. "A disaster waiting to happen," she called it. We wave to them and they drive off.

The Sloanes' front door flies open and Emma and Cassidy tumble out onto the front porch. "What took you so long?" Emma demands. "We're starting in half an hour."

"My fault, girls," says my mom. "I couldn't pry the twins out of bed."

The two of us follow them inside and hang up our coats. My mom heads for the kitchen while Emma and Cassidy and I linger in the hall, inspecting each other. Cassidy is fairly presentable for once, in black velvet pants like my mom's and a black sort of tunic sweater with a bright pattern on it that looks like maybe it's from Sweden or Norway or someplace. Her face is clean and she's even brushed her short red hair, but she's tucked it back behind her ears, which her mom hates and will try and fix the minute she spots it. Emma said she was never going to wear her snowman sweater again, not after what Becca Chadwick said about it, so today she's wearing a frilly lavender shirt and a gray skirt. Her socks have slipped down, revealing bruises on her knees and Band-Aids on both of her shins. Emma started taking figure-skating lessons a few weeks ago. She's not very good yet.

"Did you bring it?" whispers Cassidy.

I nod, and Cassidy and Emma start to giggle. Of course that has to be right when Mrs. Chadwick walks in. She sees us and frowns.

"What are you girls up to?" she demands.

"Nothing," we chorus.

"Where's Becca?"

Cassidy points upstairs. "In Courtney's room with Megan. My sister's doing their makeup."

Emma's smile fades. It's kind of awkward now that Megan is friends again with Becca Chadwick. It's not like she ignores us—she doesn't. She's still friends with us, too. But it's pretty uncomfortable sometimes, especially in the cafeteria at lunch. Megan never quite looks like she knows where to sit. Sometimes she sits with us, and sometimes she sits with the Fab Three. Emma and Cassidy and I can't bring ourselves to call them the Fab Four again the way we used to, though. We're too afraid we'll jinx things if we do. We keep hoping Megan will wake up and realize who her real friends are.

Just as Mrs. Chadwick starts up the stairs, Megan and Becca appear at the top. Megan is wearing a new red silk dress she sewed herself. The color goes perfectly with her ivory skin and shiny dark hair.

"Hey, Megs," I call up to her. "You look nice."

"Thanks," she says, flashing me a smile. "So do you. I was hoping you'd wear that dress again."

"Stop dillydallying, girls!" booms Mrs. Chadwick. "Mrs. Sloane wants to talk to us all. We'll be starting soon."

The two of them clatter downstairs and we follow Mrs. Chadwick to the kitchen. She's wearing an emerald green outfit made of some stiff embroidered fabric that makes her look kind of like a sofa. Not that I'd ever tell her that. My mom lectured me about being respectful of my elders. No more jokes about Mrs. Chadwick's size, especially now that she's taking yoga and trying to turn over a new leaf, she says. We're supposed to be supportive of her efforts.

My stomach does a flip-flop as we near the kitchen. This is worse than the stage fright I had last year right before *Beauty and the Beast*. It's not like I even have to say anything—we rehearsed last night and mostly Mrs. Sloane will do all the talking with the show's host. We're just supposed to sit there politely sipping tea and smiling and looking excited and happy so people will want to watch our *Cooking with Clementine* episode when it's broadcast later today. Still, I'm really jittery. My hand slips into my pocket again, and it occurs to me that I might be feeling nervous because of what's in there.

I grab Cassidy and Emma and hold them back for a moment just outside the kitchen door. "Maybe this isn't such a good idea," I whisper.

"Yeah," Emma whispers back. "I'm kind of anxious about it too."

Cassidy looks at us in disgust. "You two are such babies!" She holds out her hand. "Gimme it."

I look over at Emma. She shrugs. Reluctantly, I pass the contents of my pocket to Cassidy.

She grins. "Trust me, it's gonna be awesome."

*Heather Vogel Frederick*

The Sloanes' kitchen is crammed with people. My stomach does another flip-flop when I spot Darcy lounging against the refrigerator. Beside him, Stewart Chadwick is standing on one leg like a crane, gawking at the trays of food that the staff of *Cooking with Clementine* has prepared. Some of it is for our *Hello Boston!* taping and some of it is for the camera crew and the dads and everybody else who's come over to watch.

Cassidy's house is always in an uproar these days. There are cables that we're always tripping over running through most of the rooms and hallways, plus floodlights and camera equipment everywhere. Poor Cassidy took a shower the other day and came out of the bathroom with nothing but her towel wrapped around her to find she'd accidentally walked into the middle of a shot! The camera crew thought it was a riot, but she was mad as heck. She told them if they tried to put it on a blooper reel, she'd sue.

You never quite know which season it is at the Sloanes', either. Last month, the same week we filmed our holiday tea party, they also filmed Mother's Day brunch, and Cassidy's house went from winter to spring in a matter of days.

There is one benefit to having your mom in charge of a cooking show, though, Cassidy says, and that's the food. She never buys lunch in the cafeteria at school anymore, and there's always tons of good stuff around when Emma and Megan and I come over to hang out.

I look around for Cassidy's dog, Murphy, but there's no sign of him. I figure he must have been banished to the garage or something. He's kind of excitable, and he'd be going crazy right now trying to keep an eye on everything and everybody if he were in the house. Murphy is very protective of Cassidy and Courtney and their mom. Mrs. Sloane says she's planning an episode just for him, to teach viewers how to bake their own dog biscuits, because he's the one the show has been the hardest on.

"Hey, Emma. Hey, Jess."

It's Stewart. He's helped himself to a homemade donut and hot cider.

"Hey, Stewart," Emma replies, politely ignoring his powdered sugar mustache.

He pushes his glasses up nervously. "So you're going to be on *Hello Boston!*?"

We nod.

"Cool."

There's an awkward pause, then Becca and Megan appear.

"Stewart, wipe that thing off!" snaps Becca, pointing to his upper lip. "You look like an idiot. Can't you do anything without embarrassing me?"

Her brother's face turns the same shade as Megan's dress. Emma hands Stewart a napkin, glaring at Becca.

"What's gotten into you?" Becca taunts her. "Lose Waldo again?"

"Who's Waldo?" asks Stewart, looking around.

Megan tugs on Becca's sleeve. "C'mon, Becca, lay off," she says in a low voice.

*Heather Vogel Frederick*

Cassidy catches my eye and pats her pocket. I nod, suddenly glad we're going to go through with our plan.

"Let's go over things one more time," announces Mrs. Sloane, clapping her hands to get everyone's attention. As always, she looks gorgeous. She's wearing a mid-calf–length purple wool skirt, a black turtleneck, and a matching purple shawl draped artfully around her shoulders. Like my mom, she's got her hair swept up. Out of the corner of my eye I see Megan studying her. She's probably wishing she had her sketchbook right now. Mrs. Sloane is her fashion idol.

"We'll be filming in the living room in just a few minutes," Mrs. Sloane continues. "Those of you who are here to watch us are welcome to do so but from the hallway only, please. We need to keep the room clear for the Channel 5 folks." She smiles at her friend Mr. Kinkaid, who's standing with the dads, and he smiles back. She checks her watch, then gestures toward the countertop where the food is waiting. "We'll be taking our places in just a few minutes, but until then, help yourselves!"

I glance over at Darcy. He winks at me and my heart gives a happy flutter. I've known Emma's big brother forever, but about a year ago it was like I noticed him for the first time. I always thought he was really nice, but I never realized how cute he was too. He's got the warmest brown eyes, just like Emma's, and he's always laughing and joking around. Plus he's thoughtful and polite and smart too. Well, most of the time. Except when he's doing dumb gross boy stuff. Emma thinks it's hilarious that I've gotten all tongue-tied around him. "It's just Darcy," she always says, and I know it's true but I can't help it. She doesn't bug me too much, though, just like I never tease her about Zach Norton. We keep each other's secrets. That's what best friends are for.

Out of the blue I realize that I'm thinking about math, of all things. *The shortest distance between two points is a straight line.* It occurs to me that this is probably true for people, too. I take a deep breath and start to walk across the kitchen toward Darcy. Just as I do, Becca Chadwick brushes past and beats me to him.

"Hi, Darcy," she coos, batting her eyelashes.

"Oh, hey, Becca," he says politely, then glances over at me. "Hey, Jess."

"Hey," I reply.

Becca ignores me, of course. "How's high school?" she asks him in that fake voice she uses when boys are around.

"Great!" Darcy replies.

I just stand there feeling stupid as the two of them start talking. All of a sudden my dress seems babyish and I wish that I'd done something different with my hair, rather than just pull it back into its usual braid. In her plaid taffeta skirt and black V-neck sweater, Becca looks perfect, of course. The Fab Three always look perfect. Maybe if I spent ninety-seven hours a day trying on makeup and looking at fashion magazines I'd look perfect too.

I back away slowly, right into Carson Dawson, the host of *Hello Boston!*

"Whoa there, little lady," he says, "better check your rearview mirror when you're driving!" He chuckles at his little joke—Carson

*Heather Vogel Frederick*

Dawson is known for chuckling at his own little jokes—and I notice that he's a lot shorter than he looks on TV. Not much taller than me, in fact. He's older, too. Up close like this I can see the wrinkles under his tan. I also notice that he has an abundance of teeth. Very white teeth. He's baring them at me in his trademark smile.

"Pardon me," I manage to squeak.

He chuckles again and trots off toward the living room.

"Girls!" says Cassidy's mother. "We need you on the set. Five minutes until liftoff."

I follow her down the hall, my heart thumping again. Part of me hopes Darcy isn't going to watch us filming, and the other part of me hopes he does. We pick our way carefully over the camera cables to where the couch and chairs are grouped around the coffee table. At the far end is one of the three-tiered tea trays we used when we filmed the tea party. It's piled with the same goodies, too—tiny little cucumber sandwiches with the crusts cut off, mini cupcakes, scones with Devonshire cream and Half Moon Farm raspberry jam, crackers spread with goat cheese, little tarts filled with lemon mousse, truffles, and homemade cream puffs with chocolate sauce. My stomach rumbles. I was feeling too anxious to eat breakfast earlier, but now despite my jangling nerves I'm actually hungry.

Mrs. Chadwick is already seated on the sofa next to Carson Dawson. She must have gotten into the cream puffs or the truffles because there's a smear of chocolate on one side of her mouth. An assistant spots it, and hands her a tissue.

"Becca will sit here next to me," Mrs. Chadwick announces, as if this were her party and she were the hostess.

Mrs. Sloane's smile looks a little strained. "Actually, Calliope, I'm going to have to ask you to move over here to this armchair." She pats it encouragingly. "I'll need to sit next to Mr. Dawson as he'll be directing most of his questions at me."

Mrs. Chadwick looks displeased to hear this. She's used to being the boss. She's sort of like the queen bee of Concord. I guess that's where Becca gets it. She heaves herself reluctantly off the sofa and into the designated armchair.

"Two minutes!" calls one of the Channel 5 camera crew. The dads and brothers crowd around the doorway, jostling for a good view. Mr. Kinkaid blows Cassidy's mom a kiss, then gives Cassidy a thumbs-up. She scowls at him.

As we all take our assigned seats, Courtney comes in with a silver tray. On it is a large silver teapot and eleven teacups. She sets it down in the middle of the coffee table and places a teacup in front of each of us. Cassidy sits up straight, on full alert.

Beside me, Emma's knee starts jouncing up and down and she flicks me a nervous glance. Cassidy, on the other hand, isn't the least bit nervous. Her face is alight with excitement. There's nothing Cassidy likes better than a good prank. I have no idea how she's going to pull this one off, though. Not with a room full of people watching our every move.

"Ninety seconds!" calls the cameraman.

*Heather Vogel Frederick*

My palms are sweaty. I'm smiling my fake smile so hard the muscles in my cheeks are twitching. I don't dare look at Darcy.

Beside me, I see Cassidy slip the garage door opener out from behind one of the couch pillows and drop her arm casually over the back of the sofa. She aims it at the window and pushes the button. Outside, there's a rumbling sound as the garage door starts to go up. Two seconds later Murphy hurtles through the front door, barking wildly at all the strangers in his house.

"What is that dog doing in here!" cries Carson Dawson. "Get him off the set!"

"Murphy, you naughty boy, how did you get out?" scolds Mrs. Sloane. "Courtney, grab him and put him back in the garage—quick!"

Courtney springs into action. Darcy and Stewart Chadwick are right behind her. Stewart trips over one of the cables and goes sprawling, startling Murphy, who ducks under the coffee table. In their haste to grab him, Courtney and Darcy collide, and they go sprawling too. In all the confusion I see Cassidy remove the something from her pocket that I gave her earlier. Quick as lightning, she pours a few drops from it into Becca's teacup. Then just as quickly she puts it back into her pocket. She looks over at me and Emma and grins.

I lean over and peek into Becca's teacup. There's nothing to see—the few drops Cassidy added are colorless. We left the blue food coloring out this time. Suddenly it strikes me how funny it would be if there really *were* such a thing as invisibility potion, and Becca Chadwick vanished—*poof!*—right in the middle of the *Hello Boston!*

interview. I start to giggle. So do Emma and Cassidy. Megan gives us a funny look.

Fortunately, everyone else is laughing at Murphy—everyone except Mr. Dawson, who is still looking annoyed—so no one notices us.

"Ten seconds!" cries his assistant, as the Sloanes' dog is finally corralled and whisked back to exile in the garage.

The lights on the cameras go from red to green, and the expression on Carson Dawson's face goes from irritation to toothsome enthusiasm.

"And *action!*" says the Channel 5 cameraman.

"Helloooooooo, Boston!" calls Carson Dawson, launching into the show's trademark opening cry. "And greetings from the set of *Cooking with Clementine*. I'm here live this morning with the lovely Clementine Sloane in her lovely home in Concord, Massachusetts, where today's upcoming episode was filmed. Isn't that right, Clementine?"

"That's right, Carson," Mrs. Sloane responds, right on cue. "We have something special for our viewers later this morning."

"What's that, Clementine?"

"It's a mother-daughter holiday tea, Carson. We've made all sorts of goodies"—she waves her manicured hand gracefully toward the tiered tray, and the camera zooms in on the food—"and we'll show you how you can create an elegant tea party of your own, from the homemade invitations to the homemade treats."

"Sounds like good old-fashioned homemade fun!" gushes Carson Dawson, with a chuckle. "Be sure and stay tuned."

*Heather Vogel Frederick*

Mrs. Sloane is casually pouring out the tea as she talks, but before she can serve it like we rehearsed, Carson Dawson reaches out and grabs a teacup. And not just any teacup. He grabs Becca Chadwick's teacup.

Beside me, Emma sucks in her breath. Cassidy groans quietly. Her mother gives her a sharp look.

"One lump or two?" she asks, holding the sugar tongs poised above the bowl.

"Two," Carson Dawson replies.

Two lumps won't even begin to counteract the garlic-laced invisibility potion. My heart starts pounding again, and it's not just my palms that are sweating now.

"I'd like to introduce some of the guests you'll be seeing later this morning at our tea party," Mrs. Sloane continues, naming each of us by turn as she dispenses sugar and milk into our cups. Becca gives a closed-lip smile, hiding her braces from the camera. Emma looks like she's going to cry, and even Cassidy's normally cocky grin is a little uncertain.

"I have to tell you, I'm hearing good things about *Cooking with Clementine*," says Carson Dawson. "Word is that yours is the hottest new show on the Cooking Channel."

Mrs. Sloane smiles modestly. "Well, Carson, it might be premature to call it that since only a handful of episodes have aired. And I'd hardly call it *my* show—I have a lot of help from my colleagues here. Phoebe Hawthorne, our town librarian, is in charge of research, and Lily Wong consults on ingredients."

Megan's mother pipes up, "I'd like to add that it's entirely possible to create a healthy tea party."

"Is that right?" murmurs Mr. Dawson, eyeing the goodies on the tea tray greedily. He chooses a lemon tart from the middle tier, and in my mind I start reviewing everything I know about chemistry, desperately hoping that citric acid will cancel out garlic. Maybe the lemons will save us.

"All you need to do is select fresh, organic ingredients, which as you know *Cooking with Clementine* is devoted to using."

"Is that right?" the host repeats, clearly more interested in his lemon tart than in Mrs. Wong. He takes a bite. "Mmmmm," he says, raising his cup.

Emma reaches over and clutches my hand. I squeeze back, hard.

Carson Dawson pauses. Hope soars inside me. Maybe he's not going to drink it after all.

No such luck.

"Bottoms up!" he says, winking at the camera. "Or since this is a proper tea party, perhaps I should say, 'Tally ho'?" He chuckles at his little joke, then puts the cup to his lips and takes a deep sip. So does everyone else except me and Emma and Cassidy. We're too busy holding our breath.

Carson Dawson sets his teacup down with a clatter. He presses his lips together tightly, and his cheeks bulge out like he's trying to suppress an explosion. His face turns bright purple with the effort. His eyes start to water. And then all of a sudden he leans forward and

*Heather Vogel Frederick*

coughs violently, spewing tea across the table and all over the front of Mrs. Chadwick's green dress.

"Well, I never!" sputters Mrs. Chadwick.

"Oh, my," says Mrs. Sloane weakly.

"Cut!" cries the Channel 5 cameraman.

For a long moment, no one says a word. Not even Carson Dawson.

He can't. Nestled in the cream puffs, grinning to themselves, are a gleaming set of very abundant, perfectly white teeth.

# WINTER

*"Marilla, isn't it nice to think that tomorrow is a new day with no mistakes in it yet?"*

—Anne of Green Gables

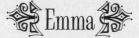 Emma

*"Kindred spirits are not so scarce as I used to think. It's splendid to find out there are so many of them in the world."*
—*Anne of Green Gables*

"Come on, Yo-Yo," I say, my words forming little puffs in the frosty air. I untie his leash from the bicycle rack outside the market on Main Street. "Time to head home."

Yo-Yo has other ideas, however. He bounds off in the opposite direction, yanking me along behind him. The light on the corner changes and he galumphs after a group of people crossing the street. I have no choice but to follow. Finally, I manage to wrestle him to a stop in front of the Concord Toy Shop.

"No, Yo-Yo!" I tell him firmly. "Sit!"

He sits down on the snow-covered sidewalk and looks up at me, tongue lolling out the side of his mouth, giving me his best doggie smile. I sigh and smile back. It's impossible to get mad at Yo-Yo. I am a pushover and he knows it.

I adjust my scarf and pull my hat more firmly down over my ears. The temperature's been dropping all day, and they're predicting snow later tonight. I hope we get a blizzard—I'm having a sleepover party, and I can't think of anything better than all of us getting snowed in together. Not that we'd miss any school, unfortunately. Tonight is New Year's Eve, so tomorrow's a holiday anyway. But it would still be fun.

The dog at the end of the leash isn't mine. He belongs to the Chadwicks. Besides writing apology letters to Carson Dawson, our other punishment for pulling the invisibility potion prank was that we had to pay for dry-cleaning Mrs. Chadwick's dress, plus do any other favors of her choosing. For me and Jess, that meant dog-sitting over the holidays. Becca's grandparents are in town, and they don't like dogs.

I don't know how anyone could not like Yo-Yo. He is all dog and not a speck of Chadwick. He's not quite as cute as Sugar and Spice, but he's cute all the same, and really sweet-tempered. He's something called a Labradoodle, which is part Labrador Retriever and part Poodle. His coat is a soft brown, like maple sugar, and curly all over. He looks sort of like a bath mat. A very friendly bath mat with big chocolate brown eyes.

Jess had him last week, and I've been taking care of him this week while she's up in New Hampshire at her aunt and uncle's for her birthday. I think Yo-Yo likes Half Moon Farm better than our house— there are a lot more interesting things to smell at Jess's house, what with all the chickens and goats—but Half Moon Farm doesn't have Melville. And Yo-Yo is enchanted with Melville.

*Heather Vogel Frederick*

"Come on," I tell him again, tugging on his leash. "Let's go see the kitty!"

Yo-Yo's ears perk up. He knows the word "kitty." He wags his tail. He gives me his most charming smile. But he doesn't move.

"Yo-Yo!" I protest. It's been like this all week. Exasperated, I huddle closer to the toy store, out of the wind. It's still decorated for Christmas, and there are dolls and puppets and toy trains and stuffed animals and all sorts of fun stuff on display. When I was little, I used to spend hours at this store. I press my nose against the window for a moment, remembering how Megan and I would save up for weeks and pool our allowances to buy a new Barbie. That was before her dad's invention, of course. After that, she could have any Barbie she wanted. It was never as much fun as the anticipation of saving up, though.

All of a sudden Yo-Yo starts barking like crazy, and I turn around to see Stewart Chadwick coming down the sidewalk. His face lights up when he spots us.

"Hey, Emma! Hey, boy!"

"Wait, Yo-Yo!" I cry, but it's too late. Yo-Yo lunges toward Stewart and pulls me off my feet. I go flying and do a face-plant in the snowbank on the curb. A moment later I feel a tug on the back of my jacket as Stewart hoists me up.

"Sorry about that," he says, looking flustered. "I shouldn't have called him."

*Stewart the dork strikes again*, I think to myself, but aloud I just tell him, "It's okay." I brush myself off and pick up the grocery bag I'd been carrying. My dad sent me downtown for whipping cream. He's making a fancy dessert for my sleepover party, and he forgot to pick it up when he went shopping earlier.

Stewart squats down beside Yo-Yo and starts to pat him. His hockey skates are slung over his shoulder, and I'm guessing he's been at the rink with Cassidy. Her punishment was that she had to give Stewart private hockey lessons.

Stewart isn't that horrible, for a Chadwick—he's always been pretty nice to me at our newspaper staff meetings—but he's an unbelievable klutz on skates. Even worse than me, and I have the bruises to prove it. Every year Stewart tries out for the school hockey team, and every year he gets cut. He ends up on the town rec league, which pretty much takes anybody with a pulse. But Mrs. Chadwick is convinced there's a pro hockey star just waiting to burst from Stewart's gangly frame, and after our *Hello Boston!* stunt, whatever Mrs. Chadwick wanted, Mrs. Chadwick got. Including private hockey lessons.

"I'll bet you miss him, huh?" I say sympathetically. I can tell Stewart loves Yo-Yo.

"Yeah," he replies, standing up. "He's a really good dog. Thanks for taking care of him. Usually my mom just puts him in a kennel when Grandma and Grandpa are here, but he's probably having a lot more fun with you and Jess."

"Probably."

We stand there awkwardly for a minute. Stewart wears glasses, just like me, and they're kind of fogged up. He takes them off and

*Heather Vogel Frederick*

swipes at them with his mitten. I've never noticed his eyes before. They're gray as snow-clouds. He flicks them nervously from me to the toy store window. "I used to love that store when I was a kid," he says, sounding kind of sheepish.

"Me too," I admit. "I think I gave them all my allowance for about five years."

Stewart's laugh turns into a squeak at the end as his voice cracks. Darcy's has been doing the same thing lately. My dad has warned me not to tease him about it. "We men are sensitive about these things," he tells me. So I pretend not to notice with Stewart.

He leans over and pats Yo-Yo again. "So, are you heading home?"

"Uh-huh."

"Me too," he says. The Chadwicks' house is just past the center of town, not too far from ours. "How about if I walk Yo-Yo for you? He's kind of a handful."

"No kidding," I reply, handing him the leash.

We cross back over Main Street. We're quiet all the way to Monument Square, just looking in the shop windows and listening to the crunch of our boots on the snow-covered sidewalk. We pass the Colonial Inn and a row of stately old houses. In keeping with our town's historic tradition, everybody keeps their holiday decorations spare and simple, the way it might have been back in the olden days. No strings of multicolored lights, no Santas on the rooftops or electric reindeer on the front lawns, just a wreath on each front door and the glow of a single electric candle in each of the windows facing the street.

It's almost dark now, and most of the candles are lit already for the New Year's Eve parties that will soon be starting. Everything looks old-fashioned and pretty. I love Concord this time of year.

As we pass the Chadwicks' house the front door flies open and Becca appears. She puts her hands on her hips.

"Stewart! Where have you been? Mom's worried. She thought maybe you got squashed by a truck or something."

Stewart gives another nervous chuckle-squawk. "Uh, no, I'm fine," he says. "I ran into Yo-Yo downtown, and I was just giving Emma a hand."

"What's the matter, can't Emma handle him on her own? Maybe her invisible friend Waldo can help."

The tips of Stewart's ears turn bright red, though whether from embarrassment or anger or just the cold wind I can't tell. "Shut up, Becca," he tells her, and she flounces back inside and slams the door. "Sorry about that," he mutters to me. "My sister is, well, she's—"

"I know," I reply, taking Yo-Yo's leash from him. "Don't worry about it."

The only good thing that came of the *Hello Boston!* disaster is the fact that Becca's not in our book club anymore. Her mother pulled her out instantly, declaring us all to be hooligans and a bad influence. Cassidy says the invisibility potion worked after all because it made Becca disappear. She only says this to Jess and me, of course. Our mothers would go ballistic if they heard her say something like that. It took them weeks to cool down as it was.

*Heather Vogel Frederick*

After things backfired that morning, Carson Dawson stormed out, threatening to sue. It didn't take everybody else long to figure out that we were behind it—Cassidy couldn't stop snickering, for one thing, which was a dead giveaway, plus her mother spotted the garage door remote and quickly put two and two together—and when the truth came out, our mothers were so furious I thought they were going to end the book club permanently right then and there. Mrs. Chadwick left in a huff with Becca and Mr. Chadwick and Stewart and a whole lot of stinging words about our hideous behavior.

Cassidy didn't help matters by bringing up *Anne of Green Gables*.

"Can't you just think of it as kind of like the time Anne served liniment cake to the minister's wife?" she'd argued. "Only we used garlic instead of liniment."

"Cassidy Ann! How *dare* you compare what you just did to a scene in a book!" Mrs. Sloane had exploded. "That was fiction. This is real life. There's a big difference!"

"And besides," added my mother severely, "what Anne Shirley did was unintentional. It was an accident, and therefore excusable. What you three did was deliberate."

"That's right," said Mrs. Delaney. "There's simply no excuse for what you girls did to poor Mr. Dawson."

Behind us there was a muffled snort. We'd all turned around to see my brother and my dad and Mr. Wong struggling not to laugh.

"Don't you start!" warned my mother. "This is not a laughing matter. Nicholas, I'm expecting you to back me up on this one."

My dad had nodded, pressing his lips together tightly. He couldn't stop his eyes from smiling, though. So were Mr. Wong's and Darcy's and even Stanley Kinkaid's.

"You have to admit it was kind of funny," said my dad. "The teeth and everything, I mean."

That did it. Darcy laughed so hard he went weak in the knees and slid to the floor. The dads quickly joined in. Murphy heard them from his exile out in the garage and started to howl.

"Out!" Mrs. Sloane had cried, furious. "All of you! Out of my sight!" She shooed them from the room and shut the door firmly behind her. Her face was flushed with anger.

"Mom," Cassidy had said after a moment, "the thing is, the tea wasn't meant for Mr. Dawson."

"Oh, really?" her mother replied icily. "And that's supposed to make it all right?"

Cassidy dropped her gaze.

"Who exactly did you think was going to drink your wonderful concoction?"

Jess and I looked at each other. Megan and her mother were sitting quietly on the sofa, watching us. Neither of them had said a word this whole time.

"Uh, Becca," said Cassidy.

Megan got a funny look on her face when she heard this.

"Because she's been so mean to Emma," Jess explained.

*Heather Vogel Frederick*

"Girls!" chided my mother. "That is absolutely no excuse for such a thoughtless prank. Besides, didn't you think about the fact that your actions might have wider repercussions? This was an important morning for Mrs. Sloane and her new show, and now you've gone and ruined it."

We were all shipped home in disgrace. The only thing that saved us was the Internet. Clips of Carson Dawson's flying dentures quickly flashed around the world, and overnight, viewership on *Hello Boston!* shot way up. All the media exposure gave *Cooking with Clementine* a boost in the ratings too, as people tuned in hoping for more comedy disasters. The producers of both shows were delighted with the results, which mollified Carson Dawson enough that he withdrew his threat of a lawsuit. He's been basking in the limelight of international celebrity ever since. My dad says he's taking full advantage of his fifteen minutes of fame, whatever that means.

We weren't completely off the hook, of course. Our moms spent our entire December book club meeting lecturing us again, and on top of that, things are really awkward with Megan. It was clear from all the drawings in her sketchbook that she still likes Becca a lot. Plus, she's been making excuses for Becca's behavior, even when she picks on me. It's like Megan has a blind spot where Becca is concerned. And it seems to have grown bigger since the *Hello Boston!* prank.

Stewart and I are still standing in front of his house.

"Brrrr," I say, because I can't think of anything else to say.

"Uh, I hope you have a happy new year," he replies, jamming his hands in his pockets and hopping from one foot to the other.

"You too," I tell him.

"I guess I'll see you next week. At the newspaper staff meeting, I mean."

"That's right."

"Well, bye then."

"Bye."

"Unless maybe you wouldn't mind if I walk, uh, Yo-Yo, back to your house," he adds, suddenly very interested in the sidewalk. "With you, I mean."

I'm not sure what to say to this. "Well, I guess—I mean, sure, that'd be okay," I manage to stammer.

Stewart looks up and flashes me a smile. It's a nice smile, almost as nice as Zach Norton's, in fact. For some reason, I'm suddenly feeling a little shy.

Stewart takes his skates off his shoulder and props them against the front gate. Then he takes the leash from me and we set off again. He gives me a sidelong glance. "So, did you really have an invisible friend?"

I scowl at him. "Yeah."

"No need to get huffy about it," he says mildly. "I had one too."

"You did?" Somehow, I never would have expected a Chadwick to have an invisible friend.

He nods, grinning. "His name was Brubby. He was always getting me into trouble. You know, breaking things and stuff. The only

*Heather Vogel Frederick*

problem was, he'd always disappear the minute my mother came into the room."

Now it's my turn to laugh. I start to tell him about Waldo, and pretty soon we're trading stories about our invisible friends like we've known each other forever.

"How are the hockey lessons going?" I ask eventually.

"Terribly," Stewart moans.

Actually, I know this already. Cassidy's been tutoring him twice a week all month. She's pretty grouchy about it, not because it's a lost cause—although Stewart is completely hopeless and should probably take up miniature golf, or bowling, according to her—but because Stanley Kinkaid has been going along to help. Stanley doesn't skate himself, but it seems he knows a fair amount about hockey. Or at least he thinks he does. He sits on the sidelines and offers advice, which doesn't endear him to Cassidy. She says he's just butting in, but it makes her mom happy and after *Hello Boston!* Cassidy needed to earn a few brownie points with her mother. More than a few brownie points, actually.

"This afternoon, at the rink?" Stewart says, "Cassidy decided it would be fun for us to scrimmage with some of her teammates against your brother and his friends."

"Uh-oh," I reply. The Concord Comets are the top-ranked team in New England's PeeWee division, and Darcy plays for the Alcott High Avengers.

"Exactly," says Stewart. "Things were going along just fine at first, and I started thinking maybe I was finally getting the hang of it. Then one leg went one way and the other leg went the other way, and I ended up sliding into the net and scoring a goal for the wrong team. Now everybody's calling me the human hockey puck."

I turn my head so he can't see me smile. Poor Stewart! That's almost as bad as Porky the Poet.

He shakes his head sadly. "I'm just not cut out for hockey."

"Then why do you play?"

He shrugs. "It's my mother, mostly. She can be kind of stubborn when she gets an idea in her head. Her dad and her brother played hockey, and she thinks I should too. You know, 'part of a New England boy's childhood'"—Stewart mimics his mother's booming voice—"and all that." He sighs. "The thing is, even though I'm terrible, it's still kind of fun."

"I know what you mean," I tell him. "I'm not very good at figure skating—about as good as you are at hockey—but I like being out on the ice."

"Exactly."

We look at each other and smile.

"Whoa!" says Stewart, as Yo-Yo suddenly breaks into a trot. "What's gotten into him?"

"Melville!" I explain breathlessly, jogging to keep up with the two of them.

"Herman Melville the author?" Stewart looks puzzled.

"No, silly—Melville my cat! Yo-Yo knows we're almost to my house,

*Heather Vogel Frederick*

and he's crazy about him." I'm puffing like a dragon now, but I notice I'm not quite as breathless as I used to be when I tried to run home from the Colonial Inn. Maybe Cassidy was right; maybe the extra exercise is helping a bit.

Stewart finally manages to rein Yo-Yo in, and we slow our pace to a walk again. "So, did you read anything good over vacation?" he asks.

"My dad gave me this book called *The Alpine Path* for Christmas," I tell him. "It's by Lucy Maud Montgomery—you know, the one who wrote *Anne of Green Gables*? We're reading her Anne stories for book club this year. We just started *Anne of Avonlea*. Anyway, it's her memoir about how she became a writer. Oh, and I got *The Hobbit*, too."

Stewart's face lights up. "I love Tolkien! Have you read *The Lord of the Rings* trilogy yet?"

We launch into a discussion of our favorite authors, and it turns out Stewart is nearly as big a bookworm as I am. He's read almost all the same books I have, except for the girl ones like *Little Women*. We both love *Treasure Island* and *The Count of Monte Cristo*, and he even likes poetry, too.

I never in a million years would have guessed that a Chadwick might actually be a kindred spirit. Stewart is completely different from Becca. I'm almost sorry when we finally reach my house and it's time for him to turn around and go home.

The Sloanes pull in just as he's saying good-bye.

"Was that Stewart Chadwick?" says Cassidy, hopping out of her minivan and gaping at him as he lopes off.

I nod.

"What the heck did he want?"

"I think he misses his dog," I tell her, reaching down and giving Yo-Yo a pat.

Mrs. Sloane pokes her head out of the window. "Happy New Year, Emma!"

I'm glad she's not mad at me anymore. I like Cassidy's mother so much, and I felt awful after *Hello Boston!* Especially after my mother pointed out that what we did reflected on her new show. That honestly never occurred to me. I was just thinking about getting even with Becca.

"Happy New Year, Mrs. Sloane," I reply. "You look really nice."

Cassidy's mother is wearing something twinkly under her winter coat. Sequins, probably. She's going to a fancy party in downtown Boston with her friend Stanley Kinkaid. The accounting firm he works for puts on a big shindig every year at the top of the Prudential Center.

"Thanks. You girls have fun now, okay?

We wave as she drives off, then race each other inside.

"There's a towel on the floor for you!" my dad calls from his office, hearing the back door slam behind Cassidy and me. "Wipe off that dog's feet!"

My dad calls Yo-Yo "that dog." He's about as thrilled with Yo-Yo as Melville is. The two of them have been sticking close together these past two weeks, hiding out in Dad's office "away from marauding paws," as my father puts it. He is not a dog person, and Melville definitely isn't a dog cat.

I asked for a puppy for Christmas, but my dad said no. He tried to be funny about it, by slipping a note under my door supposedly written by Melville. There was a silhouette of a dog on the envelope, in the middle of a red circle with a line through it.

"No dogz allowed!" was written inside, in shaky letters. "Resident feline gives two paws down to canines! Love, Melville."

Honestly, sometimes my dad still thinks of me as a little kid. He forgets that I'm almost thirteen. The note was funny and everything, but it didn't exactly cheer me up. I've wanted a puppy forever. Which is why it's nice having Yo-Yo around.

"Only seven more hours to go!" crows Cassidy, waltzing around the kitchen. "Seven more hours till freedom!"

Our punishment officially ends at midnight tonight. I planned our sleepover party to celebrate. Jess and Cassidy and I all agreed we should invite Megan, too, even though she wasn't punished since she wasn't in on the prank, and even though it felt a little awkward asking her.

"I'll get back to you about it," she'd said coolly, when I told her about the party.

I figured that meant she wouldn't come, but then she called right before she and her parents left for San Diego for the holidays and said yes, she'd be there. I'm glad we invited her, but still, I'm feeling a little nervous about the four of us being together.

"So when is everyone else getting here?" asks Cassidy.

"The party officially starts at six," I tell her, dutifully wiping off Yo-Yo's paws. Cassidy got dropped off early so her mother could leave for her date. "We could start making the pizzas, though."

Six is when New Year's Eve officially starts for my parents, too. They're not much for parties. Not fancy ones, anyway. Their New Year's Eve tradition is to hole up in the living room with *Pride and Prejudice*. The six-hour miniseries, not the movie. My father calls it "the annual marathon," and kind of drifts in and out, but my mother stays glued to the TV the whole night. She tries to time it so that the wedding scene at the end happens right at midnight. It's more romantic that way, she says. My mother has a crush on Colin Firth. He's the British actor who plays Mr. Darcy. I like the newer movie version better, but my mother says nobody beats Colin Firth as Mr. Darcy.

"What's that?" Cassidy asks me, pointing to a puffy mound on a platter on the counter.

"That, my dear Miss Sloane, is an ambrosial confection fit for the gods," says my father as he enters the kitchen. He's obviously warming up for Jane Austen mode. "You and your gentle companions are in for a rare treat this evening—I highly doubt there are any other young ladies in these environs who will be enjoying such a heavenly dainty!"

"Yeah, but what is it?" Cassidy repeats, prodding the mound cautiously.

"It's called a Chocolate Raspberry Pavlova," my dad tells her. "It's a guaranteed-to-melt-in-your-mouth chocolate meringue, which we will shortly pile with fruit and whipped cream—thanks to Emma and that dog—and, in our own unique Hawthorne family twist, drizzle with chocolate sauce."

My mouth starts watering just thinking about it. My dad makes Chocolate Raspberry Pavlova only once a year, on New Year's Eve. He takes the pizza ingredients out of the fridge and Cassidy and I wash our hands and start helping him put them together. A little while later there's a knock at the door. It's Megan and her father.

"Where's Lily?" asks my dad.

"Home getting ready," says Mr. Wong. He's wearing a tuxedo. The Wongs are going to a big party tonight too. He leans down and gives Megan a hug and a kiss. "Have fun, sweetie." He turns to the rest of us. "Happy New Year!"

"Happy New Year!" we all chorus back.

My dad has set up a table for us in the family room, and while he and Cassidy finish making the pizzas, Megan and I get out the good china and real silver. We set just four places, since this is a girls-only party. My brother is spending the night at his friend Kyle Anderson's. We get my mother's crystal goblets out too. She said we could use them for our sparkling apple cider toasts at midnight.

Megan and I are kind of quiet at first. We haven't talked since she called to say she'd come to my party. And before that, we hardly spoke for almost a month at school. She made the effort to sit with me and Jess and Cassidy a few times at lunch, but mostly she went around with the Fab Three. *Hello Boston!* still hangs over all of us like a dark cloud.

"Here's your Christmas present," I say, handing her a long slender package wrapped in bright paper. "Sorry it's kind of late."

"That's okay," she replies softly. "Now I feel bad, though, because I just brought you guys silly little souvenirs from my trip."

I shake my head. "Don't feel bad. It's nothing big."

She opens it. Inside the box is a doll.

"It's Stewardess Barbie," I tell her. "She's vintage, from the 1960s. My mom and I found her on eBay. I thought she might be good luck for your *Flashlite* interview."

Megan smiles at me. "She's perfect! Look at this cool uniform she's wearing, and the little suitcase and everything. And her hat has a tiny flight pin on it—sweet!" She gives me a hug. "Thank you, Emma."

I can tell that Megan really likes her gift, and that she's not just being polite. This makes me happy, even though I still feel a little weird about the whole Becca thing. My mom says I should be patient, and just keep trying to put myself in Megan's shoes. "She's in an uncomfortable position," she explained to me. "She likes you both. Try and see things from her point of view, instead of forcing her to choose between the two of you."

I still can't understand why anyone would want to be friends with someone like Becca, though. Maybe it's selfish of me, but underneath it all I guess I just really want to keep Megan for myself. And for Cassidy and Jess too, of course.

Cassidy joins us and she and Megan start talking about San Diego.

*Heather Vogel Frederick*

It turns out Cassidy's been there a whole lot of times before, back when she lived in California, so she and Megan compare notes on Sea World and the San Diego Zoo and someplace called the Hotel del Coronado. I mostly just listen. Nobody brings up Becca Chadwick.

The buzzer goes off and my dad takes the pizzas out of the oven for us, then disappears back into the living room where my mother is waiting with the fancy Thai takeout they ordered for their *Pride and Prejudice* marathon.

There's a knock at the back door.

"Jess is here," I say, and the three of us rush to open it.

"Happy New Year!" we all shout as she walks into the kitchen.

Jess takes one look at us and bursts into tears.

We just stand there, aghast.

"What's the matter?" I ask finally.

"This has been the worst birthday ever!" she wails. "And the worst Christmas. It's the most *tragical* thing that ever happened to me!"

Jess quoting Anne Shirley is not a good sign. Cassidy hands her a tissue and gives me a worried look. I know exactly what she's thinking. What if Mrs. Delaney moved back to New York?

"What happened?" I ask gently.

Words and tears come tumbling out of Jess. "My parents didn't want to worry me, but I've known for a while that something's going on. We finally talked about it this morning. I told them I was thirteen now and they didn't need to treat me like a baby anymore."

"Is it your mom?" asks Cassidy, handing her another tissue.

Jess blows her nose. "No. That's what I thought too. I thought maybe she was unhappy and missed acting and was leaving again. But she said no, that wasn't it."

"So what is it, then?" Megan says.

Jess collapses into a chair at the kitchen table and buries her head in her arms. "We have to sell the farm!"

For a moment I can hardly breathe. "Half Moon Farm?" I say stupidly, like maybe the Delaneys have another farm stashed away someplace that they haven't told us about.

She nods.

"No way!" says Cassidy. "Why would your parents do that?"

Jess shakes her head. "It's some tax thing," she sniffles. "My dad tried to explain it to me but I didn't quite understand. He said something about a tax exemption for a historic property being revoked. Because we're running a business on the property."

"That's dumb," says Cassidy, which is true but not exactly helpful.

"I don't get it," says Megan. "Half Moon Farm's been around since the Revolutionary War, right? Hasn't it always been a farm? And isn't a farm a business?"

Jess wipes her nose on her sleeve. "I don't know," she says miserably. "I guess my parents have been paying taxes, but not as much as they normally would because the farm is on the National Historic Register or something like that. And now they have to come up with a whole bunch of money, which they don't have." Yo-Yo trots over and rests his head on her knee. He looks up at her,

*Heather Vogel Frederick*

his big brown eyes sorrowful, like he can tell she's sad.

Cassidy and Megan and I sit down at the table beside the two of them.

"So what's going to happen?" asks Cassidy cautiously.

Jess shrugs. She reaches out and starts patting Yo-Yo. "All I know is unless my parents raise enough money for the taxes, they'll have to sell. There's already somebody interested in buying it. A developer. He wants to build condos."

I suck in my breath sharply. Condominiums? On Half Moon Farm? The pastures paved over, the woods by the creek all cut down? It hurts even to think about it.

"Isn't there anything they can do?" I ask her.

Jess's face is blotchy from crying. "My mom offered to try and get her acting job back on *HeartBeats*, but my dad said absolutely not. He said he'd rather lose the whole shebang than break up our family again. He said he'd rather live in an apartment."

I try and picture the Delaneys in an apartment, but somehow the dogs and the chickens and the goats—plus Led and Zep, their two big Belgian drafthorses that Mr. Delaney named after Led Zeppelin, his favorite rock band—keep wandering in.

"And I sure don't want her to go," adds Jess in a low voice.

"I could talk to my dad for you," offers Megan. "Maybe he could help out."

Jess gives her a weak smile. "Thanks, Megs. He already talked to my dad, but my dad said no. He can be kind of stubborn that way. My mom says he's too proud, but my dad says it's way too much money, and that he'd rather sell than take anybody's charity. Besides, he says, even if your dad gave us the money, we'd still have to come up with more again next spring. I guess the thing is with taxes, you have to pay them every year."

"That's ridiculous," says Cassidy flatly. "And unfair. Who came up with that rule?"

"I don't know," says Jess, "but there's nothing we can do about it."

We're all silent for a while. Half Moon Farm without the Delaneys? I just can't believe it could really happen.

"You know, that's not necessarily true," I say slowly, as an idea dawns. "Maybe there is something we can do about it."

"You're kidding, right?" says Megan.

I shake my head. "No, I'm serious. Remember at the end of the first Anne book, when she's about to head off to college and Marilla's eyesight starts to fail, and it looks like she'll have to sell Green Gables?"

My friends all nod.

"Remember how Anne gives up her scholarship, and stays home to teach at the Avonlea school instead, so she can help Marilla keep the farm?"

They nod again.

"Well, we can't just sit around and let this happen. We have to do something, just like Anne did."

Jess's forehead crinkles. "But I don't have a scholarship to give up."

I smile at her. "That's not what I mean, silly. I just mean we have to come up with a plan."

*Heather Vogel Frederick*

"What the heck can we do?" says Cassidy.

"Raise money," I reply. I look at Yo-Yo. "We could start a dog-walking service, for instance. Plenty of people need their dogs exercised and looked after, especially this time of year. We could use your barn to run them around in, Jess."

"Hey," says Megan. "That's not a bad idea."

Cassidy nods slowly. "I could give hockey lessons. Lots of people saw me tutoring Stewart at the rink and asked me about teaching their kids."

"And we can pool our babysitting money," I say.

"And I can sew!" Megan offers. "Winter formal is coming up, and then there's Spring Fling and the high school prom. Friends are already asking me to design dresses for them." Friends meaning Becca and Ashley and Jen, most likely, but for once I don't care.

Hope blooms on Jess's tear-streaked face. "You really think it would work?"

Megan and Cassidy and I all nod enthusiastically.

"I'm not sure what my parents would say if they found out," says Jess. "My dad is acting kind of funny about all this. I think he's embarrassed that people will think we're poor. Which we're not—we just don't have a whole lot of extra money for taxes, that's all."

"Nobody has to know," I tell her. "This will be our secret."

Jess leans over and hugs me tightly. "You are the best friend anyone could ever have! And so are you, and you," she adds, hugging Cassidy and Megan too. "And you too, Yo-Yo."

Yo-Yo wags his tail.

"Just you wait," I tell her. "This may have been your worst birthday and Christmas ever, but the New Year is going to be a whole lot better."

Cassidy reaches into the fridge and pulls out the bottle of sparkling apple juice. "Forget waiting until midnight—let's make a toast right now." We follow her into the family room. She hands us each a crystal goblet and fills them with the bubbly amber liquid. "To the new year, and to saving Half Moon Farm," she says, lifting her glass.

We lift our glasses too. "To saving Half Moon Farm!"

*Heather Vogel Frederick*

# CASSIDY

*"His memory was still green in Anne's*
*heart and always would be."*
—Anne of Green Gables

There are worse ways to spend a Saturday night.

I'm at the Garden, sitting inches away from the rink. On the ice are the Boston Bruins and the New York Rangers, my two favorite teams in the whole world. Well, besides my own team, the Concord Comets. That's the good news. The bad news is that Stanley Kinkaid is sitting next to me.

This is my birthday present from Stan the man. I wasn't too thrilled when I found out that it was only going to be the two of us here at the arena. This is the first time I've been alone with him for more than about five minutes. Still, I could hardly pass up seats right behind the team bench at a Bruins game. I hardly said a word as we drove into the city. Stan seemed pretty uncomfortable too. First he tried to make small talk by asking about school, which was stupid, because really, who wants to talk about school? Things got a little better when he started talking about hockey. He's almost as big a fan as I am.

We talked about the Bruins and about how my team's doing. Stan's gone with my mom to nearly all of my games this season, and he tells me that he thinks we can take the regional championships again this year. He says we're playing really well together—which I already know, because we've played the Minutemen twice and beaten them both times. He told me he talked to Coach Danner and gave him a few pointers. I cringed at that. I can only imagine Stan the man bragging to coach, who took Cornell to the Eastern College Athletic Conference championships two years in a row, about how he kept the stats for the Boston University hockey team back when he was a student a hundred years ago. That's kind of like bragging about being the water boy or the manager of the chess team or something. But still, I have to admit Stanley knows hockey.

Not like my dad did, though.

Most people figure I'm an Anaheim Ducks fan, since I'm from California and everything, but Dad was from Boston so I've always been a Bruins fan. He had DVDs of all their best games, and we never got tired of watching the one where Bobby Orr took the team to the Stanley Cup. Dad was just a little kid then, and he was right there in the stands with Grandpa. Every time we watched that DVD we used to look for them, but we never have been able to spot them.

So Stanley Kinkaid can reel off all the stats he wants—and he knows plenty—but he'll never rival my dad for sheer love of the game.

*Heather Vogel Frederick*

I'm not supposed to compare Stan the man to my dad, though. I promised Dr. Weisman I'd try not to anymore.

Even worse than having to spend my winter break skating with Stewart Chadwick was the fact that mom dragged me back to Dr. Weisman. He's the shrink ("family therapist" my mother calls him) she made me go to last year, after we first moved to Concord. He's nice and everything, but it's not like I needed to see him again. There's absolutely nothing wrong with me. Mom said she'd be the judge of that, and she told me that if I wanted to play hockey this season I'd better cooperate. This was right after the whole *Hello Boston!* mess, and she was really, really mad, so I decided maybe it was a good idea to play along.

I explained to Dr. Weisman all about queen bees in general and Becca Chadwick in particular, and how horrible she's been this year, especially to Emma, and he nodded and listened and took lots of notes. When I got to the part about the invisibility potion, his mouth twitched like he was trying not to smile.

"Ah, yes," he said. "I saw something about that on the Internet."

"How were we supposed to know that Mr. Dawson would grab the wrong teacup?" I said indignantly. "Or that his teeth weren't real?"

Dr. Weisman grabbed a tissue at that point and swiveled around in his chair so his back was to me. He blew his nose really loud, but I could see his shoulders shaking and I knew he was laughing. That made me feel a whole lot better, even when he swiveled around again and his face was all serious. Grown-ups always have to do that, to set an example and everything.

"I can understand your logic, Cassidy," he'd said. "But what you're not taking into consideration are the ethics of the situation." He explained that ethics are the principles or rules for how we act in the world.

"Kind of like the golden rule?" I asked him. I've been hearing a lot about the golden rule ever since *Hello Boston!*

"Exactly," he said. "The thing is, it doesn't matter whether or not Becca had it coming"—he held up his hand as I started to interrupt—"and yes, I agree with you that she certainly sounds like she can be a little pill at times. Not that her behavior isn't understandable, perhaps, given what you've told me about her family. It can't be easy growing up with a mother like that. But in the end, none of that matters. What does matter is your behavior, not hers. Your ethics, not hers. The way you conduct yourself, not the way she conducts herself. Ambushing someone like that, whether privately or publicly, is unkind and unethical."

"But Becca does it all the time!" I'd protested.

"Cassidy, we all must learn to act, not react," Dr. Weisman had replied patiently. "Remember, too, that sometimes others learn by our examples. If you consistently treat Becca with courtesy and respect, perhaps you could help her."

I made a face. "I doubt it."

"Well, you might try. It would please your mother."

I heaved a huge sigh.

"There's one other issue your mother would like me to discuss with

*Heather Vogel Frederick*

you," he said, glancing at his notebook. "Stanley Kinkaid."

I stiffened in my seat. Dr. Weisman glanced at me over his glasses. "You don't particularly want to talk about him, I take it," he said gently.

I shook my head.

Dr. Weisman didn't say anything at all. We sat there in silence. I could hear the slow ticking of the clock on the wall behind me. Finally I burst out, "We're fine just the way we are!"

"I see," said Dr. Weisman.

"Why does my mother even like him, anyway? He's short and bald and boring—he's an accountant!—and he doesn't play sports."

"Is it possible you're judging him a bit harshly, Cassidy? Comparing him to, say, your father?"

"Leave my father out of this!" I hollered.

Dr. Weisman took his glasses off and polished them. "Perhaps you could try and see things from your mother's perspective. She obviously finds qualities in Mr. Kinkaid that make up for what you consider to be his shortcomings. His kindness, for instance. His intelligence and warmth. His sense of humor. His thoughtfulness. She made me a list. Perhaps you'd like to take a look at it?"

He shoved it across the desk toward me. I shoved it right back at him. We went around like that for a while, but I wouldn't budge. No way was he going to force me to like Stan the man, although in the end I did promise—but only to keep my mother happy so she'd let me play hockey—that I would try to stop comparing him to my father.

"Just try and see him for the individual he is," said Dr. Weisman. "That's what you'd want, if you were in his shoes. It's the golden rule, pure and simple."

And then came my birthday, and the Bruins tickets.

Beside me, Stanley gets up and says he's going to buy us some hot dogs and drinks. "Don't go anywhere," he tells me.

Go anywhere? Is he kidding? Wild horses couldn't drag me away. I'm, like, three feet from the bench, where the team captain, who is six foot nine and the tallest player in NHL history, not to mention an awesome defenseman, is sitting next to one of the goalies. I could practically reach out and touch their jerseys, if the Plexiglas divider wasn't in the way.

These are really, really good seats. Amazing seats, in fact. Either Stan the man is richer than I thought, or he's got good connections.

Turns out he's got good connections.

The goalie stands up to stretch. He looks over in my direction and his face lights up. He bangs on the Plexiglas and waves. My heart stops for a split second because I think he's waving at me, then I realize his gaze is focused over my left shoulder, so I look over my left shoulder and there's Stanley heading back down the steps with our food. I can tell it's him because the stadium floodlights are bouncing off the top of his shiny bowling-ball head. He's like a human spotlight. The Garden could save millions if they hired him to help light the arena. Stan waves back with his elbow, grinning.

"You know him?" I ask, incredulous, as he takes his seat again.

"Sure," he replies casually, handing me a hotdog. "I know all the players. I do the team's taxes."

I gape at him. *Stan the man is the accountant for the Boston Bruins.* I try not to look impressed by this piece of information but I can't help it. It's pretty cool. I sip my soda thoughtfully as the referee's whistle signals the start of the second period. It's a great game, really close and really fast, and I get so excited a few times I forget who I'm sitting next to. Stanley and I even slap each other a couple of high fives when the Bruins score.

By the end of the second period, Stanley seems more relaxed. He's smiling, even. He hardly ever smiles or laughs around me. He always seems nervous. Courtney says that's because I'm always glaring at him. She says a face like mine would make anybody nervous. Maybe she's right, maybe I've been too hard on him. I think about what Dr. Weisman said, about how I should judge Stanley for who he is, instead of always comparing him to my dad. How I should treat him the way I'd want to be treated. I take another sip of soda and watch him out of the corner of my eye. Maybe he's not so bad after all. Still, though, that doesn't mean I want Stanley Kinkaid butting into my family.

As the teams disappear for their break, the Zamboni ice resurfacers rumble out onto the rink. I love watching the big machines sweep around the rink, leaving those gleaming paths of fresh ice behind them. It makes me itch for my skates—there's nothing like gliding across untouched ice.

Stanley nudges me with his elbow.

"What?"

He points wordlessly at the Jumbotron. I look up at the giant screen above center ice. My mouth falls open. So does the mouth of the image onscreen. My image. The camera has zoomed in on me and Stan the man. He smiles and waves. I snap my mouth shut so I don't look like so much of a dork. My head looks huge, like one of those enormous Macy's Thanksgiving Day parade balloons. Then my picture disappears and is replaced by the words HAPPY BIRTHDAY CASSIDY SLOANE! in flashing orange letters.

"Did you do that?" I ask Stanley, feeling embarrassed but kind of pleased.

"Uh-huh," he replies. He smiles at me, and for the first time I see that my sister is right. Stan the man does have nice eyes. They're blue—Dad's were gray, like mine—and they're crinkly around the edges. Dad's were, too. Mom used to call them his happiness lines. Somehow, I don't think Dr. Weisman's ban on comparisons counts in this case.

"Thanks," I tell him, smiling back.

My mother would be proud of me for remembering my manners for once.

Out on the rink, the Zamboni trucks are finishing their work. A voice comes over the loudspeaker, announcing the puck-shooting contest. They always have puck-shooting contests during the breaks.

"Will Miss Cassidy Ann Sloane please come to center ice!" calls the announcer.

I just about have a heart attack when I hear this.

*Heather Vogel Frederick*

"Cassidy Sloane?" the announcer repeats. "The birthday girl?"

I can't move. I'm glued to the spot. I've been to a lot of pro hockey games before, but I've never gotten to be in the contest.

Stan the man nudges me again. "That would be you," he says, his eyes crinkling again.

I manage to clamber up onto my seat and wave my arms over my head, and an official skates over and unlocks a nearby door in the Plexiglas screen. He beckons to me.

"Give me your camera," says Stanley. "I'll take some pictures for your mom."

I hand it to him and follow the official out onto the ice. I'm wearing sneakers, of course, and they slip a bit. But I manage to make it to the center of the rink without falling, and I take my place on the red line. Some other guy the announcer called down from the stands is there too. The official hands us both a stick and places a puck on the ice in front of each of us.

"Now, folks, we all know how this works!" says the announcer. "Each contestant will have three shots. Whoever gets the most goals wins!"

The other guy is bragging to the official about how he played college hockey, and how he's on the New England Senior Hockey League now, and how his team took first place in last year's Bostonfest Tournament. He doesn't even look at me.

I don't say a word. I'm too busy eyeing the goal. The puck shooting contest is harder than it looks. Most people don't even make it anywhere near the net. I'm going to have to put muscle into my shot to get it all the way to the goal from center ice.

"First up is our birthday girl, Cassidy Sloane!" calls the announcer.

The official gives me a nod. The other contestant gives me a smug grin. "Good luck, kid."

Kid? I'm thirteen as of today! Grown-ups can be such morons. Ignoring them both, I lift my stick, frowning in concentration. The noise of the arena fades. All I hear is my own breathing. All I see is the ice, the puck, and the goal.

I swing my stick down and it connects with the puck, which goes flying. Right past the net, unfortunately, and into the boards.

"Oh, too bad!" says the announcer. "So close, and yet so far. This little lady has a powerhouse swing though, that's for sure. Can our other contestant top that?"

As it turns out, he can't. His first shot isn't even close. It just peters out about halfway between where we're standing and the goal. He doesn't look too happy about it.

"Now for the birthday girl again," says the announcer.

My second shot is lined up perfectly. It slides across the ice directly toward the goal, but loses steam right at the last second and stops just barely outside the edge of the net. They even send an official over to check on it and see if it's close enough.

He shakes his head regretfully. No goal.

The other contestant's second shot gets a little farther down the ice than his first, but it still falls short of the mark.

Heather Vogel Frederick

"Let's mix it up a little here for the final shot," says the announcer. "How about you flip a coin and see who goes first?"

The official produces a quarter. I call heads. It's heads. "You first," I tell the other contestant.

"Age before beauty, eh?" jokes the official.

The other contestant is sweating now, and he looks kind of mad. I guess it's no fun to have to play against a girl, especially when you're a grown-up. His third shot almost makes it in, but it clips the edge of the goal post at the last second and skitters away.

"No goal, but the puck definitely tapped it!" cries the announcer. "Unless Miss Sloane can do better than that, folks, it looks like we may have a winner."

My mother says I'm the most competitive person she knows. I don't know about that, but it's true that I really hate to lose. I take a deep breath and try and refocus myself, then wind up and let it fly. My stick comes down and the puck shoots off like a bullet, and this time it flies straight and true, all the way down the ice and into the net. The crowd lets out a cheer.

"Score!" shouts the announcer, and the Jumbotron overhead starts flashing my name again.

"Nice job, kid," says the official, clapping me on the shoulder. "You play a little hockey, do you?"

"A little," I admit.

"Maybe you should recruit her for your league," he suggests to the other contestant. "This girl can shoot."

The other contestant looks like he wishes the Zamboni would come out and run me over. I don't care, though. I get a prize—an official Bruins game jersey—and he doesn't. I take the shirt back to my seat with me, and show it off to Stanley.

"Very cool," he agrees.

This birthday is turning out better than I thought it would, I have to admit.

The third period is a nail-biter. The score is tied, right up until the last few seconds. I keep a close eye on the Rangers' goalie, not because he's cute—I honestly don't see what the big deal is, but Mom and Courtney always seem to turn up whenever he's being interviewed on ESPN, and Courtney gave me a poster of him for Christmas mostly so she can sneak into my room and look at it—but because he's *good*. He's really on his game tonight, and almost nothing is getting by him. The Rangers have the puck. The Bruins intercept and gain possession. The puck flies across the ice between the two forwards. With just seconds to go one of them passes it to the center, who dekes left around the Ranger defenseman and takes a shot. The goalie lunges. He misses! The puck slides past him into the net. The Bruins score!

I leap to my feet. So does Stanley. We're both screaming. Everybody's screaming. The Garden is going wild! Out on the ice, the players are nearly as excited as the fans. A win like this is a real shot in the arm for everybody, fans and players alike. The Bruins haven't been doing too well these past few years, but they can turn it around. The Red Sox sure did.

When the arena finally starts to quiet down again, I reach for my jacket.

"Where are you going?" asks Stan.

I shrug. "Home, right?" I reply. "Game's over."

"It's not over quite yet," Stanley says.

He hustles me down to the end of the rink, through a passageway under the stands and down a long corridor. A few seconds later we're standing outside a closed door.

"We're going in the *locker room*?" I ask in disbelief.

Stan the man nods, grinning. "Don't worry," he tells me. "They know you're coming. They'll still have their uniforms on."

If only Dad were here to see this! I feel like I'm going to keel over any second from the thrill.

Stan holds the door for me. "Give me that camera again," he whispers as I brush past him, and I hand it over.

"There you are!" says the Bruins' head coach. "We've only got a couple of minutes before the press arrives." He looks at me. "So, I hear you were MVP for the Comets last season. Concord's own Cammi Granato."

I open my mouth to reply but nothing comes out. I'm as mute as Jess used to be. *The Bruins' coach just compared me to the greatest US women's hockey player ever.* I know he's kidding, but still. Cammi Granato!

"My neighbor's son plays for the Minutemen," he continues. "I asked him about you and even he had to admit you were good. Said you wiped the ice with them at the championship game last year."

I still can't speak, but I manage a smile.

"Better watch your step, boys," he teases the team. "She'll be after one of your jobs in a few years."

"She already has a jersey," says Stan, holding up my prize.

Everyone laughs. We line up for a picture. They put me right in front in the middle. Afterward, I get a signed hockey stick and the winning puck. I feel like I'm dreaming.

"So this is your daughter?" I hear the coach ask Stanley.

The top of Stan the man's glossy head turns bright crimson. "Uh, well, actually . . ." he stutters.

"No," I blurt, scowling.

"Tough customer on the ice and off," says the goalie, and everybody laughs again. He winks at Stan. "Just like you said. Good luck, dude."

Just like you said? I whirl around and stare at Stanley, shocked. He's been talking about me behind my back? To the *Bruins*? Oh, I get it now. This whole evening was a setup. It wasn't a birthday treat for me, it was something he cooked up to try and weasel his way into my good graces. And into my family.

Disgusted, I stomp out of the locker room and make my way angrily back to the arena. I charge up the stairs in the stands two at a time. I can hear Stanley behind me, huffing and puffing. I pause at the top only because I don't know the way to the garage.

"Cassidy, I hope you don't think I—"

*Heather Vogel Frederick*

"It doesn't matter what I think, does it?" I spit the words out like shards of ice. "Nobody really cares what I think."

"Look," he says lamely, holding out my camera. "The pictures turned out really well. Here's you making the shot, and this one of you with the team is great." He fumbles with the buttons and accidentally clicks on the only other picture I still have stored on my camera. He squints at it. "Say, is this you and your dad?"

"Don't touch that!" I scream, grabbing it away. How dare he? How dare he ruin my private picture, my private memory?

My mother was dead wrong. Stan the man isn't thoughtful, or intelligent, or kind. He's a stupid jerk.

I stare stonily out the car window all the way home. I don't care what my mother says, and I don't care what Dr. Weisman says. I am never speaking to Stanley Kinkaid again.

Final score? Stanley—0. Cassidy—0.

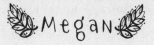# Megan

*"Oh dear, this is such a dreadful predicament. I wouldn't
mind my misfortunes so much if they were romantic . . .
but they are always just simply ridiculous."*
—*Anne of Avonlea*

Emma taps her finger on one of the drawings in the sketchbook on my lap. She's perched on the arm of my chair, looking over my shoulder. "I think you should definitely include this one," she says, pointing to a drawing of an orange-and-yellow–striped halter dress.

"I like that one too," says Jess.

Emma and Jess are helping me sort through my sketches to choose the final lineup for *Flashlite*. My designs are due by March 15, which is just two weeks from now. I'm kind of stressing about it. Cassidy's trying to help too, but since her idea of style is anything that's not actually a garbage bag, she's not much use.

The three of them have been extra nice to me recently. I'm not sure why, because I know it bothers Emma—Jess and Cassidy, too, but especially Emma—that I'm still friends with Becca Chadwick.

The thing is, I really like Becca. Ashley and Jen, too. And not because they're popular, either. Well, maybe just a little. But mostly I'm over that. I know Becca can be snotty and snarky and downright mean—and I tell her so a lot more than I used to, especially when she picks on Emma—but she can also be a lot of fun, plus she and Ashley and Jen are just as crazy about clothes as I am. I love Emma and Cassidy and Jess, but none of them really understands how I feel about fashion. They never notice what I'm wearing, never say anything about my earrings or shoes or makeup, and they'd rather do just about anything else than hang out at the mall. Is it wrong to want to have friends who like the same things I do? Even if that means Becca Chadwick?

"How about this one?" says Jess, pointing to another sketch.

"You mean the workout gear?" I reply.

Cassidy crowds closer for a look. Her brow furrows. "Workout gear? How can anyone work out with those giant sock things on their legs?"

"Those are leg warmers," I tell her.

"Whatever. They're dumb."

"They're making a comeback," I explain. "They were big in the eighties."

Cassidy grunts. I smile at Emma and Jess. The four of us are shoehorned into a small room off the kitchen at Half Moon Farm. The Delaneys call it the "keeping room." It's kind of like a tiny family room or something, and really old New England houses used to have them. Mrs. Delaney says that back in the colonial days, it would be easy to keep a room this size nice and snug in the wintertime, so this was where everyone would gather to keep warm.

We're going to have an Avonlea luncheon here in a little while. Mr. Delaney built us a fire in the fireplace, and we helped him rearrange the armchairs and loveseat facing it. Jess and her mother set up a table in the corner by the window and decorated it the way they think Anne Shirley might have. There's a white tablecloth, and a vase full of holly and evergreen and pine cones and other winter stuff in the middle, since Anne is such a nature freak, and Mrs. Delaney is even letting us use her fancy blue-and-white china.

"It may not be Marilla's rosebud spray tea set, but it will have to do," she told us.

Jess lined the mantle with pretty things, too—teapots and brass candlesticks and figurines—and even Cassidy said it looks good.

I can't believe I ever thought this house was a junk heap. Sure, it's old—Half Moon Farm was built, like, way before the Revolutionary War, sometime in the early 1700s—and it's kind of shabby, with floors that are all slanted and squeaky and a roof that sometimes leaks and ancient drafty windows, but I still like it a whole lot better than my house. Emma says it's because it's alive with history, but Emma is what my mother calls a hopeless romantic.

It will be terrible if the Delaneys have to sell. I can't imagine them living in a modern house like mine, or even in a Victorian like Cassidy's or a cozy little Cape Cod–style house like Emma's. The Delaneys belong here, at Half Moon Farm.

*Heather Vogel Frederick*

"So," says Jess, consulting the piece of paper she's holding in her hand, "counting the halter dress and the workout clothes, that makes an even dozen outfits. Perfect."

I make a face. "I'm not so sure about this one, though," I tell her, pointing to the pleated plaid mini-skirt I paired with a V-neck sweater. "I still think it looks too much like a school uniform." Becca thinks so too, but I don't tell them that.

The door opens and Mrs. Hawthorne pops her head in. "Lunch is ready, girls. Is the table set?"

We nod.

She sweeps in carrying a platter of roast chicken—I try not to think too much about where it came from—and Diana Barry's "Splendid Lettuce Salad" from *Anne of Avonlea*. Mrs. Sloane is right behind her with the baking powder biscuits we helped make earlier, just like the ones Anne made for Marilla and Mrs. Lynde, and there's some of Half Moon Farm's famous raspberry jam to go with them.

The four of us cheer when Mrs. Delaney comes in with tall frosted layer cake. She sets it down on the table with a flourish. "I promise there isn't a speck of liniment in it," she says with a smile.

"What is liniment, anyway?" asks Cassidy.

"It's a kind of medicine," says Mrs. Hawthorne, who knows everything. I think that's one of the job requirements for a librarian.

"Yuck," says Cassidy. "No wonder Anne's cake tasted so horrible."

Nobody cheers for my mother. She was worried there wouldn't be enough healthy food, of course, so she brought a tray of organic vegetables and hummus. I told her that nobody in Avonlea ever even heard of hummus, but she wouldn't budge. Sometimes I wish my mother would just chill out a little.

Jess made place cards for all of us, with little dried flowers glued next to our names, and we each find ours and sit down. Cassidy's mom pours out the raspberry cordial (apple-raspberry juice, actually, which was the closest thing we could find) and Mrs. Hawthorne raises her glass.

"To kindred spirits!" she says.

"Hear, hear!" echoes my mother.

I look around the table at Emma, whose eyes are shining in excitement behind her glasses; and at Jess, who is staring off into space like she does sometimes, which is weird but probably just means she's doing calculus in her head or something; and at Cassidy, whose cheeks are bulging already, which means she probably snuck a biscuit off the plate when her mother wasn't looking. I know Becca thinks book club is, like, totally stupid—although maybe she just says that because her mother won't let her come anymore—but I don't care, I love book club. I love that I can be dorky, and pretend I'm at Green Gables even though I'm a teenager now and too old to pretend stuff anymore and not worry that anyone's going to make fun of me.

Is it wrong of me to want to keep all of my friends, even though they don't get along? I plop some butter and jam onto a hot biscuit and think about it. How come everybody thinks I have to choose either one group or the other? Life is so confusing. Sometimes I wish there was a rule book.

The keeping room door opens again and Mr. Delaney comes in.

*Heather Vogel Frederick*

His arms are full of wood for the fire. I catch a whiff of goat—he must have been out in the barn—which used to gross me out but now it doesn't bother me. Much.

"Sorry for the interruption, ladies," he says, "but I want to make sure you stay warm. It's cold out there this afternoon."

After lunch and our book club discussion we're all going skating on Half Moon Farm's small pond. Make that "The Mirror of the Sky." Jess and Emma told me that they named it in honor of Anne Shirley, which is so Emma and Jess that it's ridiculous, but it's still kind of fun. Definitely not something I'd share with Becca, though.

"Michael, you're welcome to join us," says Mrs. Hawthorne.

"You're an honorary member of the mother-daughter book club, remember?" adds my mother. "Pull up a chair."

Mr. Delaney smiles. "And I am honored indeed," he says with a bow, "but for today I am simply shy Matthew Cuthbert, who will leave you ladies to your elegant luncheon while he feeds a pair of monkeys out in the kitchen."

I can hear Dylan and Ryan out in the hall, giggling. They've been spying on us all day. Nobody suggested invisibility potion this time around, though.

"So," says Mrs. Hawthorne a little later, after we've finished our last bites of cake and are settled around the fire. "We got a bit sidetracked these last couple of months, what with, uh, various things"—there's an uncomfortable pause at this—"but now that we're back together again, let's see where you all are. Has everyone finished *Anne of Avonlea*?"

"I'm done with the whole series," Emma blurts out.

"Sheesh, Emma, way to make us look bad," says Cassidy. "I thought I was doing good just getting through the first book."

"'Doing *well*,' darling, not 'doing good,'" her mother corrects.

"Whatever," mutters Cassidy.

Mrs. Hawthorne asks for a quick show of hands. Cassidy has barely started *Anne of Avonlea*, but says she loves the part where Anne accidentally sells her neighbor's cow. Jess is almost but not quite finished with it, and I'm about halfway through.

"I haven't had much extra time for reading," I say defensively, glad at least that I'm a bit further along than Cassidy, who barely reads anything unless she absolutely has to. Except for the sports page in the newspaper, of course.

My mother nods. "Megan's right. This *Flashlite* project is taking up all of her free time. I'm beginning to wonder if maybe it's a bit much for a seventh grader."

"Mom!"

"I know, I know, you have your heart set on it! But you didn't do so well on that last math test, and your schoolwork really must have top priority."

What is it about moms and grades?

"Why don't we finish up any loose ends from our discussion of *Anne of Green Gables*, then, and at least get started on *Anne of Avonlea*, even though not everyone has finished it," suggests Mrs. Hawthorne.

Heather Vogel Frederick

"Before we do, I brought something to show you all," says my mother, pulling out her laptop. I frown, worried that she'll have found some weird connection between Anne Shirley and recycling or the Amazon rain forest. Fortunately, it's nothing like that.

"Look at this great website," my mother says, and we all cluster around her. A map of Prince Edward Island pops up. I should have known. My mother loves maps. "See? There's Charlottetown." She points at a dot on the screen.

"Where Anne and Gilbert and Josie Pye and everybody went to Queen's College?" asks Jess.

My mother nods. "Exactly."

"Wait a minute, where's Avonlea?" asks Cassidy, peering at the screen.

"Avonlea isn't a real place, honey," her mom explains. "Lucy Maud Montgomery made it up."

"You know," adds Emma, "like Camelot, or Narnia."

Cassidy looks disappointed.

"It's based on Cavendish, though, where Maud spent her childhood," Mrs. Hawthorne consoles her, pointing to a dot on the north shore of the island.

"She didn't make up Green Gables," says my mom, clicking on a photograph of a pretty little green-trimmed house. "It's a real house that belonged to her cousins. She used to stay there a lot. It's a museum now, and look! This is the best part—you can take a virtual tour!"

Now even I'm excited. We check out all the rooms, poring over the pictures.

"The dining room looks a little bit like your keeping room, Jess," I tell her. "See? There's even a fireplace."

"And look at the dishes on the table—it's as if Marilla and Anne just stepped out," adds Mrs. Delaney.

We decide we like Anne's bedroom best of all.

"It's so cozy!" sighs Emma. "Can I have flowered wallpaper in my room someday too, Mom?"

"We'll see," Mrs. Hawthorne replies, smiling at her.

"I'll bet there's a nice view from the window," adds Jess. "With plenty of scope for the imagination, just like Anne always used to say."

"I'll bet you're right, Jess," says my mother. She clicks on the map again and points out how Green Gables is part of a chunk of Prince Edward Island that's now a national park. "The Canadian government did this to protect the landscape that Lucy Maud Montgomery loved so much," she explains. "And to preserve the island's fragile ecosystems."

Somehow, I just knew my mother would find a way to eventually bring things around to the environment.

"It looks beautiful," sighs Mrs. Sloane, looking at the pictures over her shoulder. "I sure would love to go there someday."

"What do you think it is about Lucy Maud Montgomery's books that make readers love them so much?" says Mrs. Delaney, after my mother puts her laptop away. "People have been reading *Anne of Green Gables* now for, what, almost a hundred years?"

"Since 1908," says Mrs. Hawthorne. Like I said, she knows everything. "Which brings us to our handout."

*Heather Vogel Frederick*

1. The *Anne of Green Gables* story came from something Maud jotted down in her idea notebook: "Elderly couple apply to orphan asylum for a boy. By mistake a girl is sent to them."

2. The book was rejected five times, and Maud tossed it in a hatbox and forgot about it. Later, she pulled it out again and read it over. Deciding it wasn't all that bad, she rewrote it and sent it off to a publisher in Boston, who accepted it.

3. *Anne of Green Gables* was first published in 1908. It was an instant success and was reprinted six times in the first five months.

4. The book has been translated into over twenty languages, made into movies, television shows, and a popular musical, and is still a worldwide bestseller one hundred years after its publication.

5. People everywhere loved the book. The Prime Minister of England asked to meet Maud when he was visiting Canada, and even Mark Twain wrote her a fan letter.

"Wow," says Jess. "If Maud hadn't taken the story out of her hatbox, and tried again, the book would never have gotten published."

My mother nods. "That's right, honey. It just shows you how important it is to be persistent. You can't give up."

Emma's hand shoots up. I know she's not showing off or anything, she's just enthusiastic about books, but honestly, sometimes I can see why Becca thinks she's such a goody-goody.

"Yes, Emma?" says her mother.

"I've been thinking about Mrs. Delaney's question, and I think people love the *Anne* books so much because they're about friendship, and love, and growing up, and that's something everybody thinks about. Plus, there's a little bit of Anne in everybody, even in all of us."

"Hey, Emma's right," says Jess, looking around the room. "Cassidy has red hair and freckles—"

"What's wrong with red hair and freckles?" Cassidy sounds belligerent.

"Nothing," says Jess. "I'm just saying you kind of look like Anne Shirley, that's all."

"And she's smart like you, Jess," Emma adds. "Anne's always getting the best grades on her tests and coming in first in everything, or tying with Gilbert Blythe."

"Plus she likes poetry and wants to be a writer like you do, Emma," I tell her.

"And she likes fashionable clothes, just like you!" Emma tosses back, smiling at me.

"Looks like you're right, Emma," says my mother. "There does seem to be a little bit of Anne in everybody."

My cell phone vibrates in my pocket and I sneak it out to see who's calling. It's Becca, of course. I told her that I'd be busy at book club this

*Heather Vogel Frederick*

afternoon, but she must have forgotten. Or maybe she didn't forget. Even though she makes fun of us all the time to Ashley and Jen—she says we read stupid books and who'd want to be in our stupid club anyway—I think secretly she's a little jealous. Emma sees me peeking at my phone and flushes slightly. I slip it back in my pocket. No point upsetting Emma. I'll text Becca later.

"So what were your favorite parts of the first book?" asks Mrs. Hawthorne. "Megan? How about you?"

"I liked when Matthew bought Anne that dress for Christmas. The fabric, I mean. I loved how he got so nervous and tongue-tied at the store, and bought all that other stuff first."

"I liked that too!" says Mrs. Delaney.

"I liked when she lost her temper and called Mrs. Lynde a bunch of names, and that time when Josie Pye dared her to climb the ridgepole and she did, and broke her ankle," says Cassidy. "And I especially liked when the boat got a leak while she was in it pretending to be the Lady of Shalott, and she nearly drowned."

Emma says it's impossible for her to choose, because she has too many favorite parts, and then everybody looks at Jess.

"Remember when Anne and Diana went to Charlottetown, to visit Diana's Aunt Josephine in her fancy house?" says Jess.

We all nod.

"Well, I like when Diana said she thought she was born for city life, and Aunt Josephine asks Anne what she thinks, and Anne says—here, I'll read it to you." She riffles through the pages of her book. "And Anne says, 'It's nice to be eating ice cream at brilliant restaurants at eleven o'clock at night once in a while, but as a regular thing I'd rather be in the east gable at eleven, sound asleep, but kind of knowing even in my sleep that the stars were shining outside and that the wind was blowing in the firs across the brook.'" Jess looks up. The room is quiet, except for the crackle and snap of the fire in the fireplace. "That's the way I feel about being here, at Half Moon Farm."

Her mother looks at her sadly.

There's a knock on the sitting room door and Mr. Delaney pokes his head in. "I hate to interrupt again, but it's nearly two thirty," he says. "The others will be arriving any minute."

"The others" are the rest of our families. They're going to join us for skating and a bonfire. Jess said her dad has been fussing with the pond—I mean "The Mirror of the Sky"—all week, clearing the snow off it with their tractor and hosing it down every night to try and make the ice nice and smooth.

Mrs. Delaney blows him a kiss. "I think we're about wrapped up here, sweetheart," she says. "Girls, why don't you go and get your jackets."

Pretty soon cars start to pull in the driveway—Mr. Hawthorne and Darcy first, then my dad, and then Courtney, who just got her license. Her grandparents gave her their old car for her birthday, so she could take over driving Cassidy to hockey practice now that their mom is so busy. I can't wait until I'm sixteen. I hope I get a car too.

We all walk over to the pond and sit down on the logs that Mr.

Delaney stuck around the bonfire for benches. I pull on my skates and start to lace them up.

"Watch this!" cries Emma, who's the first one out on the ice. She zooms across the pond. Frowning in concentration, she does a tiny little leap.

"Hey, nice bunny hop," says Cassidy, clapping.

"Can you show me how?" asks Courtney.

The two of them twirl off together while Darcy and Cassidy round up hockey sticks and start chasing a puck around, using an old badminton net that Mr. Delaney nailed to some scrap wood for a goal. Mr. and Mrs. Hawthorne skate around sedately, holding hands—well, mittens. Jess and I race past them, trying to see who can go faster.

"What's all that barking in the barn?" I ask her when we pause for a break.

"We have a few dogs boarding with us over the holiday weekend," Jess explains. "There's a beagle named Buddy, and this fat, mean little dachshund named Jelly Roll, and Yo-Yo, of course."

I'd forgotten that Becca's grandparents were in town again. They told Becca they might take us into Boston shopping tomorrow afternoon.

"Hey, boarders are good. More money for our secret fund, right?"

"Yup," says Jess.

We loop around the pond again, trying to skate backward this time. I manage to get my skate tip caught in Jess's blade and we tumble over in a heap. I lie there for a minute, laughing, then sit up and look out over the snowy fields, trying to imagine them covered with condominiums. I sure hope we can help the Delaneys save their farm.

There's a loud bang behind us and we scramble to our feet in time to see the side door of the barn slam open. Jess's brothers scamper out, clutching brooms to use as hockey sticks.

"Close the door, boys!" hollers Mr. Delaney, but it's too late. There's an explosion of squawks and feathers as a handful of chickens make their escape. Right behind them come the dogs in hot pursuit. Buddy the beagle is at the head of the pack, Yo-Yo is chasing Buddy, and the chubby little dachshund is nipping at both their heels. Sugar and Spice are trying to herd the three of them plus the chickens back into the barn, but of course none of the other dogs is paying the least bit of attention. For some reason the chickens all make a beeline for the pond.

"Look! The chickens are skating!" cries Dylan as they slide out onto the ice.

Not exactly. In a panic because of the dogs, the chickens are trying to run, but on the ice their little legs just thrash around like those cartoon characters on TV. Buddy's legs, on the other hand, go out from under him as he dives after them, and he slides across the pond on his belly, yowling. Yo-Yo's scrambling to stay upright, and Jelly Roll, who may be mean but who at least has some sense, stays put on the bank, yapping furiously.

Cassidy comes flying down the ice, herding chickens with her hockey stick. The chickens don't like this idea at all, and scrabble around even harder to get away. Cassidy manages to scoop one up on the blade of her stick, and carrying it gingerly she glides toward us to give it to

*Heather Vogel Frederick*

Jess. Before she can, though, the chicken gives an indignant squawk and hops off—straight into the goal net.

"Score!" cries Darcy, and everybody laughs except the dogs, who start to howl.

"Chicken hockey!" shouts Ryan. He and Dylan slip-slide across the ice clutching their brooms, bent on cornering a plump, blondish hen.

"Leave Dolly Parton alone, boys," warns their mother.

Mr. Delaney skates over and grabs the back of a jacket in each hand. "It's the penalty box for you two," he says firmly, hustling the twins off the ice and back to the log benches by the bonfire. "Get the dogs first," he says to the rest of us. "The chickens can take care of themselves."

With the help of Sugar and Spice, we eventually manage to corral Yo-Yo and Buddy and Jelly Roll. Mrs. Delaney lures the chickens back to the barn with a slice of bread.

"That was exciting," says Mrs. Hawthorne, after the animals are all finally put away.

"Not something you see every day," agrees Mr. Hawthorne, winking at me.

My dad skates over. "Have you seen your mother?"

I shake my head.

"She might be in the kitchen," says Mrs. Delaney. "I think she was planning to make some hot chocolate."

We all skate around for a while longer. Mr. Delaney rounds up a few more brooms for Jess and Emma and me, and Darcy and Cassidy teach us a few hockey moves. It's actually pretty fun. Especially when Courtney and the grown-ups join in.

And then it happens.

"Yoo-hoo!" calls my mother.

We look up from our scrimmage. There's no sign of her.

"Yoo-hoo! Up here!"

I finally spot her. My mother is in the twins' tree house, on the far side of the pond near the barn. She waves cheerfully.

Dylan and Ryan scramble across the snow to go investigate. My dad follows them.

"Hey, no fair!" shouts Ryan. "She pulled up the rope ladder."

"Rapunzel, Rapunzel, let down your long hair! I mean ladder!" jokes my dad.

But my mother isn't joking. She shakes her head. "Not for a while, hon."

My father laughs nervously. "Uh, Lily, it's February. It's cold, and it will be dark before long."

"I know, isn't it great?" my mother calls down to him—to all of us, because we've all trooped over to her by now. "Carson Dawson's dentures gave me the idea."

Carson Dawson's *dentures*? Emma, Jess, Cassidy and I exchange puzzled glances.

"Mom, what are you talking about?" I say.

She taps her watch and smiles. "You'll find out soon."

Five minutes later, trucks start arriving.

News trucks.

"Uh-oh," I mutter.

"What the heck is going on?" says Emma.

"I don't think I want to know."

The twins spot the camera crews and race over, dancing around them as they lug their equipment across the pasture. I pull my hat down and hope nobody puts two and two together and figures out that I'm the daughter of the crazy woman in the tree house.

Fat chance of that, since we're the only Asian Americans at Half Moon Farm today.

"Is that your mom?" asks one of the reporters. I recognize her from the six o'clock news.

"Uh," I reply, stalling for time.

"Can you tell me more about what she's protesting? She sent over a fax that said something about saving historic Half Moon Farm."

"Oh, man," I groan. Only my mother could hatch such a harebrained scheme. Climbing a tree to save Half Moon Farm? It's one thing if you're one of those nutty Hollywood actresses. They're always pulling crazy stunts to protest global warming and stuff. You can do that sort of thing in California. In New England, in February, a person could freeze to death.

A person could also humiliate her family.

An SUV pulls into the driveway. It's the Chadwicks. This is just so not my lucky day.

"We're here to pick up Yo-Yo," booms Becca's mother, rolling down the window. Becca and Stewart roll their windows down too.

Mrs. Chadwick's eyes narrow as she spots the news trucks. "What's going on?" she demands, getting out of her car.

My dad walks over to her and I see the two of them talking. Becca and Stewart get out too. Becca looks over at us and smirks.

"If it isn't Josie Pye," says Jess. "Just what we need."

My cell phone vibrates. I pull it out of my pocket. Becca has sent me a text message: WHAT IS UR MOM DOING?

I text her back: NO CLUE!

Mrs. Chadwick marches over to the base of the tree.

"Come down this instant, Lily!" she bellows to my mother. "You're embarrassing yourself!"

I hunch into my jacket and pull my hat down even farther. Talk about embarrassing—I don't know who's worse, my mother or Calliope Chadwick, the human megaphone.

"Please, you don't need to do this," pleads Jess's mom. "I mean, we appreciate the idea and everything, but honey, it's COLD out here!"

My mother holds up a sleeping bag and a backpack. "I have everything I need right here," she says. "Hot cocoa, too! I'll be fine."

"Nonsense," hollers Mrs. Chadwick again. "You won't be fine. You'll catch your death of cold, and then where will you be?"

"Dead, duh," whispers Cassidy.

Emma and Jess both giggle.

"Shut up," I snap. This is not funny at all.

*Heather Vogel Frederick*

In response to Mrs. Chadwick's question, my mother pulls a set of handcuffs from her backpack and holds them up in the air. We all gasp. The camera crews rush closer for a better shot. The reporters are eating this up too, of course.

"Uh, we admire your passion, but are those really necessary?" calls Mrs. Delaney.

"Please, sweetheart, come down," says my dad. His voice is wobbly, and I can't tell if he's embarrassed or angry or if maybe he's going to cry.

My mother shakes her head. "No," she says firmly. "I'm on a mission here."

There's a loud *click!* and I gape up at her in disbelief.

My phone vibrates again. Another text message from Becca: NO WAY!

But it's true. My mother has handcuffed herself to a branch of the tree. She pulls a piece of paper from her backpack. "Silence, everyone," she commands. As if we're not already quiet enough to hear a pine needle fall in the snow. No one quite knows what to say. It's not every day you see someone handcuff themself to a tree in Concord, Massachusetts.

My mother begins to read in a loud, dramatic voice, "I am here this afternoon not to protest, but to mourn. To mourn the possible passing of a way of life. To grieve for the potential passing of a piece of our history and our tradition. To lament the prospective passing of Half Moon Farm."

*Why does it always have to be* my *mother?* I wonder in despair. She's babbling on about Henry David Thoreau now, and something he wrote called *Civil Disobedience*, and how he spent a night in jail once to protest taxes. "Like our own bard of the woods, I, too, protest an unfair tax!" she cries. "The tax on Half Moon Farm!"

Anger wells up in me. Why can't my mother just be normal for once? Why does she always have to be the poster child for conservation, and world peace, and animal rights, and global warming, and every other cause under the sun? Why couldn't it be someone else for a change—Mrs. Hawthorne, say?

I glance over at Mrs. Hawthorne, who is standing beside Emma with her arm around her. Never in a million years could I picture Mrs. H handcuffing herself to a tree.

How did I end up in this family? I look over at Mrs. Chadwick. Right now, I'd think seriously about trading my mother for a snapping turtle.

Becca is lounging against their car, keeping her distance. She's got her cell phone out, but mine isn't vibrating, so it's not me she's texting this time. She's probably letting Ashley and Jen know what a loony tune I have for a mother.

I peer up at the tree house again. My mother is happily answering questions from the reporters. Forget snapping turtles—right now, I'd even think seriously about running away and joining the circus.

On second thought, I realize bitterly, I don't need to go anywhere to do that. My life is already a circus.

*Heather Vogel Frederick*

# Jess

"Easy, Sundance," I murmur.

It's early, just before six, and both of us are sleepy. Promising fresh grain, I lead her across the barn to the milking stand. "That's it," I tell her as she jumps up into position. I give her an encouraging pat.

Sundance is my very own goat. She's a Nubian, brown mostly, with a black streak down her nose and long silvery ears that frame her face. I think she's beautiful. I raised her from a kid for a 4-H project last year. While she's distracted by breakfast, I move down to what my dad calls her "business end" and get to work. First I dip a rag in warm water and wash down her udder and teats. Then I put the bucket in position, pull up the old kitchen chair we use for a milking stool, and lean my forehead against her warm flank. Her coat is soft as velvet and smells like sweet hay.

*Squeeze, squeeze. Squeeze, squeeze. Squeeze, squeeze.* There's a rhythm to hand-milking, and I find myself humming along. I haven't done much singing lately—I just haven't felt like it. I didn't even try out for the school musical this year, even though Mrs. Adams, our drama teacher, asked me to. It's hard to think about anything these days but Half Moon Farm.

I can't stand the thought of having to leave our home. What would we do with Sundance and the rest of our goats? And what about Led and Zep? I glance over to their stalls, where only our horses' broad backs are visible. But I can hear them patiently chewing the hay I forked into their troughs a few minutes ago. I'd miss them terribly. I'd even miss our chickens.

Five minutes of worrying and squeezing later I'm done with Sundance. "One down, six to go," I tell her as I lead her back to her pen. Next up is Matilda. She's a Saanen, which is a breed from Switzerland. Matilda is creamy white and my dad's favorite, because she's such a dependable milker.

"Come on, girlfriend," I coax, grabbing her by the collar. Sundance thinks I'm her mother, so she'll follow me anywhere, but Matilda can be a little stubborn sometimes.

Some people think farming is romantic, but the truth is it's a lot of hard work. We have to milk the goats in the morning and the evening, and we have to feed them and clean their stalls, just like we do for the horses. Plus there are the chickens to take care of, and the garden—although this time of year it's mostly just herbs in the greenhouse. And everything's organic, which for my dad means more work because he likes

Heather Vogel Frederick

to use as little machinery as possible, even for plowing, which he does with Led and Zep. My parents hardly ever go on vacation—there aren't too many people we can ask to help out with all the chores—but they love it, especially my dad. He says this is what he was born to do.

I'm not sure what I was born to do. I know I love animals, and I'm thinking about being a veterinarian. And I could always be a farmer. But I like to sing, too. And then again I like math and science. Good thing I don't have to decide yet.

An hour later, I'm done. I carry the buckets of milk to the dairy room and put them in one of the big refrigerators. My parents will process everything later. Some people think the idea of milk from a goat is gross, but I think it tastes better than cow's milk. It's sweet and creamy and we make all sorts of stuff from it besides cheese—butter, for example, and even ice cream.

I pause for a minute as I'm leaving the barn and lean against the door frame. I gaze out across the pond to the far edge of the back pasture. The trees look beautiful silhouetted against the delicate pink of dawn, and I feel a sharp pang again at the thought of leaving this place. So many of my best memories are here! I close my eyes and breathe deeply, trying to shut out the worry that won't stop gnawing at me. It seems to me there's a hint of spring in the air, a tiny note of warmth hovering in the chilly breeze, but it's probably just my imagination. Winter tends to hold on tight through March and sometimes into April here in New England.

It can hold on as long as it wants to this year, as far as I'm concerned.

Spring only means we're that much closer to June, when the taxes are due. We were supposed to pay them in April, but my parents got an extension. Even with the extra time, though, it's not looking good.

I cross the yard to our house and glance at the clock as I enter the kitchen. I'm ahead of schedule for once. Sometimes I don't have enough time to cram down breakfast, shower, get dressed, and make it to the school bus. Which explains why sometimes I skip the shower and just head to school in my barn clothes. I try not to do that anymore, though. I've had enough of people calling me "Goat Girl."

My parents are sitting at the kitchen table drinking tea. Mom's still in her pajamas, but Dad's dressed in his jeans and barn jacket. He's been up all night with one of our does who's expecting.

"Anything?" I ask him, hanging up my own jacket on its hook by the back door.

He shakes his head. "Not yet. Should be soon, though. Maybe by the time you get home from school today."

New baby goats are always fun. Dylan and Ryan will be beside themselves with excitement. Especially since Dad said they could name this one.

My mother pats the chair beside her. "Have a seat, sweetheart. I'll scramble you some eggs."

I watch her as she moves around the kitchen fixing my breakfast. Looking at her in her fuzzy blue robe, it's hard to believe she ever played the role of the glamorous Larissa LaRue. I like my mother much better this way, though.

*Heather Vogel Frederick*

She pours me some orange juice and smiles. "Whatcha thinking about?"

I shake my head. "Nothing."

My parents exchange a glance.

"What is it?" I ask, my heart skipping a beat. "More bad news?"

"Not necessarily," says my mom lightly. "Your dad and I were just talking—"

"—about selling the farm?"

"Now don't get all worked up. It's just an idea. The thing is, I've been in touch with the producers at *HeartBeats*, and they said if I want to come back they'd bring Larissa LaRue out of her coma."

I pluck at my dad's sleeve. "But I thought you said we were going to keep the family together, no matter what!"

He gives me a wry smile. "We are, Jess. If your mom takes the acting job again, we'll all move to New York this time."

I feel like I've just been butted in the stomach by one of our goats. For a few seconds I can hardly breathe. New York City?

"But what about our farm?" I reply, stunned. "What about all our animals?"

"This would only be as a last resort, honey," my mother says gently. "We'd be able to keep Sugar and Spice, though. Acting pays well, and with the money from selling the farm I think we could find a big enough place. Maybe even with a view of the river, or of Central Park."

I stare at them, stricken.

"Now, Jess," says my father. "I seem to remember a certain young lady begging us recently to treat her like a grown-up since she's reached the ripe old age of thirteen."

I drop my gaze. Right now I feel about two years old. I just want to climb onto his lap and have him wrap his arms around me and tell me everything's going to be fine.

"I hate the idea of losing this place as much as you do," my father continues. "Maybe even more—remember, I've lived here a lot longer than you have. I grew up on this farm." He runs his hand through his hair. His eyes are bleary from lack of sleep. "We just don't have a lot of options at this point."

"Can't you get a loan or something to pay the taxes?" I ask.

My mother shakes her head. "We can't take on any more debt. We have too much already, what with the new roof last winter, and then on top of that adding the greenhouse, and the new commercial refrigerators this fall."

"But what about our goat cheese? I thought you said the Half Moon Farm brand was starting to take off."

"It is," Mom tells me. "More and more restaurants are placing orders, and it's selling like hotcakes at all the local farmers' markets and organic grocery stores."

"But—"

My dad reaches over and pats my hand. "It seems to be a case of too little, too late," he says. "We have to face facts here, Jess, and the fact is that we may not be able to keep this place. Besides, your mother

*Heather Vogel Frederick*

and I want to be able to offer you kids a better life—money for your college educations, vacations, that sort of thing. Aren't you tired of being Princess Jess of Ramshackle Farm?"

This has been our little private joke ever since the school play last year when Mrs. Chadwick insulted us, but I don't smile this time. "I will never, ever get tired of being Princess Jess of Ramshackle Farm," I tell him, my voice quivering with emotion. "I don't ever want to be anything else!"

I push back from the table and run upstairs to my room.

The day goes downhill from there. Even without showering or changing I barely make the bus, and we have a pop quiz in math class, which I completely tank. How am I supposed to remember the Pythagorean theorem when I'm worried about losing Half Moon Farm?

There's more bad news at lunchtime. Emma and Cassidy and I are the first ones at our table in the cafeteria and it turns out Emma chose today of all days to add up the money in our secret fund. She pulls a big manila envelope out of her backpack and dumps a pile of bills and coins onto the table.

"Let's see," she says, frowning at a piece of paper that was in the envelope too, and comparing it to the money on the table. "With the seventy-five from your hockey lessons, Cassidy, and a hundred and eighty-two from all of our babysitting, and a hundred and ten from dog-walking and doggie daycare, plus all of our combined allowances and Christmas and birthday money, that makes, um—"

"Four hundred ninety-seven dollars and forty-six cents," I announce, adding rapidly.

"This sum brought to you by Jessica Delaney, the human calculator," says Cassidy.

Nobody laughs. We stare at the pile of money on the lunch table in glum silence. Four hundred ninety-seven dollars and forty-six cents is not going to save Half Moon Farm.

"I wish you had a rich Aunt Josephine, like Diana Barry," says Emma.

"Things like that only happen in books," I tell them sadly. Not that I haven't spent the last few weeks wishing madly for a miracle too.

But there aren't any on the horizon. Mrs. Wong's stunt last month didn't quite have the effect she wanted. She got on TV, all right, but her handcuffs weren't the sensation that Carson Dawson's flying teeth were. I guess because it wasn't particularly funny, just weird. My parents got a bunch of phone calls from friends and neighbors offering us their sympathy, and a few people even sent checks. But that was it. And while Dad said it gave our savings account a boost, it didn't solve the problem. A person doesn't need to be a math genius to figure that out. Because even if we do manage somehow to come up with the money for the taxes this year, what about next year, and the year after that?

"Well, we can't give up yet," says Emma firmly. "We've still got, what, four months to go before the deadline?"

I shake my head and hold up three fingers.

*Heather Vogel Frederick*

"Oh." Emma stares at the bills and coins again and chews her lip.

I scoop up the money and stuff it back into the envelope, then give the envelope to Emma. I don't want to look at it anymore. She puts it away and we eat our lunches in silence.

Kevin Mullins materializes. "Can I eat with you?" he asks me. He asks me this every single day, and every single day I tell him the same thing: "Of course." I am Kevin's security blanket. I guess I can understand why. Middle school is hard enough when you're a normal kid—or mostly normal—but it's especially tough on someone like Kevin. My goat Sundance weighs more than he does. Kevin is, like, barely four feet tall and he already knows Latin and Greek and all the constellations and he's learning calculus in his spare time. Plus he looks like an owl, a really pale owl with dark hair and these huge dark eyes that blink at you when he's thinking. Which is most of the time. A ten-year-old like Kevin deserves a security blanket.

Zach and Ethan set their trays down across from us. Ethan slides in beside Cassidy. He looks at our faces and frowns.

"Who died?" he says. "You three look like you've just come from a funeral."

Cassidy punches him in the arm. "Shut up, Tater."

"Nobody died," says Emma. "We're just worried about the Delaneys' farm."

"Oh, yeah, I saw something about that on the news the other night," says Zach, taking a bite of burrito. "Sorry, Jess."

Third comes up behind him and starts to snicker. "Hey, was

that really Megan Wong's mother handcuffed to the tree?"

Before any of us can reply, the Fab Three stroll over.

"Oh, great, just what I need on top of everything else," I mutter. "Josie Pye."

"Hi, Zach," Becca coos.

"Hi, Zach," Cassidy mimics, her voice all high and flirty just like Becca's.

Zach blushes. Becca glares at Cassidy, but she keeps her distance. Becca is a little bit afraid of Cassidy.

"Uh, hi, Becca," mumbles Zach to his burrito.

Becca looks over at me. She wrinkles her nose in disgust, and I'm suddenly acutely aware of the fact that I'm still in my barn clothes. Becca doesn't say anything—probably because Cassidy is sitting next to me—but she gives Ashley and Jen a nudge and jerks her head toward me, holding her nose. Ashley and Jen, who had been all smiles a second before, looking at Zach, quickly rearrange their expressions into sneers.

Beside me, Kevin Mullins turns beet red. He jumps to his feet. Unfortunately, he's so short nobody notices. "You take that back!" he demands.

Becca looks at him, startled. So does everyone else. Kevin rarely makes a peep. Becca holds up her hands in mock horror. "It speaks!" she says, and Ashley and Jen laugh right on cue. Becca's eyes narrow. "Take what back, twerp?"

"What you were thinking," Kevin mumbles.

Becca glares at him. "How could you possibly know what I was thinking? What, are you a mind reader in addition to being a twerp?"

Kevin plunges on. "I saw you making fun of Jess to your friends. She can't help it if she smells."

Becca's mouth drops open. Ethan starts to howl, and Third laughs so hard milk comes out of his nose. Zach is biting his lip, trying really hard not to join in. Even Cassidy and Emma are smothering grins.

I'm wishing I were anywhere but here.

"I mean it!" squeaks Kevin. His thin chest is rising and falling really fast, and I can tell he's upset. "Jess doesn't get to sleep in until the last minute the way you do. She gets up way before all of us to do her chores, and sometimes she doesn't have time to change her clothes. Sometimes she's so tired she falls asleep on the bus when we go to the high school for math. She works really, really hard—a lot harder than any of you. And none of you guys have to worry about losing your homes."

The boys stop laughing. I stare at Kevin, astonished.

"Sticking up for your girlfriend, huh?" Becca taunts him. "Why don't you just go back to your playpen like a good boy."

Kevin sits down again and stares at his tray. He looks like he might cry.

"Leave him alone, Becca," I tell her.

"Whatever." Becca starts to walk away. Then she changes her mind and comes back to the table. "By the way, I just read your article in the paper about Friday night's basketball game," she chirps to Zach. "I don't know anything about basketball, but you made it sound sooooo exciting!"

Zach looks up from his plate. "The paper's here already?"

Becca nods. "They're by the front office."

"Awesome. I'll pick one up after lunch."

"It was an amazing game," says Ethan. "Really close score, which is the best kind. You should have seen us, in the fourth quarter, when the Buccaneers were ahead by eleven points . . ."

As he gives her an enthusiastic shot-by-shot account of the game, Becca's eyes glaze over, but she still pretends to be interested, laughing and tossing her head so her hair flips around and her earrings jangle. Cassidy grabs a handful of carrot sticks off of Third's tray and spells out PYE on the table. Emma and I giggle.

Suddenly, there's a commotion behind us.

"EMMA HAWTHORNE!"

Water starts to freeze at exactly thirty-two degrees Fahrenheit—zero degrees Celsius—and the tone in Megan's voice is far, far colder than that. I turn around to see her standing behind us with her hands on her hips.

"Hey, Megs," Emma says, but her smile falters when she sees the expression on Megan's face.

Megan slaps a copy of the *Walden Woodsman* onto the lunch table. "How could you?" she demands.

Emma stares blankly at the front page. We all do. Right smack dab in the middle is a huge picture of Megan's mother in the Delaneys' tree house, waving at the camera. Above it a headline screams "PTA CHAIR LILY 'HANDCUFFS' WONG STAGES PROTEST AT LOCAL FARM!"

"I thought you were my *friends*," says Megan, her voice flinty.

"But—I—I am your friend," Emma stammers. "I don't—I wouldn't—I mean, I didn't have anything to do with this."

"Oh, really?" Megan stabs at the top of the article with her fingernail. "What's that doing there, then?"

The byline reads "Emma J. Hawthorne."

Emma's face goes as white as the milk in the carton on her tray. "But I didn't write it!" she protests. "Honest, Megan, you know I would never do something like that."

"And how about you, *Carrots*?" says Megan, turning to Cassidy. She thrusts the paper under Cassidy's nose. The photo credit reads "Cassidy Sloane."

Cassidy starts to sputter. "That's a lie! I never took that picture!"

"I know my mom isn't a famous supermodel," Megan says to her, her voice dripping with sarcasm. "And I know she isn't smart like your mother, Emma, or talented like yours, Jess. She dresses in stupid clothes and eats stupid food and gets all involved in stupid causes, and she embarrasses me to death most of the time and I hate it, but she's my *mom*, and now I have to go around school and have everybody stare at me and think she's crazy."

"Megan!" Cassidy yells at her. "Are you deaf? We didn't do it!"

A crowd has gathered around our table, including the Fab Three. Megan ignores them all. "Then who did?" she snaps. "The tooth fairy?"

"You don't have to get all snotty about it," I say.

"Somebody played a prank," Cassidy tells her. "And it wasn't us. Honest."

"She's right, Megs, you have to believe us," pleads Emma. "I would never do something like this, and neither would Cassidy."

"That's not true," says Megan frostily. "You would do something like that and you did. Or have you forgotten what you tried to do to Becca on *Hello Boston!*?"

Behind her, Becca nods triumphantly. So do Jen and Ashley, of course.

"That's so not fair!" Cassidy protests.

"Isn't it?"

"This is just ridiculous," I say. "You know them—you know us—better than that."

"Do I?" she says bitterly, slamming the paper down on the table and stalking away. The Fab Three flounce off behind her.

"Sheesh," says Zach. "I've never seen Megan get mad like that."

Beside me, Emma is shaking.

"Did you guys really not do it?" Ethan asks.

Cassidy shakes her head. "No way. That is absolutely not my picture."

I look at it more closely. Even if I hadn't been standing beside her that day, and known for a fact that she didn't have a camera with her, I would still be able to tell right away that the picture wasn't Cassidy's. The pictures Cassidy takes for the *Woodsman* are full of energy and life, just like her, and this one is flat and dull and out of focus.

"Somebody must have changed the proofs," says Zach. "I was the last one at the news meeting last Thursday—well, besides Stewart—

*Heather Vogel Frederick*

right before we turned them in. The front page was completely different. The basketball game was the lead story, and Katie had that big long article about the new lunch menu they're proposing."

"I had to leave early that day, to go to the dentist, remember?" says Emma. "That proves I couldn't have done it."

"And I had hockey practice and wasn't there at all," adds Cassidy.

"So somebody else definitely switched the articles," says Zach.

"Who?" Third asks. "Stewart?"

Emma shakes her head. "Stewart may be a nerd, but he's not mean."

"Yeah," Kevin pipes up. "He's even nice to me."

Suddenly I know exactly who made the switch. I turn around in my seat. Megan is in the hall outside the cafeteria, talking to the Fab Three. Becca has her arm around her shoulder, the picture of sympathy. She glances back at our table. Our eyes meet. She smiles. It's not a friendly smile.

It doesn't take a math genius to add two and two and get four. I turn back to my friends. "It was Becca Chadwick," I tell them. "She had her cell phone with her that day, remember? She took the picture. And I'll bet she wrote the article, too. It's called payback, queen bee style."

"Or Pye style," says Cassidy, picking up a carrot stick. "You've gotta be right, Jess. The only problem is, how are we going to get Megan to believe us?"

# SPRING

"Oh, Anne, things are so mixed-up in real life. They aren't as clear-cut and trimmed off, as they are in novels."

—Anne of Green Gables

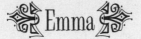

# Emma

*"Sometimes I think it is of no use to make friends. They only go out of your life after awhile and leave a hurt that is worse than the emptiness before they came."*
—*Anne of Avonlea*

I still can't believe that Megan quit book club.

She's really, really mad. She won't talk to me at school—she won't even look at me—and she hasn't returned any of my phone calls. Or Cassidy's, or Jess's. It's like we don't even exist.

It's so unfair! We didn't even do anything! But of course Becca and Jen and Ashley are busy working overtime convincing her that we did, and that we don't deserve her friendship and that she's better off with them.

I even tried writing a letter. I wrote it on my best stationery—the pink paper with the roses along the edge, which my Aunt Sarah sent me for Christmas—and tucked it inside Megan's social studies notebook when she wasn't looking. But I found it in my locker the next day, all wadded up. She hadn't even opened the envelope.

And then when she didn't show up at last night's book club meeting, and my mom explained to us all that Mrs. Wong had called and said that Megan was feeling too much pressure at the moment with her *Flashlite* deadline and wouldn't be joining us, and in fact might not be able to fit book club in any more at all, well, it was like somebody threw a bucket of cold water on our group.

We still went ahead with the meeting, and we talked about *Anne of Avonlea*, which Cassidy and Jess finally finished, and ate the homemade shortbread cookies that my dad and I baked, just like the ones that Paul Irving's grandmother made for Anne in the book. We got our "Fun Facts About Maud" handouts, and learned that Lucy Maud Montgomery's favorite of all her books was *The Story Girl*, which I haven't read yet and want to, and that she didn't think she was anything like Anne in *Anne of Green Gables*, but that she was a bit like Emily in *Emily of New Moon*, which I also want to read. But it wasn't the same. Mrs. Sloane and Mrs. Delaney and my mom tried extra hard to be cheerful and normal, but you could tell their hearts weren't really in it. And mine sure wasn't.

"Emma?"

Startled, I blink at Ms. Nielson. She has a worried expression on her face.

"You look like you're a million miles away," she says. "Is everything okay?"

My gaze darts over to where Becca is sitting with Katie Malone, then back to Ms. Nielson. "Uh, yeah," I lie. Everything is not okay,

*Heather Vogel Frederick*

everything is horrible in fact, but I'm not going to let Becca Chadwick know that. For once, she's not going to get the better of me.

We're at our first newspaper staff meeting since the "Handcuffs Wong" article. Becca's brother isn't here this afternoon because he's home with a cold. But everyone else is seated around the table, including Zach Norton.

Ms. Nielson shuffles some papers. "As you know, people, we had a little incident with last month's issue of the *Walden Woodsman*, an incident about which there is conflicting information." She gives Cassidy and Becca and me a significant look. "While I realize that it was all probably meant as a harmless prank, I just want to reiterate that from now on, our agreed-upon guidelines must be followed, including obtaining my approval for any last-minute changes. No exceptions."

"But Ms. Nielson!" I start to protest.

She holds up her hand. "What's done is done," she says briskly. "Let's move on, shall we?"

What's almost as bad as Megan not believing me is the fact that Ms. Nielson doesn't either. Somehow, Becca managed to cast enough doubt on the whole thing that Ms. Nielson said she wasn't sure what to think. So she decided we'd all have to face the consequences.

"I've found that the best way to deal with these kinds of disagreements is to tackle them head-on," she continues. "Therefore, I'm assigning a special team of reporters to cover a new story about one of our students here at Walden Middle School." She glances down at her notes. "Apparently Megan Wong and her fashion designs are going to be featured this summer in the premiere issue of a new magazine called *Flashlite*. This is certainly newsworthy, and I'm sure our readers would like to hear more."

*Uh-oh*, I think. Somehow I know what's coming. Sure enough, Ms. Nielson looks straight at me.

"Emma, I want you and Becca to work together on this piece. You'll need to interview Megan, and possibly try to get a quote or two from the editors at *Flashlite*. And Cassidy, you're in charge of taking the pictures."

Cassidy groans. "Who's going to cover the basketball playoffs?"

"I'm sure Zach can handle it, right, Zach?"

Zach doesn't look happy to be caught in the middle. "Uh, sure, I guess."

"You can borrow my digital camera if you need to," Ms. Nielson tells him. "It'll be a snap."

"Can't I team up with Katie instead?" pleads Becca, who looks equally horrified at the prospect of us working together. "She knows a lot more about fashion than Emma does."

"Now, Becca, I'm sure you didn't mean that the way it sounded," says Ms. Nielson.

Obviously Ms. Nielson doesn't know Becca very well. Of course Becca meant that exactly the way it sounded. I look down at my clothes, baffled and frustrated. This whole fashion thing is maddening. Honestly, what's wrong with purple corduroy pants? Or with my sweater? They're not even hand-me-downs, for once.

*Heather Vogel Frederick*

"Emma is perfectly well-equipped to write about fashion," continues Ms. Nielson, giving me an encouraging smile. "She's one of our best reporters."

My pleasure at this compliment is quickly punctured when I see Becca lean over and whisper something to Katie. The two of them look at me and laugh, and I feel my face turning red. So much for not letting Becca get the best of me.

Cassidy leaves early because she has to go home and get changed for Courtney's birthday dinner—"My mom's making me wear a dress," she reports glumly, "because Stan the man is taking us to some fancy restaurant"—leaving me stuck by myself with Becca as she and Ms. Nielson and I draft some interview questions for the article about Megan.

Later, as everyone files out of the room after the meeting, Zach pauses by my chair. "Cheer up, Emma," he whispers. "Just remember what Cassidy always says—buzz, buzz, buzz."

He grins at me. After Megan's meltdown in the cafeteria about the "Handcuffs Wong" article, Cassidy explained all about queen bees to him and Ethan and Third.

"Buzz buzz," I reply halfheartedly.

"That's more like it," he says, punching me lightly on the shoulder.

I reach down to gather up my jacket and backpack, then stand up and smile shyly at him. In that instant when our eyes meet, I suddenly know two things for sure. First, I know that Zach likes me. Second, I know that he doesn't *like* like me. Not that way.

Zach Norton thinks of me as a friend. That's it. No more, no less. Just a friend, the same way he thinks of Cassidy, and Jess, and Ethan, and Third. A boy who really likes you doesn't punch you on the arm, the way he does a teammate. To Zach, I'm just one of the guys.

He saunters off and I stand there, stunned. Becca says something to me but I don't even hear her. She and Katie laugh as I push past them and stumble down the hallway. Outside, the after-school activities bus is waiting. I climb on and take a seat, staring blindly out the window. I hardly know what to think. I can't even remember a time when I haven't had a crush on Zach Norton. It started way back in kindergarten. I've always hoped that maybe he secretly liked me, too. But now I know he doesn't. Not that way.

*There's one consolation I suppose,* I tell myself as the bus doors close. *Zach Norton doesn't like Becca Chadwick at all. Not even as a friend.*

I continue to stare out the window as we bump our way toward town. I don't want to go home just yet. If I go home right now, my mother will take one look at me and know something's wrong, and then she'll want to talk about it. My mother says she can read me like a book. She loves to quote Lucy Maud Montgomery to me, the part in *Anne of Avonlea* where Mr. Harrison says, "You've got a very expressive face, Anne; your thoughts just come out on it like print." That's what I'm like, she says.

I don't feel like being an open book for my mother right now, so when the bus reaches downtown Concord I get off and head for the rink instead.

*Heather Vogel Frederick*

You can't grow up in New England and not know how to skate. Mr. Delaney got me and Jess started by pushing old kitchen chairs around their frozen pond when we were only five or six, but I didn't think it would be something I'd be interested in as an actual sport. I've just never thought of myself as the athletic type. Not unless they suddenly decide to make reading an Olympic sport. Which is why I'm still kind of surprised at how much I'm enjoying figure skating.

When Cassidy first suggested it, right away I thought of the *Shoes* books for some reason. My mother gave them to me way back in elementary school. Noel Streatfield was one of her favorite authors when she was growing up, and she thought maybe I'd like the stories too. Like them? I *loved* them. Especially *Ballet Shoes*, *Theater Shoes*, and *Skating Shoes*. I read them over and over again.

Maybe that's why I decided to go ahead and give figure skating a try, I don't know. Maybe because it seemed familiar somehow, after all that time I spent reading about Harriet and Lalla. At any rate, I'm glad I did, even though I'm still pretty awful at it and I still fall down a lot, especially when I try toe loops and spins. Skating is just plain fun.

When I get to the rink, I call home to let my dad know my change of plans and he offers to pick me up afterward. I tell him that would be great. Then I dig my skates out of my locker and stuff my backpack in their place, and lace up as quickly as I can to head out for what's left of the free skate session.

Push glide, push glide, arms out for balance, I swoop left, then right, then skate as fast as I can down to the far end of the rink. I make the turn with inches to spare, gathering speed as I round the curve, placing one foot over the other, practicing my crossovers. I repeat the same pattern back to the other end of the rink to complete my warm-up. By now I'm breathing hard and feeling loose enough to attempt a little spin, which lands me squarely on my behind.

I can almost hear Eva Bergson laughing. "Remember Thomas Edison, Emma," she'd say if she were here. I thought she was nuts the first time she brought him up during class. What could a guy who invented the lightbulb have to do with figure skating?

"When one of his experiments went bust," she had gone on to explain, "Mr. Edison always told people that he hadn't failed, he'd just found ten thousand ways that didn't work!"

"That makes about nine thousand more to go," I mutter to myself, but I pick myself up and brush myself off and head across the rink again. Because if there's one thing I've learned from Eva Bergson, who may be ancient but who's actually still pretty cool, it's not to get discouraged. A few tries later I finally manage the spin. Feeling ridiculously pleased with myself, considering all the little kids who are whirling effortlessly around me like tops, I skate my way down the rink again, humming. Cassidy is right—exercise always helps. No matter how horrible things get, no matter how cranky or tired I am, just getting out and moving makes a difference. My mom says that's why she and my father try and go for a long walk every day.

By the time free skate is over, I'm drenched with sweat and feeling a whole lot better. My dad doesn't bring up school on our ride home,

*Heather Vogel Frederick*

and best of all there are no comments at dinner about me being like an open book. I'm glad. I don't really want anybody trying to "read" me right now.

By Saturday morning, though, I'm feeling sorry for myself again. I prop my chin on my hand and stare out our kitchen window, mindlessly tapping my spoon against my bowl. Rain drips from the eaves and the bare tree branches, melting the snow and turning everything to sloppy brown soup. I hate this time of year, when winter's not quite over and spring hasn't quite started and the half-melted piles of snow are covered with dirt and everything looks dead and forlorn. Mud season, my dad calls it. The Ides of March. A fine old New England tradition. Ha! This time of year, Mother Nature is as mixed-up as my thoughts. Why does life have to be so complicated?

As if the mess with Megan and Becca isn't enough, in addition to my disappointment over Zach, it turns out that he is going to Spring Fling with Katie Malone. Cassidy called me last night to check something on our math homework, and it turns out she ran into Zach after her hockey game and he told her that Katie had asked him to go to the dance and he said yes. Cassidy didn't tell me this to be mean or anything—she has no clue about what happened after our newspaper meeting—but it just brought everything crashing down again.

And on top of all that, I haven't written a single poem in months. Every time I try, all I hear ringing in my head is Becca calling me "Porky the Poet"—even though I'm a lot less porky these days. Cassidy was right about exercise helping with that, too.

"You're awfully quiet this morning," says my mother.

The two of us are sitting alone at the breakfast table, where I'm brooding over my oatmeal.

"In fact," my mother continues, "you've been awfully quiet lately, period."

I shrug.

"How's school?"

"Fine," I tell her.

"And the newspaper?"

"Fine." I don't feel like explaining about what happened on Thursday.

"Figure-skating lessons?"

"Fine."

"Is Becca Chadwick acting up again? Should I have a talk with Calliope?"

I shake my head.

My mother gives me a long, thoughtful look. I scrape my spoon listlessly across my bowl, plowing a shallow trench in the oatmeal. I can tell she's in the mood for one of those heart-to-heart kind of mother-daughter chats. Which is exactly what I'm *not* in the mood for. I really don't want to talk about it.

"You're still upset about book club, aren't you?" she says gently.

I put my spoon down. Maybe I really *do* want to talk about it. "I just feel so awful," I tell her. "Remember in the first Anne book, when Mrs. Barry wouldn't believe that Anne hadn't deliberately tried to get Diana tipsy on the raspberry cordial? And she wouldn't let them be friends

*Heather Vogel Frederick*

anymore? That's how awful I feel. Megan just won't believe me."

My mother nods sympathetically.

"And now Ms. Nielson won't either."

My mother raises an eyebrow. Suddenly the words tumble out in a rush, and I explain about Ms. Nielson making me work with Becca on the article about Megan, and how Becca tried to weasel out of it and made snide remarks about my clothes, which made me feel even worse.

"And most of all I still can't believe that Megan doesn't want to be friends with us anymore," I finish miserably.

My mother nods again. "Just try and be patient, Emma. Often these things have a way of sorting themselves out. I think there's more to this than what's on the surface. Megan is probably feeling a lot of pressure right now with this upcoming magazine feature. She's pretty young for that kind of attention. Lily told me she's spent every waking hour this past month either sketching or sewing, so she probably didn't get enough sleep, and that can certainly affect one's attitude."

Moms are really good at finding excuses to make their kids feel better.

"So how about the rest of your life besides Megan?" she asks. "Everything going okay?"

I pick up my spoon and poke at my oatmeal again. My mother waits quietly for my reply. She's really good at just listening, too. "Mom," I say finally, "what do you do when a boy you like doesn't like you back?"

"Oh, sweetheart," she says, reaching over and giving my hand a squeeze. "That's a tough one. I wish I had an easy answer."

I guess I was kind of hoping she did too. I think about Anne Shirley, and how she secretly liked Gilbert Blythe but wouldn't admit it to herself for ages and ages. I guess I was kind of hoping that it might be that way for Zach Norton, that maybe he really did like me deep down underneath. But now I know that's not true and never will be. We're friends, that's all. His stomach doesn't get all fluttery when he sees me coming down the hall at school, the way mine does when I see him.

"Emma, you're twelve—"

"Almost thirteen."

My mother smiles. "Almost thirteen, then. My point is, you've got plenty of time to worry about boys, and dating, and all that."

Why is it that grown-ups always tell us stuff like this? That we've got plenty of time? It sure doesn't feel that way. Can't they remember what it felt like when they were our age?

"Don't you worry," she adds. "One of these days your knight in shining armor will come along."

This is mom-code for you're probably going to be an ugly duckling for a while longer before you turn into a swan so get used to it. I know she's doing her best to comfort me, though, and actually she has managed to make me feel a little better. Make that a whole lot better. I don't know what I'd do without my mother to talk to.

She reaches over and gives me a hug. "Finish your oatmeal," she tells me, smoothing my hair.

*Maybe she's right,* I think, spooning up a bite. Maybe I shouldn't be worrying about all this stuff so much. But still, it would so be nice to have a Gilbert Blythe all my own!

*Heather Vogel Frederick*

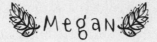

# Megan

*"Anne, you certainly have a genius for getting into trouble."*
—*Anne of Green Gables*

Field trip day.

This used to be my favorite day of the whole school year. When I was little, I couldn't wait to go to Boston to the Aquarium, or to Paul Revere's house, or Plymouth Plantation where you got to talk to a real live Pilgrim (okay, so I was dumb back in elementary school and I thought there were actual Pilgrims at Plymouth Plantation, not actors dressed up as Pilgrims). Field trips used to be so much fun.

Not this year.

Right after Thanksgiving, when they told us where we were going, I burst out laughing. I actually thought they were kidding! I still can't believe we're only going to Walden Pond.

I guess it's some big tradition at Walden Middle School. It's called "Namesake Day," and we've been preparing for it for months. They made us all read *Walden* in English class—which is such a boring book my eyes nearly fell out of my head—and then in science we've been studying the wildlife that Henry David Thoreau observed when he was living in his stupid cabin at the pond, and of course we had to make models of the cabin for social studies. My mother thinks this is all just about the greatest idea in the history of the world, naturally, and she volunteered right away to go along as a chaperone. Fortunately, she has a board meeting today for the Concord Riverkeepers, so she couldn't come. I don't think I could stand one more crack about "Handcuffs Wong."

I wish I were an eighth grader. They're so lucky—they get to go to Washington, DC, and tour the White House and the Capitol and the Smithsonian and all that stuff. Even though I've been to Washington already with my parents, given a choice between going there again and having to tromp around Walden Pond, which is exactly five miles from my house, and where I've spent nearly every day of every summer since before I can remember, I'd pick DC in a flash.

I climb reluctantly on to the bus and head down the aisle toward the back where Becca and Jen and Ashley are saving me a seat. They like to sit as close to the boys as possible. Emma and Jess and Cassidy are sitting together near the front, but I don't look at them as I pass by. *Traitors.*

They tried to convince me that Becca masterminded the whole "Handcuffs Wong" thing, but Becca said I shouldn't believe them. Not after that mean trick they tried to play on her on *Hello Boston!*

*Heather Vogel Frederick*

And after all I did for them too, helping with their stupid fund to try and save Half Moon Farm.

A little spark of guilt flares up inside me when I think about Half Moon Farm, but I push it away. Becca smiles and pats the seat beside her and I slide in. Becca is the only one who really understands how humiliated I was by the *Woodsman* article. Emma and Jess and Cassidy all have normal mothers—well, mostly. Not many people have moms as famous as Cassidy's, and Jess's mom running off to be an actress last year was pretty weird. Still, neither of those things compare to the stunt my mother pulled.

My mother still doesn't understand why I was so upset. She actually thought the whole "Handcuffs Wong" thing was funny. I tried to explain to her how it made me feel, but she didn't get it.

"Remember when Anne Shirley accidentally dyed her hair green?" I told her. "Remember how she was so mortified that she wouldn't leave the house for a whole week?"

My mother had just stared at me, puzzled. Then she told me it was a faulty analogy, whatever that means, because *she* was the one who had handcuffed herself to the Delaneys' tree, not me. And that I shouldn't be embarrassed because of something she'd done.

She just doesn't get it, just like she doesn't get me.

Becca understands, though. "I am so not looking forward to sitting in that boring old cabin, and listening to Ms. Nielson read boring old *Walden* to us," she says to me and Ashley and Jen.

"No kidding," I reply.

"At least it's a warm day," Ashley points out.

This is true. The last week of April in Concord isn't usually this warm. The sun is streaming in through the bus windows, and I've already taken off my hoodie.

"Maybe it won't be so bad," Jen says. "We aren't stuck at school, for one thing. Besides," she adds, turning to Becca, "your brother said it was a fun field trip."

Becca gives a little snort of disgust. "He would. You know my brother. He's worse than Kevin Mullins. Stewart loves this sort of stuff. He's all into history and poetry and he's read *Walden* about a hundred times. Don't listen to him—Stewart's like the Emma Hawthorne of boys."

I feel that hot flicker of guilt again, just like I do whenever Becca says snide things about Emma, but I shove it away.

It's a short ride to Walden Pond, and in no time we're milling around the parking lot, shrieking and laughing as Ms. Nielson and Mr. Doolittle, our science teacher, try and get us organized.

"Let's make sure we're in Zach's group," says Becca, drifting closer to where he's standing with Ethan and Third. Ashley and Jen and I trail along after her, trying to look inconspicuous. I haven't had much time to think about Zach lately. I've been too busy with all the *Flashlite* stuff. I sent my sketches in over a month ago, and Wolfgang called to tell me that he loved them, and had sent them along to the design department. It's pretty cool, actually—they have a staff of tailors and seamstresses who are going to take my sample prototypes and

*Heather Vogel Frederick*

make professional clothes out of them for the photo shoot. We set up a date for the interview next month, and I'm already nervous. Being interviewed for *Flashlite* is way different from being interviewed for our school newspaper. What if I end up sounding dorky? What if everybody thinks my designs are dumb?

"Listen up, people! I'd like all the girls over here, please!" hollers Mr. Doolittle, holding up his clipboard and waving it like a flag. He's exasperated and red-faced and sweaty already, and we haven't even started yet.

"And all you boys come over here with me!" orders Ms. Nielson, moving to the far side of the parking lot.

"What?" Becca bursts out indignantly. "No way—they're going to split us up!"

"That is so not fair," moans Jen.

Disappointed, the four of us watch as the boys head over toward Ms. Nielson, pushing and shoving each other as they go. Then we line up reluctantly in front of Mr. Doolittle with the rest of the seventh-grade girls. He passes handouts to the chaperones, who consult their clipboards and start calling out names. Emma and Cassidy and Jess and a few other girls are assigned to Mr. Hawthorne. The four of us end up with Mrs. Chadwick, who is dressed like she's going on an African safari, with a hiking stick and a big hat and binoculars and everything. I can tell just by looking at Becca that she's dying of embarrassment. I feel a rush of sympathy. When it comes to weird mothers, Becca definitely gets it.

As we pass the bus where Mr. Hawthorne is standing with Emma and the others, I hear him cracking jokes and for a split second I find myself wishing I were in his group. But I push the thought away. I'm getting used to pushing those thoughts away. *Traitors*, I remind myself.

"Does anyone need to go to the bathroom before we start?" trumpets Mrs. Chadwick. "Remember, there are no toilets in the woods!"

Becca turns bright red at this announcement. Cringing, she looks over to see if any of the boys heard, but they aren't paying the least bit of attention to us. They're too busy stuffing Kevin into the recycling bin by the visitor's booth. Ms. Nielson spots them and races to the rescue.

Meanwhile, Mrs. Chadwick sets off at a brisk pace. With a last lingering look at Zach Norton—who is heading in the opposite direction with Third's mother—we follow her. The plan is that the boys will hike one way around the pond looking for wildlife while we girls hike the other way. We'll tour Thoreau's cabin along the way and then meet up for lunch back here at the amphitheater, where Ms. Nielson will read to us from *Walden*.

"I'm bored already," whispers Ashley, before we're even out of the parking lot.

Jen and I giggle. Becca manages a smile.

Mrs. Chadwick, who in addition to her loudspeaker vocal cords must have ears like a fox, turns around and frowns at us. "Now, girls,"

*Heather Vogel Frederick*

she chides, "Walden Pond is a national treasure, and an important part of Concord's heritage. Do you realize how fortunate you are to be able to so easily appreciate its splendors? Visitors travel from all over the world to walk these hallowed trails."

Behind us, there's a burst of laughter from Mr. Hawthorne's group. I feel that little twinge of regret again. Mr. Hawthorne is probably telling funny stories about Thoreau. He knows lots of good stories about Concord's famous authors.

Under Mrs. Chadwick's grim supervision, we plow our way through the checklist of wildlife from science class. We scour the woods for signs of mice, and squint at the sky for hawks or loons or geese or even blue jays. All I manage to spot is a squirrel. Halfway around the pond Mrs. Chadwick makes us stop and listen to see if we can hear some of the same things Thoreau heard when he lived here: Cows? No. Owls? No. Whippoorwills? No. The rattle of railroad cars? No. Church bells? No.

Mrs. Chadwick squinches her eyes closed. "Listen harder, girls!" she orders.

Jen and Ashley and I collapse in silent giggles. Becca glares at us.

Mrs. Chadwick's eyes pop open. "There! Did you hear that?" she cries in triumph.

"What?" snarls Becca.

"The trill of a sparrow!"

"If you say so, Mom." Becca makes a mark on her checklist.

In the end, the only other things I check off are "baying of dogs" and "croaking of frog."

Then it's on to plant life, and we spend a while trying to identify blackberry bushes, shrub oaks, sumac, pine trees—that at least is a no-brainer—goldenrod, and something called sand cherry.

I'm starting to get hungry. It must be close to noon by now. It feels like we've been wandering around out here for hours. I don't say a word, though. I don't want another of Mrs. Chadwick's lectures about appreciating the glories of Concord's heritage.

Finally, we reach Thoreau's cabin—well, the replica cabin. Like the Pilgrims at Plymouth Plantation, it's not the real thing. I guess the original was taken down a long time ago. A park ranger is inside, waiting to give us a tour.

"Cozy, isn't it?" she says with a smile, as the six of us squeeze inside the tiny one-room cabin. "Henry David Thoreau moved into this cabin on July 4, 1845. He lived here for two years, two months, and two days."

"I wouldn't have lasted two minutes," whispers Becca.

Her mother shushes her.

The park ranger continues her spiel. "It was Thoreau who wrote, 'There is some of the same fitness in a man's building his own house that there is in a bird's building its own nest.' He was quite proud of his cabin and of the furniture he crafted for it."

We glance around. There's nothing to get excited about, just a bed, a table, a small desk, and three chairs.

"Big deal," whispers Ashley, and Becca and Jen and I all snicker.

Mrs. Chadwick shoots us what my dad calls the evil witch-mother

*Heather Vogel Frederick*

eye of death. Mrs. Chadwick's eyes are ice blue, and her version is even scarier than my mom's. We quickly wipe the smiles off our faces.

"Many of Concord's townspeople considered Thoreau to be somewhat of an odd duck," the park ranger tells us. "But in the end he had the last laugh. His book *Walden* has come to be known and loved the world over, and many of its quotes are deservedly famous." She glances down at the notecard she's carrying. "Quotes such as: 'Beware of all enterprises that require new clothes,' and 'Simplify, simplify.' And my personal favorite, 'If a man does not keep pace with his companions, perhaps it is because he hears a different drummer. Let him step to the music which he hears, however measured or far away.'"

I don't know about the clothes one—Thoreau probably wouldn't think too much of *Flashlite*, which would help explain why my mother admires him so much—but I kind of like the sound of that last quote. I turn to say something about it to Becca, but she's rolling her eyes at Jen and Ashley. Again I feel a nip of regret, and find myself wishing for a split second that Emma were here. Emma would know what I mean.

As usual, though, I push the thought away.

After our tour is over we wander around a bit more and then head for the amphitheater. The others are already there, and Ms. Nielson tells us to find our seats quickly.

"Boys and girls!" she shouts, clapping her hands together to get our attention. "Before I start reading to you, does anybody have any questions about what they've seen here this morning?"

Somebody makes a wisecrack in the boys' section, and Ms. Nielson frowns. "People! I want you to be serious here. Don't forget, you'll be journaling about your experience here today, so you need to pay attention."

Emma raises her hand.

"Teacher's pet," Becca whispers to me.

"Rebecca! Hush!" says her mother.

"How come Thoreau is so famous for being a hermit and this big outdoorsman and everything?" Emma asks. "We're only a mile from Concord, and people used to visit him all the time. Plus, it's a well-known fact that he used to walk into town often for dinner with his family and friends."

"Uh," says Ms. Nielson, looking a little flustered.

"And my mother says his mom and his sister did his laundry for him too," adds Emma.

I've heard Emma's parents arguing about this before, when I was over at the Hawthornes' for dinner. Her parents love to talk about books. I guess it's only natural, since Mrs. Hawthorne is a librarian and Mr. Hawthorne is a writer.

"Well, uh . . ." Ms. Nielson flounders, looking around for support.

"Nonsense," states Mrs. Chadwick flatly. "Henry David Thoreau was a true bard of the wilderness."

"Actually, Calliope, my daughter is correct," says Mr. Hawthorne. "Thoreau was as fond of a good home-cooked meal and a little company as any of us. And his family did keep an eye out for him."

Mrs. Chadwick doesn't like to be contradicted. She swells up indignantly, but before she can say anything else Mr. Hawthorne continues smoothly, "However, I think we can all agree that whether or not his time here at Walden Pond was a truly solitary sojourn, Henry David Thoreau is still one of our country's premier naturalists, and his book *Walden* is as ardent a plea for the preservation of the environment as any that has ever been written. In addition, his philosophy of simplicity has influenced many lives, including my own."

Mr. Hawthorne's little speech seems to satisfy Mrs. Chadwick, and Ms. Nielson looks relieved. I notice she doesn't ask if there are any more questions. She opens *Walden* and starts to read: "I went to the woods because I wished to live deliberately...."

We eat in silence as she drones on. The sun filters through the trees overhead, warming my shoulders. I'm wearing a pale yellow, sleeveless T-shirt with jeans today, and the matching hoodie is tied around my waist. I look out at the sparkling water. At least we'll get to have a little fun when we all go canoeing.

After Ms. Nielson is finished, we troop down to the boat launch and line up with our chaperones.

"Three or four per boat, maximum!" hollers Mr. Doolittle, waving his clipboard again. "And make sure your life jackets are securely fastened!"

"He sounds like a flight attendant," says Becca.

"Maybe he'll pass out peanuts and soda later," Jen replies, and we laugh.

The four of us scramble to be in the same canoe.

"Don't get too far ahead, girls!" Becca's mother orders, as she wedges herself into a canoe with Mr. Hawthorne.

"Relax, Calliope," I hear him tell her. "How much trouble can they get into on such a beautiful day?"

It's really warm out now, and I start to perspire as we stroke down the pond toward the shelter of a small cove. Out of the corner of my eye I see a flash of red, and I look over to see another canoe approaching. Fast. Cassidy Sloane is in the front, and behind her are Emma and Jess. They're all paddling hard, like they think they're warriors or something. Their canoe is aimed straight for us.

"Hey!" I shout. "Watch where you're going!"

They veer away at the last second. As their canoe flashes by, Cassidy grins and swipes her paddle across the surface of the pond, sending up a huge spray of ice-cold water. The sun may be warm today, but Walden Pond sure isn't.

"You moron!" shrieks Becca as it engulfs us.

We dig our paddles in and chase after them. Cassidy is laughing, of course, which makes us even madder, so we paddle even harder. Meanwhile Zach and Ethan and Third have rounded the corner of the cove. Kevin Mullins is with them, his head barely visible over the edge of the boat. They paddle over to see what's going on.

When we come up alongside Cassidy's canoe, Becca reaches out and gives it a shove, trying to topple it over, but Cassidy grabs hold of her arm. She yanks, hard. With another shriek, Becca tumbles forward.

*Heather Vogel Frederick*

*KER-SPLASH!*

"Man overboard!" hollers Ethan, just as Mr. Hawthorne and Mrs. Chadwick appear at the mouth of the cove.

Becca surfaces, gasping for air.

"Rebecca!" bellows her mother, waving her paddle. "Swim for your life! I'm coming to save you!"

In response, Becca stands up. We're close enough to shore that the water is only up to her waist. She's dripping and shivering, and there's murder in her eye. Cassidy stops laughing as Becca wades over, grabs the edge of her canoe and pushes down on it with all her might. The boat tips over, dumping Cassidy and Emma and Jess into the pond.

For once in her life, Becca has the attention of all the boys, who are howling with laughter by this point.

"Go, Becca!" shouts Zach.

"Attaway, Chadwick!" encourages Third.

Suddenly I realize that Cassidy and Emma are nowhere to be seen. Next thing I know, they've surfaced on the far side of our canoe and in a flash, they've flipped it over and sent Ashley and Jen and me tumbling into the water too. Now it's our turn to shriek. The water is *freezing*.

"Why'd you do that?" I scream at Emma.

"Why have you been so mean to me?" she screams back.

"Because you're a traitor!"

"I didn't write that stupid article!"

"You did too!"

"Did not!"

"That's a lie and you know it!"

We're both dripping wet and mad as heck and neither of us cares that everybody is staring at us.

"It's a lie," Emma repeats, more quietly this time. "Becca was the one who wrote it." She's looking me straight in the eye, and in that instant the spark of guilt I've been feeling for the past few weeks flames up inside me again.

"Don't listen to her!" yells Becca.

Jess turns on her. "Why don't you tell the truth for once! Even your brother knows you did it, Becca. He told Emma he found the picture of Mrs. Wong on your cell phone."

"Shut up, Goat Girl!"

"Don't you call me Goat Girl," says Jess, giving her a shove. Becca topples over backward into the water again and comes up spluttering.

I wrap my arms around my sodden middle. "Is this true?" I ask Becca, shivering. Stewart might be an uber-nerd, his pants might be high-waters, and he might read poetry like, well, Emma, but he's not a liar.

Becca pushes her wet hair back off her face. She shrugs. "Does it really matter? Listen, if you'd rather be friends with . . . with stupid Goat Girl here, and Carrots, and, and *Waldo*, go right ahead! See if I care!"

By now, her mother and Mr. Hawthorne have made their way across the cove. Mr. Doolittle and Third's mother are right behind them, and Mr. Doolittle does not look very happy.

*Heather Vogel Frederick*

"You girls are in detention for the rest of the day!" he yells. "I want you back at the bus on the double!"

The seven of us manage to slither back into our canoes, and cold, wet, and shivering, we paddle our way to the boat landing.

"You'll dry off faster out here in the sun," suggests Mr. Hawthorne, as we start to climb onto the bus.

"Someone will need to keep an eye on them if they're not with the driver," says Mr. Doolittle.

"I will," barks Mrs. Chadwick, who looks only too eager to volunteer as our jailer.

"I think you're better at this chaperone thing than I am, Calliope," says Mr. Hawthorne mildly. "Why don't you go help the teachers with the other kids. I've got a book in the car that I'm supposed to review. I can stay here with the girls and read while they're drying off."

Mr. Doolittle agrees that this is a good plan, and he and Mrs. Bartlett rearrange themselves to make room for Mrs. Chadwick in their canoe. As they paddle off, Mr. Hawthorne heads for his car.

"I'll be right back," he tells us.

"You are such creeps," says Becca bitterly, crossing the grass and spreading her jacket out on the beach. She sits down.

"Look who's talking!" says Cassidy. "At least we're not big fat liars."

"Some of you are plenty fat," Becca zings back, looking straight at Emma.

Suddenly I am just sick and tired of this whole thing. "Would you all please just SHUT UP!" I yell. Mr. Hawthorne looks back over his shoulder and I lower my voice. "Can't we just stop this stupid fighting? How did it ever get started, anyway?"

Everyone looks at Becca.

"What?" she cries. "Why are you all looking at me?"

"Because you, you—" I take a deep breath. "Look. The thing is, you guys, we're all really different. Cassidy, you like sports, and none of the rest of us do. Well, maybe Emma a tiny bit since she started figure skating. Jess, you love animals"—I glare at Becca, daring her to say a word about goats—"plus, you're the smartest one of all of us. A whole heck of a lot smarter than me, that's for sure. Emma, you've read every book under the sun and can write circles around most of the kids at school. Jen, you're an amazing artist, and Ashley, you and Becca and I really like fashion. So we're different, so what? We don't have to be best friends, but can't we just quit picking on each other for five minutes?"

The only sound for a long moment is the slam of Mr. Hawthorne's car door on the other side of the parking lot. Emma traces her finger in the sand.

"I'm tired of always feeling like I have to be at war with somebody!" I tell them, flopping down on my jacket beside Becca. "It's just so stupid."

Out on the pond, there isn't a canoe in sight. The sun is sparkling on the water, and a faint breeze has sprung up, rustling the leaves in the woods behind us. The quiet is soothing. Mr. Hawthorne has returned and is sitting a short distance away against a tree. His book is open but his baseball cap is tipped over his eyes, and I think maybe he's falling asleep.

*Heather Vogel Frederick*

"D'you mean we should call a truce?" asks Cassidy cautiously.

"A what?" says Becca.

"You know, a truce," Cassidy repeats. "No more saying nasty things, no more being mean."

We all eye each other. No way on earth is that going to happen, I think. Impossible.

"Maybe," says Emma, surprising me. "On one condition, though. Only if Becca tells the truth about the article in the *Walden Woodsman*. And if she apologizes."

"That's two conditions," says Jen.

"Whatever."

"Well, you said one."

"Gimme a break, you guys!" Cassidy tells them.

Emma looks questioningly at Becca. Becca shrugs. "Okay, okay," she says. "So it was me—so what? Big deal. I only did it to get back at you three for that horrible potion you were going to make me drink on live TV."

Somehow, somewhere deep down inside I think I always knew that it was Becca. I just didn't want to believe it, so I kept pushing the truth away.

"I didn't think you were all going to get so bent out of shape about it," she continues. "It was just a dumb joke."

"Some joke," says Jess. "You really embarrassed Megan, for one thing. And then you go around pretending to be her friend."

"I am her friend," Becca retorts. "And it's not like you're so innocent.

How come it's okay that you three tried to trick me, but when I do it you're all over my case?"

"What we did wasn't okay," Emma admits. "It was mean, and we apologized—to you, to your mom, and to Mr. Dawson. And we got punished for it big-time, or have you forgotten?"

"Look, I'm sorry, okay?" says Becca.

It's not much of an apology. I look at her, not sure what to think. Jess is right about Becca embarrassing me. People at school are still talking about "Handcuffs Wong." What's worse, though, is the fact that she lied to me. And on top of everything, I feel awful for all the mean things I've said and done to Emma and Cassidy and Jess these past few weeks.

"So is everybody happy now?" Becca adds.

Nobody replies. She flops back onto the sand. "Fat lot of good that did."

"Apology accepted," says Emma stiffly.

Everybody looks over at me. But I'm still feeling confused and a little angry, and my expression gives me away..

"I thought you liked the idea of a truce," says Cassidy, puzzled.

I lift a shoulder. "I guess you're right. Okay, then, apology accepted."

"So now what?" asks Jess.

"So now we lie here and work on our tans, while the rest of our class has to look for stupid pond insects and listen to more stupid *Walden*," says Ashley.

The tension in the air breaks and we all laugh.

*Heather Vogel Frederick*

"Lucky us," says Cassidy.

"What's the deal with the farm anyway, Jess? Is your family really going to sell?" asks Jen.

Jess nods unhappily. "Right after school gets out, unless there's a miracle."

I explain to them about the secret fund to try and save Half Moon Farm.

"Wait a minute—you mean to tell us you four thought you were going to save the farm with your *babysitting* money?" Becca scoffs.

"And dog-walking," Jess replies defensively.

"And tutoring kids like your klutz of a brother at the rink," adds Cassidy.

"Hey, you bought one of my dresses for Spring Fling," I point out.

"I know, but come on, you guys, can't you think any bigger than that?" says Becca.

"Bigger how?" Emma wonders.

"Well, if my mother were here, she'd say shoot for the top," Becca explains. "I know you all think my mother is crazy and weird, and okay, sometimes she is, but she's also really, really good at thinking big. Remember that library renovation a couple of years ago?"

Emma nods slowly. "Yeah, I remember my mom saying something about her helping with the fundraising for that."

"Helping with it?" Becca snorts. "It was my mom's baby from start to finish."

"It was not!" Emma retorts. "The library staff did most of the work."

"Hey, guys, truce, remember?" says Ashley.

"So we get it, your mom is good at thinking big," says Cassidy. "So you think we should brainstorm something big."

Becca nods.

"Maybe we could write to some famous movie stars and ask them for donations," says Jen. "They've got lots of money."

We all groan.

"At least she's thinking in the right direction," Becca notes. "She's shooting for the top, like my mother says."

"Well then, how about asking some country stars to give a concert?" says Ashley. "You know, like singers and rock stars are always doing to raise money for global warming and starving kids in Africa and stuff. Didn't they do one called 'Farm Aid'?"

"Nashville might not be so flattered that you named your chickens after them," I tell Jess.

"She did what?" A smirk hovers on Becca's lips.

"It was my mother's idea," Jess explains. "She's a big country music fan."

"Maybe I should call you Chicken Girl instead of Goat Girl," says Becca.

Cassidy pokes her in the ribs.

"I'm kidding! Can't any of you take a joke?" Becca rolls back over on the sand and we're all quiet again. After a while, she sits up. "You know, what Ashley said about Farm Aid and movie stars is giving me an idea. What if you guys put on a fashion show? As a fundraiser, I mean. Emma,

*Heather Vogel Frederick*

you and I could write about it for that article Ms. Nielson is making us do for the *Woodsman*, and Megan, you could call *Flashlite* and see if maybe they want to write about it when they interview you."

I sit up too. So does everyone else.

"Wow," I say.

"That is a seriously great idea," agrees Ashley, and Emma and Jen both nod enthusiastically too.

"Score, Chadwick!" says Cassidy.

"Do you really think it could work?" Jess looks around at all of us, her expression hopeful.

"Of course it could work," snaps Becca, sounding a lot like her mother. Softening her tone, she continues, "I mean, why not? It could be really big. Can you imagine the headlines? 'CONCORD TEENS SAVE HISTORIC FARM WITH FASHION SHOW!'"

"I could handle the publicity," says Emma, getting excited. "My dad gets press releases from publishers all the time about the books he reviews, and I'm sure I could use one as a guideline. We could probably get some newspapers to cover the show, and maybe even a few TV and radio stations." She glances quickly at me. "I mean, it worked for your mom and everything, with the, uh, tree house, even if her plan didn't quite take off."

"That's because it was a lamebrain idea, just like most of the ideas she comes up with," I reply.

"Handcuffs Wong," says Cassidy quietly.

Ashley snickers. So does Jen. Emma and Jess are both trying hard not to. Becca and I exchange a glance. My lips start to twitch. So do hers. She smiles, and I smile back, and her smile gets bigger and bigger until it's so wide her braces flash in the sun. Suddenly we're all howling with laughter. We laugh so hard we wake up Mr. Hawthorne, who gets up and moves to a tree a little farther away.

Becca leans over and gives me a hug. "I'm really, really sorry I hurt your feelings, Megs," she says. "I shouldn't have made fun of your mother like that."

"It's okay," I tell her, and this time I mean it.

"Your mom's heart was in the right place," Jess says to console me. "It really meant a lot to us that she was willing to do that to help try and save the farm."

"I just wish it had worked," I reply.

"Well, the fashion show is going to," promises Cassidy. "But we'd better get busy. We don't have much time to pull this off."

*Heather Vogel Frederick*

# CASSIDY

*"It is ever so much easier to be good*
*if your clothes are fashionable."*
—Anne of Green Gables

"Will the meeting of the Half Moon Farm Fashion Fundraiser please come to order," says Emma, knocking on the windowsill to get our attention.

She's perched on the circular window seat in my turret room, notebook open and pen in hand. Emma can be kind of prissy sometimes. But at least one of us is organized. I'm lounging on the floor alongside Jess and Murphy, my dog, while Megan and the Fab Three are up on the window seat with Emma. It's the first time Becca and Jen and Ashley have ever been up here, and they're squealing like piglets about the view, and how cool the old windows are, with their diamond-shaped crisscross pattern, and about how much they wish they had turrets too.

It's an awesome room, that's for sure. I didn't like this old Victorian much when we first moved here from California two years ago. Mostly because I was homesick for Laguna Beach, where we used to live when

Dad was alive. Now I can't imagine living anyplace else. For one thing, my mom is really good at making things homey. Plus, how many houses are there in this world with actual turrets? It's too bad they went out of style. Every house should have a turret.

My mom looked surprised to see the Fab Three on our doorstep after school, but we told her we were working together on a project for the school newspaper. Which is technically true, since Ms. Nielson is making me and Emma and Becca work on that article about Megan.

We told Ms. Nielson about our idea for the fundraiser and swore her to secrecy, since we don't want to tell our parents about it yet. Especially not Mrs. Chadwick. Despite all of our apology notes and favors, Becca's mother hasn't entirely forgiven us. My mother says it's a mama-bear thing. I guess she still sees us as a threat to her cub. At any rate, when Becca first told her about being forced to work together with Emma, Mrs. Chadwick was not happy about it one bit. She marched right down to the school and demanded to talk to Ms. Nielson. Emma heard her parents discussing it afterward—I guess Mrs. Chadwick called Mrs. Hawthorne and gave her an earful—and Emma's dad said he was glad somebody in town finally stood up to the old battleax. Ms. Nielson wouldn't give an inch. She said if Becca didn't want to work with Emma that was fine, but she would have to resign from the newspaper. Becca didn't want to do that, of course, so Mrs. Chadwick had no choice but to back down.

Ms. Nielson told us she was okay with us keeping the fundraiser a secret for now. She's pretty cool, for an English teacher.

*Heather Vogel Frederick*

"But you have to promise me you'll give your parents plenty of advance notice," she'd said. "Especially since you're planning to put it on at Half Moon Farm."

We all promised. We explained that mostly we just wanted to see if the whole idea was even possible first. We didn't want to get everyone all excited and then find out that people thought it was a stupid idea and that *Flashlite* and the newspapers weren't interested in covering it. Amazingly, though, it looks like they are. The people at *Flashlite* were wild about the idea when Megan called and told them about it, and we've already gotten nibbles from the *Boston Post* and a couple of the local TV stations.

The truce is working pretty well so far too. Not perfectly, but I can tell Megan's relieved that we're all sort of getting along. It probably wasn't much fun being stuck in the middle of everything. She seems a whole lot happier since our field trip.

"So," says Emma, once everybody is settled. "Can we have an update on publicity?"

"I got the *Concord Journal* and the *Lexington Minuteman* to agree to run ads for the show for free," I report.

Jen holds up a big piece of paper. "I finished the poster. I thought we could make copies and hang them up around town."

"Wow," says Jess.

"No kidding," Emma agrees.

Megan was right—Jen really is a good artist. The background is a dark purple sky sprinkled with stars, and she drew this big moon that looks like a spotlight shining down on the barn. There's a silhouette of a model standing in the doorway, striking a pose, and a hand-lettered banner above her reads COME TO A FASHION FUNDRAISER AND HELP SAVE HISTORIC HALF MOON FARM!

"And I've got the press release almost finished," Emma says. "Stewart said he'd help proofread it before I send it out." She turns a little pink when she says this last part. Weird. But before I can think any more about it, Megan pulls out a stack of pictures.

"The designers at *Flashlite* have almost finished the runway lineup," she says. "Take a look and see what you think." She passes the photos around and everybody *oohs* and *aahs*. Well, everybody but me. They just look like clothes to me.

"Since there are twelve outfits, you'll each get to model twice," Megan continues.

I frown. "Wait a minute—who said anything about modeling?"

"Who else did you think was going to do it?" says Emma. "Murphy?"

Hearing his name, my dog cracks open an eye and wags his tail.

"No way," I tell them. "Not even for Half Moon Farm. Sorry, Jess."

Megan sighs, and starts scratching something out in her sketchbook. "How about if I promise you'll only have to wear pants, not dresses?" she asks.

"How about if you do it instead?"

"The designer never goes out on the catwalk," Megan explains. "Except at the end, to take a bow. Besides, there'll be way too much for me to do backstage."

*Heather Vogel Frederick*

"Did you talk to the boys yet?" Ashley asks her.

She nods. "Well, Zach anyway. We saw him today after lunch. He's going to talk to Ethan and Third, but we figured we'd start with him since he and Jess are friends."

Becca's mouth pinches up a little at this, but she doesn't say anything. She still thinks Zach is her personal property.

"He wasn't too wild about the idea, but we twisted his arm," Jess says, tugging on the end of her braid. "He finally said okay, since it's for a good cause. He's going to talk to Ethan and Third. He said he didn't think they'd want to be escorts, but he could probably talk them into being ushers."

"And he knows it's a secret, right?" asks Emma.

Jess and Megan both nod.

For some reason Megan thinks all of the models need to be escorted on and off the stage by guys in tuxedos. I think this is a ridiculous idea, but hey, it's her show.

"Just as long as I don't have to be up there with Tater," says Becca.

"Maybe he's not so wild about being up there with you, Metalmouth," I tell her. Ethan is my friend, and somebody's got to defend him.

"C'mon, you guys, you promised!" says Megan.

"Sorry," I reply gruffly.

"So if Ethan and Third don't go for the idea, who else could we ask?" Megan continues, tapping her sketchbook with her pencil.

"There's always Kevin," Jess suggests.

Nobody seems very excited at this idea.

"Kevin Mullins is a twerp," says Becca flatly. "We'd get laughed off the stage."

"I guess I kind of agree," I add. "It would be like walking onstage with Dylan and Ryan."

"How about I ask my brother?" says Emma.

She winks at Jess and I frown, wondering what that's all about. Does Jess like Darcy? I just don't get this whole crush thing. My mother says don't worry, one of these days love will hit me over the head like a baseball bat, but that doesn't sound like much fun. I've been hit in the head with a baseball bat before—accidentally, of course, during practice—and it hurts like heck. I'm happy to keep things just the way they are. I like just being friends with everybody. None of this boyfriend/girlfriend stuff for me.

"Perfect," says Megan. "Now, how about seating?"

"Emma and I did a little rough measuring in the barn," says Jess, "and we think we can probably fit a hundred people in there."

"And if we charge ten dollars a seat—" Emma begins.

"Hold it right there," says Becca. "Ten bucks? Are you kidding me? What happened to thinking big? Shoot for the top, remember? You should charge a hundred dollars."

The turret falls silent.

"A hundred dollars a seat?" whispers Emma. "For our little fashion show?"

"Sure," Becca replies. "I told you, my mother does these fundraiser

*Heather Vogel Frederick*

things all the time around town. I've heard her talking about it to my dad and her friends—the more you charge, she says, the more exclusive it makes the event seem, and the more people will be falling all over themselves to get in."

"A hundred seats at a hundred dollars apiece would be $10,000!" Jess calculates.

I give a low whistle. "Whoa!"

"And then on top of that, whatever we auction the outfits for," says Ashley, getting excited. "We could raise a ton of money."

"But what if nobody comes?" asks Megan, looking anxiously at her pile of photographs. "What if nobody bids on any of my designs?"

"Of course people are going to bid on them," says Becca. "They're awesome."

One thing you have to say about Becca Chadwick—she's got confidence.

"Becca's right," I announce. "If there's one thing I've learned in sports—when you decide to go for it, you have to give it all you've got. All those in favor of charging a hundred bucks per seat, raise your hand."

Becca's hand shoots up along with mine. She looks over at Jen and Ashley and narrows her eyes. They're so used to doing whatever she says, they raise theirs, too.

"That seems like too much to me," says Jess.

"Me too," says Megan, shaking her head.

Emma bites her nails, undecided. I grab Murphy's paw and hold it up.

"Majority rules!" I announce.

Emma takes a deep breath. "Okay," she says, jotting it down in her notebook. "A hundred dollars it is."

Megan opens the gym bag on the window seat beside her. "*Flashlite* sent back some of my samples," she says. "The finished products they're working on will be a little different, of course, but this will still give you the idea." The Fab Three start squealing again as she pulls out a pile of clothes.

"Can we try them on?" begs Becca.

"Sure," says Megan.

"You can change in my room," I tell Becca, and she and Ashley and Jen rush out of the turret.

"Do you really think this is going to work?" asks Megan, sounding worried. "I mean, a hundred dollars a seat is a heck of a lot of money."

"Absolutely," I tell her, with more confidence than I feel. "It's like hockey. You just have to skate out there with everything you've got. No point holding back. If you're going to fall, fall big, Coach Danner always says."

"I wasn't really planning on falling," mutters Megan, still looking worried.

Becca and Jen and Ashley reappear and twirl around the turret. From the grin on Becca's face I can tell she likes her outfit. She's not even bothering to try and hide her braces. I guess it's nice—it's a pair of black jeans, with a long-sleeved, black-and-white swirly-patterned shirt thing on top. There's a band of black ribbon around the neckline and under what my mother always refers to as "the bustline." And there's a ruffle of black-and-white fabric in a different print around the bottom hem of the shirt.

"Cute babydoll!" Jess nods approvingly.

"Huh?" I say.

"That style with the Empire waist is called a 'babydoll,'" Megan explains.

I'm still mystified. Umpire waist? Who'd want to look like an umpire? Or a doll, let alone a baby one? This fashion stuff is beyond me.

"I love this one, Megan!" says Jen, stroking the bright orange and yellow stripes on her sundress. There's not much to it—just a tube of fabric that flares out at the bottom at her knees, like an upside-down ice cream cone, and two strappy things that go around her neck and tie in back. "This halter style is really popular right now."

*Halter as in horse?* I wonder, frowning. I look over at Jess, tempted to ask her. If it has to do with animals, she's the expert. But I don't want to say anything stupid—not in front of Becca Chadwick.

Ashley is wearing a dress too, but hers is obviously designed for winter. The bottom part of it is solid red wool or some sort of warm-looking fabric, and the top is a white satiny material with little red heart-shaped polka dots all over it.

"Wow!" says Jess. "Nice dress. For Valentine's Day?"

Megan nods.

"And that cherry red looks really pretty with your hair, Ashley," adds Emma.

Ashley does have nice hair. Even I've noticed that. Her family adopted her from Guatemala when she was a baby, and her hair is really glossy dark brown. It goes just right with her skin, which looks tan all year round. I would kill for skin like that. My mother is always slathering me with sunscreen, which I hate, but which is actually probably a good idea since I burn like crazy. My mother says all redheads do, and that my dad was the same way.

Ashley turns around, revealing a big bow on the back of the dress, and everybody *ooh*s and *aah*s again. I stare at my friends. I feel like I'm from a different planet. Planet I-Don't-Get-Fashion. How can people tell what looks good on somebody? I never pay attention to colors or styles or anything like that—I just grab whatever's clean. Jeans and T-shirts mostly. And if nothing is clean, I grab something out of the hamper. My mother hates it when she catches me doing that.

"What are you guys doing up here?"

We all freeze. My sister Courtney pokes her head in the door and smiles at us.

"Uh," I reply, stalling for time.

"Hey! Cute clothes!" she says, coming into the turret for a closer look. "Did you make them, Megan?"

Megan nods.

"These are just the samples. The production department at *Flashlite* will sew the finished ones for the magazine layout."

"Really? That is so cool. These are awesome, though."

*Heather Vogel Frederick*

Megan looks at the rest of us inquiringly. I shrug. So do Emma and Jess.

"Can you keep a secret?" Megan asks Courtney.

"Sure," my sister replies. Megan explains about the fashion show and Courtney gets all excited. "If the rest of the clothes are anything like these, I think it will be a big hit."

"You really think so?" Megan says shyly.

"They're going to sell like hotcakes," Courtney promises.

My sister can be a pain—especially when she's lecturing me about being nice to Stanley Kinkaid—but sometimes she's pretty nice. By the time my mother shouts upstairs that Mrs. Wong and Mrs. Hawthorne and Mrs. Delaney are here, and that it's time for book club, we're all feeling a lot more confident.

"Maybe you can come to book club again sometime," says Megan to Becca, after the Fab Three change back into their school clothes.

"Maybe," says Becca. "I'm not sure I can talk my mother into it, though. She's still fuming about what happened at Walden Pond. Between that and *Hello Boston!*, she's pretty convinced you guys are a bad influence."

I do a little dance around the turret. "Bad Influences R Us!" I chant, and everybody laughs.

Emma consults her notebook. "Our next meeting will be this weekend, at Megan's house," she announces. "All hands on deck to help with the final preparations. Remember to tell your mothers that it's a sleepover."

"Don't forget I have to leave early for a baseball game."

"You and your stupid baseball games," says Becca.

"Shut up," I reply.

"Guys!" pleads Megan.

"It's so nice to see you girls all getting along," says Mrs. Delaney, as we troop downstairs. She smiles, but it's kind of a wobbly smile. Poor Mrs. Delaney has been looking really, really tired and sad lately. Jess says she's just heartbroken about selling the farm.

*Little does she know,* I think smugly.

"What are you girls so tickled about?" asks my mother, after the Fab Three leave.

"They've been looking enormously pleased with themselves lately, haven't they?" says Mrs. Hawthorne. "You'd almost think they were plotting something."

"No kidding," says Mrs. Wong, shaking her head. "All this giggling and whispering and late-night phone calls!"

We just smile.

Our book club meeting ends up being a little shorter than usual. My mother decided at the last minute that since it's such a nice warm spring evening it would be fun to have a barbecue afterward, especially since she had tons of leftover food from the week's taping. Even though it's the middle of May, she and the crew are already working on the Labor Day episode, and they made ribs and homemade barbecue sauce and cole slaw and baked beans and cornbread and yummy stuff like that.

*Heather Vogel Frederick*

Just thinking about it makes me hungry, and my stomach growls as Mrs. Hawthorne passes us our handouts.

## Fun Facts About Maud

1. Lucy Maud Montgomery was petite and lively, loved books, animals (especially cats), gardening, photography, and pretty clothes.

2. Like her character Anne Shirley, Maud earned a teaching degree and taught on Prince Edward Island. She also worked for a year as a newspaper reporter at the *Halifax Daily Echo*.

3. After her grandfather died, she returned to Cavendish to help her grandmother. She lived at home for the next thirteen years, and it was during this time that she wrote *Anne of Green Gables*.

4. Although she promised her grandmother she wouldn't marry while she was still alive, she became secretly engaged to a local Presbyterian minister, Ewan MacDonald. She married him on July 5, 1911, four months after her grandmother's death, and they eventually had two sons, Chester and Stuart.

5. Maud loved to write letters, and she wrote to two of her favorite pen pals, a farmer from Alberta and a Scottish journalist, for forty years.

*Lucy Maud Montgomery had a Concord connection!* In 1910, she spent two weeks in Boston as the guest of her publisher. While she was in New England, she came to Concord and visited the homes of Emerson, Hawthorne, Thoreau, and Louisa May Alcott.

"Gee," says Jess, "She was right here in Concord. I wonder if she ever drove by Half Moon Farm?"

"If she did, I'm sure she thought it was just as pretty as Green Gables," my mother tells her.

Mrs. Delaney gets that sad look on her face again, and Mrs. Hawthorne quickly changes the subject. We talk for a while about what she calls "a sense of place" and how Lucy Maud Montgomery's love of Prince Edward Island comes through in her books.

"You mean the way reading her stories makes you feel almost like you've been there?" I ask her.

"That's exactly what I mean," says Mrs. Hawthorne.

I'm still kind of embarrassed that I thought Avonlea was a real place. But how was I supposed to know? The author sure made it seem real. As real as Concord, in fact. I wonder if maybe someday somebody will write a story set here in our town, like Maud set hers in Prince Edward Island. *Maybe Emma will,* I think, looking over at her. She's scribbling something in her notebook. A poem, probably.

*Heather Vogel Frederick*

"Hey, Mom, the grill's ready," says Courtney, poking her head in the living room. "Mr. Wong is starting the ribs. Everybody's hungry."

"I'd better get the tofu hot dogs out of the fridge," says Mrs. Wong, jumping up.

We follow my sister out onto the patio. The dads are all there, along with Darcy and the twins, who are chasing Murphy around the gazebo. And Stanley Kinkaid is there too, of course. He spends so much time at our house he could practically be part of the furniture.

"Hey, Cassidy," he says, handing me a soda.

"Hey," I reply.

The two of us are back on speaking terms again. Courtney sat me down after the Bruins game and chewed me out for being so selfish. I'm still not sure why it's so selfish of me to want things to stay the way they are, but she keeps telling me I need to think of somebody else besides myself for a change. The thing is, I do want Mom to be happy, I really do, but does that mean we have to have Stanley Kinkaid stuck to us all the time like gum on the bottom of a shoe? Why can't my mom just be happy being my mom?

Dr. Weisman says it's complicated. He's right about that. Anyway, I promised Courtney I'd try to be more unselfish, but it's hard. Stan the man is nice enough, and I know Mom is pretty crazy about him and everything, but I still like our family just the way it is. Just me, and Courtney, and Mom.

"So Little League's off to a good start, huh?" says Stanley.

"Yup," I reply politely.

"You pitching again this year?"

"Yup."

"Planning on doing summer baseball camp?"

"Yup."

Stanley's smile is starting to look a little strained. "I, uh, have some tickets to next weekend's home game at Fenway Park," he tells me. "You wouldn't want to go, would you?"

I hesitate.

"You could bring a friend along," he adds quickly. "I have three seats. Clemmie can't go that night—she said she has an early taping the next morning."

I resist the urge to gag. I hate it when he calls my mother "Clemmie."

"Maybe Courtney could come with us?" he suggests.

My sister would rather eat glass than watch baseball. Zach Norton, on the other hand, would think he'd died and gone to heaven if I could get him into a Red Sox game. So would Darcy Hawthorne.

"Let me think about it," I tell him. "You don't by any chance do the taxes for the Sox, too, do you?"

It takes Stanley a minute to realize that I'm joking. He smiles. "No, I'm not their accountant. You don't need to worry about that this time around." He claps me on the shoulder awkwardly. "You think about it, okay? Let me know when you've made up your mind."

"So, do you think they suspect anything?" says Emma in a low voice, after he wanders off.

"Who, the Red Sox?" I reply, startled.

"No, you dork, our parents! I'm talking about the fashion show."

I shrug. "Probably. We have been acting kind of strange, after all. But I don't think they have a clue what we're up to."

"We're going to have to tell them soon."

Emma's right, of course. We can't keep it a secret forever. And actually, I'm looking forward to telling them. I can't wait to see the expressions on everybody's faces. Especially the Delaneys.

I look over at the picnic table, where everyone's gathering around the food. Mr. and Mrs. Delaney are standing slightly apart from the group, quietly holding hands. Jess is leaning up against her mom.

"Emma, what if our plan doesn't work?" I ask, gripped with a sudden panic. "What if they have to sell Half Moon Farm?"

Emma turns and looks at me. Her round face is serious. "It has to work," she says solemnly. "It just has to."

## ❦ Jess ❦

*"True friendship is a very helpful thing indeed."*
—*Anne of Avonlea*

I awaken to the sound of a bulldozer.

My heart clutches with fear. *Has it started already?* Throwing back the covers and racing to my bedroom window, I open it wide and lean out as far as I can, craning to find the source of the noise.

The bulldozer is on our neighbor's property, not ours. The Thompsons must be starting to dig the foundation for their new addition.

I kneel down and rest my arms on the windowsill with a sigh of relief. The early morning sun is warm on my face, and I close my eyes and soak it in. It's going to be a beautiful day. The lilacs growing next to the porch below me are in full bloom, and I inhale their sweet, familiar scent, trying to calm my pounding pulse. Spring has always been my favorite time of year. I love how everything is fresh and new, and I love to watch the trees and fields slowly turn from brown to green.

Emma always says they're "putting on their spring clothes," which is very poetical, as Anne Shirley would say.

I open my eyes and gaze out at the barn and the fields beyond, and my anxiety returns. What if this is my last springtime at Half Moon Farm? What if today is a big failure?

I stand up and cross the room, shutting out the hateful mental image of our fields being plowed up to make space for condominiums. Propped against the mirror on my dresser is a notecard with a picture of Green Gables on the front. Mrs. Sloane sent away to Canada for them, and she gave us each a packet of them at our last book club meeting, along with these cool little pens that have a tiny wagon floating inside. Anne Shirley and Matthew Cuthbert are in the wagon, and when you tilt the pen, they drive from the railroad station home to Green Gables. Cassidy thinks they're dumb but I love mine.

I open the notecard. Inside, I wrote down one of my favorite Lucy Maud Montgomery quotes: *Green Gables is the dearest, loveliest spot in the world*. That's exactly how I feel about Half Moon Farm. I close the notecard again and give the picture on the front a kiss for luck. Today just *has* to be a success.

There's a tap at my door. My mother pops her head in. So do Sugar and Spice. "You awake?" she asks.

I nod. Dad offered to do my chores for me today so I could sleep in and get plenty of "beauty rest," as he called it, for the fashion show. "I don't want my princess looking too ramshackle today of all days," he joked last night.

The dogs push their way into my room, tails wagging happily. Why is it that dogs are always so cheerful, no matter what? I wish I could be more like our Shelties.

"Better get dressed, then," my mother says, smiling at me. "It's going to be a long day, and there's still a lot to do before tonight."

"Okay."

She glances at the notecard on my dresser, then back at me. Sometimes I swear my mother can read my thoughts.

"Everything okay?" she asks.

I shrug.

"Jess," she says, smoothing my hair back off my forehead, "no matter what happens today, our family will be fine. You know that, don't you?"

"I guess," I reply. "It's just that . . ." my voice trails off.

"Just that what?"

"It's just that I don't ever want to have to leave here."

My mother puts her arms around me and pulls me close. "I don't ever want to have to leave here either, sweetheart," she whispers. "But if I do, there's no one I'd rather be with than you, and your dad, and the boys."

I breathe her in for a moment. She smells like lavender.

"Now pull your socks up, and let's try and be positive about all this, okay? It's going to be a great day, whatever happens. All the hard work you girls have put into planning this—well, I couldn't be prouder of you, that's all."

*Heather Vogel Frederick*

Somehow we managed to keep the fashion show a secret until right before Emma and Becca's article came out in the *Walden Woodsman*. After Emma accidentally left a galley proof out on her desk and Mrs. Hawthorne spotted it, though, the cat was out of the bag. Mrs. Hawthorne e-mailed Mrs. Wong and Mrs. Sloane and my mom, and the four of them called an emergency session of the Mother-Daughter Book Club that day after school in the Hawthornes' pink kitchen.

"You planned this all by yourselves?"

Mrs. Wong looked incredulous after we explained.

"Yup," Cassidy said smugly. "Well, actually, it was Becca's idea. She and Jen and Ashley helped out too."

"The Fab Three?" Mrs. Hawthorne's eyebrows disappeared behind her bangs.

"So this is what all the secrecy has been about," said Mrs. Sloane, shaking her head.

For a minute there we couldn't tell if our mothers were mad or glad. And then my mom burst into tears.

"You girls are amazing!" she kept saying.

And of course once she started crying, the other mothers all started crying too.

"So I guess you like the idea?" I'd said.

"Like it?" my mother had replied, giving me a big hug. "We love it! It's fantastic!"

Of course they wanted to know all the details of how we came up with the idea, and what *Flashlite* had said, and how we'd planned everything.

"Well, I think it's going to be a huge success," said Mrs. Wong when we were done. She beamed at Megan. "And such a worthy cause!"

"A chip off the old block, eh, Lily?" said Mrs. Hawthorne, and Mrs. Wong nodded proudly.

As soon as the secret was out, our families all pitched in to help. Mrs. Delaney called her actor friends in New York, and half the cast of *HeartBeats* reserved tickets for the show. Mrs. Sloane insisted on doing the catering—"You can't have a fashion show without a party," she'd insisted, "and you can't have a party without good food"—plus she offered to put in a surprise appearance on the runway if Megan wanted her to. Megan is so excited she can hardly stand it. She's been going around school bragging that the world-famous Clementine will be modeling one of her outfits. She's even designing a special dress just for Mrs. Sloane, and she won't let any of us see it.

Mrs. Wong, who is on the board of trustees for just about every charitable organization in Concord, used all her connections to help get the word out, and so did Mrs. Sloane's boyfriend, Stanley Kinkaid. He sold a bunch of tickets to his clients, and some of the Boston Bruins are even going to come and bring their families. When Emma heard about the hockey players and the actors from *HeartBeats*, she decided to write another press release. Now she's calling it a "star-studded gala," and her plan worked, because a lot of the newspapers around Boston have run articles about our show, and are sending reporters to cover

*Heather Vogel Frederick*

it. So are most of the local TV stations, including Channel 5, who managed to talk Carson Dawson into giving us another chance. He said okay, as long as nobody expected him to eat or drink anything on camera.

At first when Mrs. Chadwick found out Becca was involved, she wasn't too happy. She still thinks we're a bad influence. Then she discovered that half the tickets had been sold already, and that the show was going to be on the news and featured in *Flashlite*, and that Becca was going to be one of the models. Suddenly she changed her mind and started barking orders at us.

"You can't have a fashion show in a barn, for goodness' sake," she'd decreed. "The goats might eat the clothes."

Actually, she had a point. It wouldn't be the first time. Sundance once devoured a T-shirt that I accidentally left in her pen.

So Mrs. Chadwick made a few calls—twisting arms comes naturally to snapping turtles, Mr. Wong joked—and badgered somebody into letting us use this huge tent for free, along with a portable stage and a hundred folding chairs.

A truck delivered everything last night, and all of us—plus our dads and Darcy and his best friend Kyle Anderson, and Cameron and Third and Zach Norton and Kevin Mullins and the Chadwicks and the Websters and the Sanborns—helped set it up. Mrs. Sloane and Courtney brought over these huge platters of enchiladas and chips and salsa and guacamole and stuff, and fed us while we worked. My little brothers mostly got in the way, until Mrs. Wong made Mr. Wong take them downtown to Vanderhoof's Hardware Store for twinkle lights. He came back with about a mile of them, which we twined around the tent poles and across the canopy. When we were done, my mom let the twins plug them in and the whole inside of the tent lit up. It looked absolutely amazing—like something out of a movie. Everybody clapped and cheered, and then we all piled in our cars and drove to Kimball Farm for ice cream.

There's still a ton of work to do to get ready, though. The fashion show's not until this evening, but the gates are going to open at noon so people can tour the house and barn beforehand. Mrs. Wong was the one who suggested this.

"So visitors can see what all the fuss is about," she'd said. "If they can see how special Half Moon Farm is, it will help them understand what we're trying to save."

Plus, she'd pointed out, if some people didn't want to buy tickets to the fashion show but still wanted to support our fundraiser, it might encourage them to make a donation.

By the time I take my shower and pull up a chair at the kitchen table to scarf down a bowl of cereal, people are already starting to arrive.

The screen door squeaks open. "Hey, Jess," says Darcy. One of the chickens—Tammy Wynette, I think—tries to dart past him, but Darcy's too quick for her. "You need to stay outside," he tells her firmly, shooing her off the back porch.

"Thanks."

*Heather Vogel Frederick*

He grins. "No problem. Have you seen your dad? Your mom says we should get started roping off the parking area."

I point down the hall toward the front door. "He just went that way."

"Thanks."

Darcy must have just taken a shower too, because his brown curls are still damp. He gives my braid a yank as he passes by. I wonder if he'll ever think of me as anything but a kid. I'm not that much younger than he is, but I guess when you're fifteen and a freshman in high school, a thirteen-year-old is still practically a baby.

The back door squeaks open again. This time it's Mrs. Chadwick. Mr. Chadwick is right behind her, like a shadow. Becca's father is as quiet as Becca's mother is loud, and as thin as she is, well, large. Although the yoga classes must be working, because there's less of her these days than there used to be. My dad still calls them Jack Sprat and his wife, though—at least when my mom's not around to hear it.

"Henry!" Mrs. Chadwick barks.

"Yes, dear?" Mr. Chadwick replies meekly.

"Make a note that something needs to be done about those ridiculous chickens. One of them just tried to peck my toes."

"Yes, dear." Mr. Chadwick obediently pulls a small notebook out of his shirt pocket.

"Where's your mother?" Mrs. Chadwick demands.

"Uh, I'm not sure," I tell her. "She was just here a minute ago."

"When you see her, tell her we need her in the tent."

"Okay."

The Chadwicks retreat, and I finish my cereal in peace. By the time I finally get outside, almost everybody is here. Darcy must have found my dad, because he and Kyle and some of the other fathers are with him out front, roping off a section of the front pasture for cars. Jen and Ashley are painting signs—a big one to hang on the front fence that says FASHION SHOW TONIGHT! and another that says FARM TOURS TODAY! plus two smaller ones for parking and tickets.

"This is turning into quite the community effort," says Mrs. Hawthorne, coming up behind me. She puts her arm around my shoulders. "But then, it's places like Half Moon Farm that make a community special, right?"

Cassidy appears just then, holding a clipboard. "Gather around, everybody!" she hollers.

"You sound just like Mr. Doolittle," I tease her.

She sticks out her tongue at me, then grins.

Our moms decided that since we girls planned the fashion show, we should be the ones to direct everything.

"We'll just be on hand to offer suggestions and support," said Mrs. Sloane. "This is your baby, after all, since you are now officially the 'Concord teen fashion divas.'"

That's what one of the local newspapers dubbed us, and even though it's not technically true—Emma doesn't turn thirteen for a couple of weeks, so she's not quite a teenager yet—the name

*Heather Vogel Frederick*

stuck, and our families are getting a lot of mileage out of it.

"Okay, everybody, listen up!" shouts Cassidy, consulting her clipboard. "The parking lot is almost ready, right?"

My dad nods, and she checks it off her list. It turns out Cassidy is really good at bossing everybody around. Almost as good as Mrs. Chadwick. "How about the signs?" she asks.

"We'll hang them as soon as the paint is dry," Ashley reports.

"Ticket sales?"

"Stanley should be here any minute," says her mother.

Since he's an accountant, Stanley Kinkaid has been put in charge of the ticket booth and the auction.

"How about the food? Is that under control?" Cassidy asks her mother.

"Yes, sir," Mrs. Sloane replies, saluting, and everybody laughs.

Megan is nowhere to be seen, but Mrs. Wong tells us that she's backstage in the tent, making some last-minute alterations. "She could use some help ironing," Mrs. Wong says, and Mrs. Hawthorne offers to go.

"Now all we need is for people to come," Cassidy says to me, as everyone scatters to their assigned chores.

"Do you think they will?" I ask her nervously.

Cassidy doesn't even hesitate. "Absolutely."

I wish I felt so sure.

A couple of hours later, a big black limousine pulls through the front gates. Mrs. Sloane emerges from the kitchen, wiping her hands on her apron.

"Wolfgang! Isabelle!" she calls, as a tall, skinny man dressed completely in black and a tiny woman with bright orange hair and oversize electric-blue glasses get out of the back of the car. It's the editors from *Flashlite* magazine. They have the photographer and the stylist with them too.

"Clementine!" trills the tiny woman.

They all give each other air kisses. Mrs. Sloane's friends gaze around at the farm. Isabelle d'Azur's nose wrinkles slightly, and I suddenly wish that my dad hadn't decided to spread manure on the back pasture last week.

"My," she says, "how quaint."

Mrs. Sloane quickly steers her toward the tent, which my mother and Becca and Emma are in the process of heaping with lilacs to help counteract any stray farm aromas.

Meanwhile, I head for the barn to make sure that all the animals are where they're supposed to be. I don't want a repeat of last year, when Sundance got loose during our middle school musical and practically ruined the performance. Not that it was my fault—Becca masterminded that stunt. I put Led and Zep out in the pasture, where visitors can admire them, and then, when I'm satisfied that everything else is under control animal-wise, I head for my assigned spot in the ticket booth, where I'm supposed to help Mr. Kinkaid.

As I cross the yard, Emma comes flying out of the tent.

"Jess!"

"What's the matter?" I ask.

"Come quick," she says breathlessly. "It's Megan."

She runs back toward the tent and I follow her. Backstage, Cassidy and the Fab Three are already there, standing next to the table where the stylist from *Flashlite* and my mom will be doing our hair and makeup.

"She's having a meltdown," Cassidy whispers, lifting up a corner of the tablecloth. "She won't come out."

I squat down and peek underneath. Sure enough, Megan is huddled on the ground with her knees drawn up to her chest.

"Megs," I ask her. "What's the matter?"

Megan doesn't say a word. She just shakes her head.

The stage curtain flaps open and Wolfgang pokes his head in. Cassidy quickly drops the tablecloth.

"Darlings!" he cries. Wolfgang is one of those people who only goes by his first name. He's very dramatic, and calls everyone "darling" and "sweetheart." "Has anyone seen our star of the day?" he says. "We're ready to start the interview!"

"Uh, she's around here somewhere," Becca tells him.

*Flashlite* decided to combine Megan's interview and our fashion show feature into one big article, and the plan is for Wolfgang and the photographer to follow Megan around all afternoon, taking pictures and asking questions as they go.

Wolfgang withdraws, and Cassidy lifts up the tablecloth again.

"C'mon, Megan, you have to come out," Emma coaxes.

"She's right," I tell her. "You've been looking forward to this for months."

Megan shakes her head vigorously. "No," she tells us. "I'm not going to come out. I can't believe I let anyone talk me into this. My designs are stupid and the dresses are stupid and I'm stupid. It's all going to be a horrible flop, and I'm going to look like a great big idiot."

"That's ridiculous," says Cassidy. "Your dresses are awesome, and so are you."

"You're just saying that to make me feel better," mutters Megan. "This whole fashion show idea is worse than my mother handcuffing herself to the tree."

"Um, no, actually it's not," says Becca.

There's a long silence from under the table. "Well, okay, maybe not," Megan admits. "But still—what if nobody comes? What if nobody bids on anything? What if people laugh at me? *Flashlite* will have brought the photographer here for nothing. They'll change their minds and they won't want to write an article about me at all."

The curtain twitches behind us and Cassidy quickly drops the tablecloth again. This time it's Mrs. Chadwick. She sees us all kneeling on the floor of the tent and frowns. "Did you girls lose something?"

"A contact lens," says Jen, thinking quickly. She blinks one of her eyes rapidly and makes a big show of feeling around on the floor.

"I didn't know you wore lenses, Jennifer. Well, hurry up and find it. We need to hunt for Megan. She's gone missing."

I lift up the tablecloth again after Mrs. Chadwick leaves. "Megan,"

*Heather Vogel Frederick*

I tell her, "I know how you're feeling. It's called stage fright. Remember last year? When we were in *Beauty and the Beast* together?"

There's a little grunt from under the table.

"Well, it's the same thing. Opening night, I actually thought I was going to barf. Before the curtain went up I couldn't remember a single one of my lines. But guess what? Once the show was underway, I was fine. You will be too, you'll see."

There's another pause.

"No, I won't," says Megan.

The stage curtain wafts aside again. I drop the tablecloth.

"Now who?" says Cassidy, annoyed.

It's Zach and Ethan and Third.

"Hi guys!" says Ethan. "What's going on?"

"Nothing," says Cassidy.

"Doesn't look like nothing," says Third.

The boys saunter over. Cassidy and Emma and me and the Fab Three stand up. We form a line in front of the table.

"What are you hiding under there?" asks Zach, craning his neck to see past Cassidy.

She pushes him away. He pushes back. She pushes him again, harder.

"Honestly, kids!" It's Mrs. Hawthorne. She puts her hands on her hips, frowning. "We do not have time for this today," she tells Zach and Cassidy sternly. "Boys, outside with you now. And girls, don't you have assigned jobs to do?"

"Mom, it's Megan," Emma says, as the boys leave the tent.

Her mother frowns again. "Did you find her yet? Mrs. Sloane's friends are getting a little worried."

In reply I lift up the tablecloth.

"Why, Megan Wong, what are you doing under there?" Mrs. Hawthorne's voice is gentle. She kneels down on the grass by the table.

"I don't want to come out, Mrs. H," says Megan in a small voice.

Emma's mother reaches out and strokes her hair. "Oh, honey, you don't have to be scared."

Megan bursts into tears.

"Go get Mrs. Wong," Mrs. Hawthorne whispers to Cassidy, who runs out of the tent.

The two of them return a minute later. Mrs. Wong is wearing shorts and a T-shirt with a picture of a bunch of carrots and ORGANIC FARMERS DESERVE A BUNCH OF SUPPORT on it. I hope she's planning to change before the fashion show, especially since she's the emcee.

"What's the matter, Megs?" she says, kneeling down beside Mrs. Hawthorne.

"I'm afraid," Megan replies, sniffling.

"Of what?" says her mother.

"That everyone will laugh at me."

"Laugh at you!" Mrs. Wong looks mystified. "For heaven's sake, why would anyone laugh at you? The clothes you've made are beautiful, and you've helped organize an amazing event for a worthy cause!"

"But what if they do?" Megan persists. "What if they think my

*Heather Vogel Frederick*

designs are dumb? And what if my interview with *Flashlite* sounds dumb? It'll be in print for thousands of people to read! I could never go back to school again—I could never show my face again. I'd have to become a hermit, like stupid Henry David Thoreau."

We all start to laugh, and Mrs. Hawthorne shushes us.

Mrs. Wong crawls under the table and puts her arms around her daughter. "Megan Rose Wong," she says firmly. "No one is going to laugh at you. You have more talent and gumption in your little finger"—she picks up one of Megan's pinkies and wags it in the air—"than most people twice your age. *I am incredibly proud of you.*" She peers out at us. "And that goes for all of you girls. You've done a fabulous job here today—and because of it, the Delaneys are going to get to stay here at Half Moon Farm where they belong. I just know it. You can take that from Handcuffs Wong."

Her confidence gives me a jolt of hope. Could she be right?

Megan starts to giggle. Her mother kisses the top of her head. "There's my girl. Come on out now and blow your nose."

The two of them emerge. Mrs. Hawthorne passes Megan a tissue, then turns to me. "Take her inside and help her get cleaned up, would you, Jess? Lily and I will distract the *Flashlite* folks until you get back. The rest of you girls—back to work now."

While she and Mrs. Wong go to head off Wolfgang and the photographer, I manage to sneak Megan out of the tent and into the house. I deliver her backstage again a few minutes later—face washed, hair brushed, and smiling again, though her smile is still a bit wobbly.

"There's our star!" crows Wolfgang. He sweeps his hand over the rack of clothes. "I've just been showing your lineup to our photographer, and he agrees with me completely, darling—you've done a brilliant job!"

Megan relaxes visibly.

"But what is this one here, in the garment bag?"

"Please don't touch that!" Megan says. "It's Mrs. Sloane's dress—and I want it to be a surprise."

"Ah," says Wolfgang. "Well, I'm sure it's brilliant, just like all the others."

"See?" I whisper to Megan. "You're brilliant. Everything's going to be fine."

I only wish I felt convinced of that. Even after Mrs. Wong's pep talk, worry still gnaws at me as I head off to the ticket booth. I can see cars lined up all along Old Bedford Road, though, waiting to get in, which is a good sign, so I tell myself to pull my socks up, like my mother said. I wave at Zach and Ethan and Third, who are helping Darcy and Kyle direct traffic. They wave back.

Inside the ticket booth—actually our farmstand, which my mother has practically buried under bouquets of flowers—Kevin Mullins is perched on a stool behind the counter next to Mr. Kinkaid.

"Hey, Jess," he says, his matchstick legs swinging back and forth like skinny wind chimes.

"Hey."

"This young man here tells me you're the smartest girl at Walden Middle School," Mr. Kinkaid says.

"Uh, I don't know about that," I reply, embarrassed.

"It's true," Kevin says. "We're both taking high school math."

It turns out Mr. Kinkaid is really good at math too—naturally, since he's an accountant—and between customers we talk about statistics and stuff. Mrs. Sloane stops by a little while later with lemonade and sandwiches for us. "This should tide you over until the after-party," she says.

"Thanks, Clemmie," says Mr. Kinkaid, giving her a kiss. Cassidy hates his pet name for her mother, but I think it's kind of cute. So is the look Mr. Kinkaid gets on his face whenever Mrs. Sloane is around. It's kind of how I imagine Gilbert Blythe looking at Anne Shirley. Thinking of Gilbert Blythe makes me think of Darcy Hawthorne, and I peek out the ticket booth over to the parking lot. Cassidy's older sister Courtney is perched on the top rail of the fence, taking a break and talking to him and Kyle. The three of them are laughing. I sigh and wish I hadn't looked. My little daydream is utterly hopeless.

The rest of the afternoon flies by. Cars just keep coming and coming, and Mr. Kinkaid and Kevin and I sell more and more tickets. Mr. Kinkaid is really funny and nice, and he jokes around a lot with me and Kevin and the customers. I can see why Mrs. Sloane likes him. I'm not exactly sure why Cassidy doesn't.

As the light begins to fade, Mr. Kinkaid glances at his watch. "It's nearly time, kids. You'd better round up the others."

Kevin and I find the rest of the boys and head for the tent. Inside, my little brothers spot us and come running.

"Ta-da!" they shout.

Behind me, someone starts to clap. I turn around. It's Isabelle d'Azur.

"*C'est adorable!*" she says. She's beaming, so I guess that means she approves. Isabelle d'Azur is from Paris.

The twins are dressed in tiny tuxedos. Megan calls them "pest suits." She thought it would be funny. They're not going to be escorts—nobody in their right mind would trust my brothers with that responsibility—but they're going to take tickets at the door and help the older boys with the ushering. With my brothers in hot pursuit, Zach and Ethan and Third and Kevin follow Darcy and Kyle and Stewart toward the barn to get changed. I head backstage to the girls' dressing room, which is actually just a corner of the tent that's been sectioned off with a sheet.

"Here's your first outfit, Jess," Megan says, handing me a hanger from the rack. I can tell she's back to her normal self now that things are underway. "You'll be going sixth, just like we rehearsed."

"Okay." I duck into the changing area and pull off my shorts and T-shirt. We've titled our show "The Four Seasons of Fashion." Emma made that up, and she wrote the script for the emcee too. The emcee was originally going to be my mother, but she said she'd rather just have a supporting role this time, and volunteered to help the stylist backstage. So Mrs. Wong is going to emcee.

I pull Megan's dress on over my head. Each of us has been assigned a month, and I'm supposed to be June, so naturally my first outfit is a

238                                            *Heather Vogel Frederick*

summer dress. It's short—it just reaches my knees—and designed in a loose, flowy style made of blue gingham with smocking on the top.

Cassidy plucks at the fabric when I emerge. "It looks like a tablecloth," she says.

"Cassidy!" says Emma. "It does not."

I look from one of them to the other, not sure who to believe. Fortunately, Wolfgang appears just then.

"Perfect!" he decrees. "Very farmgirl chic! And tell the stylists to keep your hair exactly the way it is, darling." He waggles his hands in the air. "It's so—you know, Dorothy! Oz!"

I'm not sure if I like this remark any better than Cassidy's, but I trudge dutifully over to the makeup table that Megan was hiding under earlier.

"Oh, sweetie, that looks gorgeous on you!" my mother says. She's wearing an apron, and there are curling irons and brushes and combs sticking out of all the pockets.

"Thanks," I reply, relieved to hear that I'm not about to go out on stage dressed in a tablecloth. I trust my mom's opinion more than anyone's. The photographer snaps a bunch of pictures as she and the *Flashlite* stylist fuss with my makeup and my hair. In the end they decide to put it in a French braid instead of just leaving it in my regular braid down the back.

"This is a fashion show, after all," says my mother.

"Knock knock!" calls a voice on the other side of the stage curtains. "Can we come in?"

"Sure," Cassidy calls back. "Everybody's dressed."

The curtains part with a flourish and Zach Norton steps through. The Fab Three start whispering in excitement. Zach is wearing his tuxedo. He takes a bow, and Cassidy gives him a wolf whistle. The rest of the boys all file in behind him. None of them are dressed in tuxedos, because in the end Megan decided that one escort would be enough. They're dressed more casually, in white polo shirts and khaki pants. Stewart's are about three inches too short, of course, but that's just Stewart.

"Very nice, gentlemen, very nice," says Wolfgang. He claps his hands. "And now, places everyone! We're just about ready to start!"

The boys turn to go.

"You look like a penguin," Ethan says to Zach, grinning at him.

"I do not," Zach retorts, putting him in a headlock. Ethan struggles to break free, and the two of them start mock wrestling.

"Knock it off, guys," warns Mrs. Hawthorne. "Remember what I said earlier."

Ethan manages to escape Zach's grip, and as he does he gives Zach one final shove.

"Whoa!" cries Zach, teetering on the edge of the stage. He waves his arms over his head, desperately trying to regain his balance. He falls into the clothes rack with a *crash!*

Everybody rushes over.

"Ooo, Zach, are you hurt?" asks Becca in that special chirpy voice she reserves for boys.

Zach winces, though I can't tell whether it's from embarrassment

*Heather Vogel Frederick*

or pain. "It's my ankle," he says. "I think I twisted it."

"We told you to quit horsing around, you morons," says Cassidy.

Ethan looks stricken. "I'm sorry, dude," he says to Zach.

"No big deal," Zach replies.

But it is a big deal. If Zach can't walk, he can't be our escort.

"We're going to need a replacement," says Wolfgang, looking around.

"Not me," says Ethan, backing away.

Wolfgang narrows his eyes, sizing him up. "Wouldn't work anyway," he replies. "Too husky." He turns to Third and Kevin. "Too short, and w-a-y too short. None of you would fit into the tux."

"How about Kyle, then, or Darcy?" Emma suggests, pointing to her brother and his friend.

My heart does a little somersault. Walking arm in arm across the stage with Darcy Hawthorne would be heaven.

"Far too tall, both of them," says Wolfgang dismissively. "We need someone the same height as this boy, so the pants fit." His gaze wanders over to Stewart, who is standing on one leg, sucking on the end of a pencil, watching the proceedings.

"Don't even think about it," says Becca flatly.

Wolfgang sighs. "Well, he is about the right height, and apparently we have no other choice. Young man!"

Stewart gapes at him. "Me?"

"Yes, you. Come here!"

Stewart lopes over.

"Consider yourself the cavalry," Wolfgang tells him.

"Huh?" says Stewart.

"You're our replacement escort."

Stewart's eyes widen behind his glasses. "Me?" he squawks, his voice cracking.

Becca snickers.

"Shut up," says Cassidy. She turns to Stewart. "Dude, remember what I told you last December, out on the rink? About what my dad always used to tell me?"

"You mean about bringing my best to every game?" Stewart's Adam's apple bobs up and down nervously.

Cassidy nods. "This is it, dude. This is the game, and this is the time to bring it."

"But I—"

"Just go put the tuxedo on and stop arguing," says Wolfgang, waving him away.

"Come on, Stewart," says my mother, hooking her arm through his and tugging him toward the makeup table. "Time to work some stylist magic."

I can't imagine any kind of magic powerful enough to transform Stewart Chadwick, but I don't say anything.

With Ethan and Third on either side of him for support, Zach hobbles off to the barn to take off the tuxedo. He returns a few minutes later in his jeans again, looking sheepish.

"Sorry if I messed things up for you, Beauty," he says, handing me the tux.

*Heather Vogel Frederick*

"It's okay, Beast," I tell him. I can't help but be disappointed, though. And a little worried. I sure hope having Stewart onstage isn't going to ruin our show. What if he trips over his feet or something, and makes us look like amateurs?

I give Zach's tux to my mom, who passes it over the dressing room curtain to Stewart. With my twin brothers in tow, the ushers all head for their posts, depositing Zach in a chair in the front row on their way. We can hear the excited murmurs from the audience as they start to file into the tent. The twinkle lights are on and everything looks amazing.

"Places, everyone!" says Wolfgang

The *Flashlite* photographer snaps away as the six of us models line up by the short flight of steps leading to the stage. I wonder if real models ever get used to having cameras flashing in their faces every three seconds. It's very annoying. But I grit my teeth and smile.

"Oh. My. Gosh." Ashley is staring over my shoulder, open-mouthed.

"What?"

She shakes her head and points. I turn around to see my mother leading Stewart Chadwick toward us.

"I can't see a thing," he complains, squinting.

My mother tucks his glasses into her apron pocket. "You don't need to," she says firmly. "And don't squint. The girls will guide you."

"But I thought I was supposed to be escorting them."

"Just relax, Stewart. Everything will be fine."

Stewart Chadwick looks completely different. I've never noticed his eyes before. His glasses are so thick and scratched-up they kind of mask them. Stewart's eyes are a really intense gray, and my mom and the *Flashlite* makeup person slicked his hair back so that his bangs don't cover his forehead, and in the tuxedo he looks, well—

"Fabulous!" says Wolfgang. "Quite the Cinderfella, aren't we?" He cocks his head to one side and gives Stewart a thoughtful look. "And quite the brooding poet type too. I never would have guessed." He pokes him between the shoulder blades and Stewart jumps. "Stand up straight, young man. Posture is essential."

Mrs. Chadwick barges through the curtain. "Has anybody seen— *Stewart?*" She looks at her son and blinks. "What are you doing in that tuxedo?"

"I, uh, I'm going to escort Emma—the girls, I mean," he stammers. "Onstage."

"Your son has quite a unique look, madam," says Wolfgang. "We'll have to see how he photographs, but it's entirely possible we might be able to use him."

"Use him?" Mrs. Chadwick's eyes narrow. "What on earth are you talking about?"

"As a model," Wolfgang replies.

For once, Mrs. Chadwick is speechless.

"Of course, the tuxedo helps," Wolfgang continues. "Every man looks handsome in a tuxedo."

"I do?" says Stewart, his voice breaking into a squeak again.

*Heather Vogel Frederick*

"Absolutely," my mother says. "Don't you think so, girls?"

I nod. Emma does too, vigorously. Becca looks disgusted, especially when Ashley and Jen start nodding as well. Cassidy just shrugs.

The curtains part again and Isabelle d'Azur walks backstage. "Who wrote this?" she asks, holding up a copy of the emcee's script.

"I did," says Emma, looking worried. "Is something wrong?"

"Where did you learn to write fashion copy?" the petite editor demands.

Emma turns red. "I, uh, kind of followed the style in your magazine."

"Aha," says Isabelle d'Azur. "Well, they say imitation is the sincerest form of flattery. You did a marvelous job, *chérie*. Truly astounding for one so young. You should think about a career in journalism. The fashion industry could use you."

Emma stares at her, openmouthed. She finally manages to stammer a thank-you.

"I helped her write the article in our school newspaper about Megan," blurts Becca.

Isabelle d'Azur nods vaguely. "*Oui, oui*. I'm sure you did." She disappears through the curtains again.

Becca glares at Emma. "You think you're so smart!"

Emma looks flustered. "What'd I do? I barely said a thing."

"Sheesh, what's eating you, Chadwick?" says Cassidy.

I know exactly what's eating Becca. First Zach twists his ankle and can't be her escort, then her brother is told he's male-model material, and now Emma's in the spotlight for her "Four Seasons of Fashion" script. Becca doesn't like it when she doesn't get what she wants, and she definitely doesn't like to share the spotlight.

All of a sudden there's a drumroll. My stomach lurches. We're starting! Megan's dad sticks his head through the curtains, grins, and gives us the thumbs-up. He's in charge of the music, and he brought over a fancy CD player and these huge speakers from his music room at home.

Becca looks Emma up and down. "That dress makes you look fat," she says spitefully.

"Yours makes you look like Josie Pye," I retort.

Stewart Chadwick takes his sister by the arm and hauls her toward the curtain. He looks over at Emma. "Becca is dead wrong," he says. "You look fine in that dress. Really pretty, in fact."

"How would you know?" snaps Becca. "You're blind as a bat without your glasses."

"For heaven's sake, stop bickering!" says Mrs. Hawthorne. "Please, everyone!"

"I hope Becca trips and falls on her face," mutters Emma.

"Don't listen to a word she says," I say, consoling her. "She's just jealous. At least Stewart stuck up for you. He's pretty nice, you know."

Emma turns pink. "I know," she says.

On the other side of the curtains, there's a roar of applause from the audience. We peek through the curtains and watch as Mrs. Wong greets the audience, thanking them for their support for Half Moon

*Heather Vogel Frederick*

Farm. Her organic T-shirt is gone, thank heavens, and she's wearing black pants and the red silk dragon-lady top she bought on our trip to New York last summer. She's even wearing lipstick.

"I've just been told that not only do we have a sellout crowd here tonight, but that we have standing room only!" she cries. After the applause dies down she continues, "Looking out at you all this afternoon I see a lot of familiar faces—some from the TV screen, others from the hockey arena, and even one from the Internet." There's a ripple of laughter as the audience realizes she's talking about Carson Dawson. He frowns, but as the audience starts clapping and cheering for him, his glower changes to a grin. Getting into the spirit of things, he stands up, takes out his dentures and waves them in the air. The audience howls with laughter.

"Megan's mom is really funny," I tell Emma and Cassidy, surprised.

"No kidding," says Emma.

"We have a very special show for you here tonight," Mrs. Wong continues, after the crowd settles down again. She explains that the fashions they'll be seeing are prototypes, and will be made up in any size the winning bidder requests. "So there's no excuse for not bidding," she says. "I'm expecting you all to dig deep into your pockets—and not in search of gum, either. I'm talking about digging for the kind of support that will help save this historic farm. And why not have some fun while we're doing it? Without any further ado, let's celebrate the 'Four Seasons of Fashion' with Concord's own teen fashion divas!"

Mr. Wong fiddles with the CD player and the opening music starts. Mrs. Hawthorne pushes Becca and Stewart through the curtains. Becca struts across the stage, dragging her brother with her.

"Kicking off tonight's stellar lineup is Miss Rebecca Chadwick," says Mrs. Wong. "Becca takes a walk on the wild side here in this wintry January ensemble. Note the sophisticated mix of metaphors as the designer pairs casual black leggings and a long-sleeved leopard-print top with the uptown glamour of a black quilted mink-trimmed vest. It's faux fur, of course. All of my daughter's designs are cruelty-free."

"Hey, I didn't write that last bit," says Emma. "She must have added it."

"Mrs. Wong wouldn't be Mrs. Wong if she didn't manage to squeeze her favorite subjects in somehow," I reply with a smile.

We watch Becca wiggle her way around the stage, trying to look like a fashion model.

"She looks ridiculous," says Emma.

"Yeah, but the audience loves it," says Cassidy.

It's true. Hands are shooting up all over the tent as Mr. Kinkaid gets the bidding started. I can tell he's enjoying being the auctioneer—we made sure he had a little gavel and everything.

A minute later, Becca reappears through the curtains. "Carson Dawson's wife just paid five hundred dollars for my outfit!" she says triumphantly. "See if you can top that!"

This is the wrong thing to say to Cassidy Sloane.

"Watch me," she says, and suddenly our fashion show is about more than just modeling. Cassidy bounds out onto the stage like she's hitting

*Heather Vogel Frederick*

the rink for the championship game. The bidding for her powder-blue ski ensemble heats up quickly, thanks to her antics. Pretending to be skiing, she squats down and tucks imaginary ski poles under arms, rocking from side to side. Stewart looks like he doesn't quite know what to do, so he sticks his arms out and pretends to be a tree, blowing in the wind. At least I guess that's what he's doing. It's kind of hard to tell.

The audience eats it up, whatever it is, and Cassidy's outfit finally sells for $475, not quite enough to knock Becca out of the lead.

"Tough luck, Carrots," says Becca smugly.

Cassidy ignores her. "Go get 'em, Ashley," she says, handing Stewart over.

Ashley's red-and-white polka dot Valentine's Day outfit raises $350. Then it's Emma's turn. She gives me a nervous wave as Mr. Wong changes the music—it's supposed to be springtime now, so he's playing a waltz or something. Stewart's right, Emma does look really pretty. Megan designed a cheerful daffodil yellow dress for April, and it's flouncy and feminine and nipped in at the waist to show off the fact that Emma isn't as round as she used to be. All that figure skating is making a difference.

Onstage, Becca's brother has this huge goofy grin on his face and he keeps beaming at Emma. Something dawns on me as I watch the two of them.

"I think Stewart Chadwick likes Emma," I whisper to Cassidy in amazement.

"Whatever," Cassidy replies. She hates it when we talk about boys.

"Note the puffed sleeves," says Mrs. Wong, reading from Emma's script. "As all of you Lucy Maud Montgomery fans will recall, Anne Shirley always wanted puffed sleeves, and this romantic springtime confection harks back to a more elegant time—a time of tea parties at Green Gables, kindred spirits, and innocent romance with a young man named Gilbert Blythe."

The ladies in the audience all sigh when Mrs. Wong mentions Gilbert Blythe, and Emma's dress sells for four hundred dollars.

"Nobody's going to beat my price," crows Becca, as Stewart and Emma come back offstage.

"We'll see about that," says Jen, showing more spirit than usual.

"Looks like somebody forgot to bring the remote control," Cassidy whispers to Emma and me, and we giggle.

Jen is modeling a pair of capris made from a bright patchwork fabric in shades of pink and orange and yellow and blue and green. Over it she's wearing a long, fitted white camisole edged in pale green lace, and topping it off is a short jacket whose floral print is in the same colors as the capris.

"Saucy, sassy, and utterly scintillating, this perky trio in cupcake shades is just right for Spring's in-between days," says Mrs. Wong.

Cassidy shakes her head. "Man, Emma, I can't believe you wrote this stuff."

"What'd you expect me to write, a poem?" says Emma defensively. "It's just like in the fashion magazines. Isabella d'Azur even said so."

Cassidy snorts.

*Heather Vogel Frederick*

"Five hundred and fifty dollars!" shouts Mr. Kinkaid, the auctioneer, and Jen returns backstage smiling.

"Now who's queen of the hill?" says Emma to Becca.

"Big deal," Becca retorts.

It's finally my turn. I take Stewart's arm and he leads me onstage. I'm incredibly nervous standing there in my blue gingham "tablecloth." Not because of the design, but because I'm wondering if we'll make enough money to keep my parents from having to sell Half Moon Farm. Usually I can add things up in my head no problem, but tonight I can't seem to get my brain to focus.

My dress goes for $425. After Stewart deposits me backstage, I run over to the stylist's table. "Mom, do you have any paper? And a pen?"

She digs around in her apron pockets. "Somewhere in here, I think," she says, fishing them out and handing them to me. I do some quick addition.

"Mom!" I cry. "We made twenty-seven hundred dollars for the first six outfits!"

"Really?"

I nod in excitement, then I dash back into the dressing room and change into my next outfit. As I do, it occurs to me that it's probably a good thing Becca decided to start a little fashion show war. I say so to Emma and Cassidy.

Cassidy grins. "Good point," she says. "We should thank her. See what you think of this." She turns to Becca, who is preparing to go onstage again. She's representing July this time around, and she's wearing white shorts, a red-white-and-blue-spangled halter top, and oversize white sunglasses.

"Hey, Old Glory!" Cassidy calls to her. "Where's the flagpole?"

"Cassidy Ann!" says Mrs. Sloane, popping up from behind the dress rack. "Where are your manners? You apologize immediately."

"Sorry, Becca," says Cassidy cheerfully, not sounding sorry at all.

Becca sticks her nose in the air. Mr. Wong starts the music, and it turns out to be "Stars and Stripes Forever." We all collapse in giggles, even Stewart. Becca shoots us a murderous look and flounces onstage. Stewart scrambles after her. Becca may be furious at us, but she's all smiles for the audience, and by the end of the auction she's regained her first-place position with a winning bid of six hundred dollars.

"I can't believe my stuff is selling for this much money," whispers Megan, looking dazed.

With Ashley waiting in the wings, Cassidy heads off to get changed. Ashley is wearing the black-and-white babydoll outfit that Becca tried on last month at the Sloanes' house.

"Wow," I tell her, as Becca and Stewart exit the stage. "That looks even prettier on you than it did on Becca."

"Thanks, Jess," Ashley replies.

Becca gives us a sharp look. "The audience might not think so," she says loftily.

Fortunately the audience does think so, and Ashley's ensemble sells for $525. She looks disappointed as she comes back through the curtains, though.

"I was hoping to beat Becca," she tells us.

"You were great," Emma consoles her. "Don't worry about it."

Cassidy appears behind us, scowling. "Megan pulled a fast one on me," she grumbles, plucking at the poufy little cap sleeves of the dress she's wearing. It's a back-to-school outfit, because she's supposed to be September. "She promised I wouldn't have to wear a dress. Besides, there's no way I would be caught dead in this at school."

Emma glances down at her scabby knees. "Maybe you should pull it down a little lower," she whispers.

"Maybe you should shut up," Cassidy whispers back. She stumps out onstage, looking surly. The audience doesn't seem to notice, however, because one of the Bruins players buys the dress for his daughter, with a winning bid of four hundred dollars.

Becca gives her a superior smile as Cassidy comes through the curtains. Cassidy looks like she wants to smack her, but Mrs. Hawthorne is watching so she ignores her instead.

Just three more designs to go. Jen is up next. "In this fresh twist on the schoolgirl look, the designer updates a classic plaid pleated skirt with a fresh autumn palette of eggplant and gold. Note the witty nod to menswear—French cuffs on the companion shirt, and a matching necktie."

"Why couldn't I have gotten that outfit? I'd rather wear a tie than a dress," says Cassidy, still grumbling, as Jen emerges backstage, pleased with the $450 winning bid.

"Here's one way to show your school spirit," says Mrs. Wong, as Stewart and Emma take to the stage again. I watch them closely. Stewart is holding Emma's arm like she's a piece of my mother's best china, and he can't keep his eyes off her outfit. She's supposed to be November, and she's dressed as if she's going to a football game, in brown corduroy pants, brown boots, and a turtleneck the same creamy shade as one of our Saanen goats. Over it all is a big, fluffy wraparound sweater that's more the soft brown of Sundance. The collar is turned up and it frames Emma's round face perfectly. She looks—

"Adorable!" says someone behind me. It's Isabelle d'Azur, who has popped backstage to help Mrs. Sloane get ready. "Simply *magnifique*—Megan, your collection is a triumph!" She kisses Megan on both cheeks and disappears into the dressing area.

I'm still watching Stewart and Emma. "He definitely likes Emma," I report in a whisper to Cassidy, who pretends not to hear me. The question is, though, does Emma like Stewart? She hasn't said a word to me about it if she does. I frown. Aren't we best friends? Don't best friends tell each other everything?

Finally, it's my turn again. I'm December, the last month of the year, and the last model in our Four Seasons of Fashion show. Well, except for Mrs. Sloane. My mother and the *Flashlite* stylist brushed my hair out and let it fall loose around my shoulders. It's wavy from being in a braid all day, and I'm wearing a necklace of crystal stars that look like diamonds. Emma tells me I look like a dream.

I'm still trying to add everything in my head as Stewart tugs me onstage. I'm pretty sure we're close to our goal, but the numbers keep swimming around in my head and I can't seem to pin them down. I try not to worry about Half Moon Farm, and instead concentrate on showing off my dress, which is a deep navy blue, instead of one of the usual holiday colors, and cut very simply and elegantly.

I never understood before tonight what the expression "your heart is in your throat" meant. Tonight I get it. I can hardly breathe. What if people don't like the dress? What if they don't bid? What if nothing we've done here today makes any difference at all?

The bidding starts, and it's low. Only a hundred dollars. I grip Stewart's arm tighter, trying not to let my anxiety show. *Come on*, I think. *Come on.*

Mr. Kincaid is a good auctioneer. He sweet talks the audience the way I sweet talk our goats, squeezing every last drop out of them.

"We're coming down the finish line here, folks," he says. "And it's a close race. Surely you can do better than that. What am I bid now, do I hear two hundred?"

He does. Then two fifty. Three hundred. I tune everybody out and let Stewart steer me around the stage. Mr. Wong is playing *When You Wish Upon a Star* for background music, and the twinkle lights envelop all of us in the tent in a warm glow. I start to hum along. *Makes no difference who you are— Anything your heart desires will come to you . . .*

There's only one thing my heart desires here tonight. I shut my eyes tight, wishing with all my might.

The gavel bangs down and my eyes fly open.

"Sold!" cries Mr. Kincaid. "For seven hundred and fifty dollars!" And then he brings the gavel down again with another resounding *thump* and adds, "And that, ladies and gentlemen, puts us over the top. Half Moon Farm is safe!"

The tent erupts in cheers. My friends all crowd onstage and surround me, including Becca, who gives me a grudging thumbs-up. Then my dad is there and so is my mother, thanking the audience while my little brothers dash down the aisle, doing silly dances. The news cameras are rolling and bulbs are flashing and everyone is calling for the designer.

Megan comes out smiling shyly. Mrs. Hawthorne presents her with a huge bouquet of flowers, and Wolfgang and Isabelle d'Azur praise her and everybody claps, and then we all get bouquets too. My parents thank everybody for their incredible generosity, and then Megan's mother gives a little speech about the importance of preserving our town's history, and about how amazing it is to pull together as a community, only this time it's a nice speech and not a goofy one like the one she gave in the tree house last winter, and even Megan looks proud of her.

"And now," says Wolfgang dramatically, grabbing the microphone away from Mrs. Wong, "we have something very special for all of you folks here tonight."

He waits for the audience to quiet down before he continues. "Historic Concord is the perfect setting for this historic event! Making her first runway appearance in over a decade, it's the one, the only— *Clementine!*"

*Heather Vogel Frederick*

We all move instinctively to the sides of the stage as the curtain parts and Mrs. Sloane appears. The audience gasps. I know I'm staring too, which isn't polite but it's hard not to. Mrs. Sloane looks—well, she looks like a queen. A real one. Queen Clementine. She's wearing Megan's mystery dress, the one she wouldn't let us see. It's absolutely the most beautiful dress I've ever seen. It's romantic and elegant and could have come straight from Avonlea, with its bustle in the back and its yards and yards of pale peach fabric that tumble to the floor. There's lace at the throat and cuffs, and tiny little pearl buttons all down the center of the back, and Mrs. Sloane's long blond hair is swept up in one of those poufy, old-fashioned styles that suits it perfectly. So *that's* how a model is supposed to walk, I think, watching her. The dress seems to float as she moves. Unhurried and smiling, she crosses to one edge of the stage and strikes a pose, then turns and crosses to the other edge and strikes another pose. The whole time, the audience watches her silently, transfixed.

"And what am I bid for this gorgeous creation?" Wolfgang asks.

Stanley Kinkaid leaps onto the stage. "I'll give you one thousand dollars!" he cries.

"Do I hear any other bids?" says Wolfgang, scanning the tent. He brings the gavel down with a bang. "Sold! To the gentleman in the front row for one thousand dollars."

Mr. Kinkaid crosses toward Cassidy's mother. He takes her by the hand and drops down on one knee. An excited murmur ripples through the audience. Beside me, Cassidy goes completely rigid.

"Clementine," says Mr. Kinkaid, as the murmur dies away, "will you do me the honor—the *immense* honor—of making me the happiest man in the world?"

Cassidy makes a small noise in the back of her throat.

Mr. Kinkaid gazes adoringly at her mother. "Will you marry me?"

For a long moment no one makes a sound. It feels like all of Half Moon Farm is holding its breath.

Mrs. Sloane beams down at him. She nods. "Yes, Stanley," she says. "I will."

The audience erupts in cheers again. All except Cassidy. She slams her bouquet to the floor of the stage and runs out of the tent.

SUMMER

"It's a serious thing to grow up,

isn't it, Marilla?"

—*Anne of Green Gables*

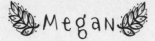

# Megan

*"I think these engagements are dreadfully unsettling things!"*
—*Anne of Avonlea*

Cassidy Sloane is a moron.

I still can't believe she blames me for her mother getting engaged to Stanley Kinkaid. It's just so stupid. She says if I hadn't made a wedding dress and gotten her mom to model it, he never would have proposed. For one thing, it wasn't supposed to be a wedding dress. Was it white? Did it have a train? Was there a veil? And for another thing, not that I'm an expert or anything, but it seems to me either a guy is going to propose or he isn't. A dress has nothing to do with it.

My mother and I are in the car on our way to the Hawthornes'. We're having a surprise wedding shower tonight for Mrs. Sloane. She thinks we're just getting together for our last book club meeting of the year, but Mrs. Hawthorne and Emma cooked this up instead. Mrs. Hawthorne said there'll be a bigger shower later, with a bunch of Mrs. Sloane's friends from yoga class and her TV show. Even a few of her friends from California and New York are flying in. But this one is just for us. I wish I were more excited about it. I've never been to a wedding shower before, but it's hard to be excited with Cassidy treating me like I'm her worst enemy.

I pull my cell phone out of my pocket and text Becca: CARROTS STILL FURIOUS. Cassidy would be furious if she knew we called her that, of course. Which is kind of the point. Becca texts me right back: CARROTS IS NUTS. She adds a smiley face.

"Everything okay?" asks my mom. "You're awfully quiet tonight."

I shrug.

She reaches over and pats my hand. "You did an amazing job with the fashion show, honey," she tells me. She's told me this at least once a day now for the past three weeks. Not that I mind hearing it. "Your dad and I are so proud of you."

Even though I suspect my mom secretly wishes I'd suddenly develop a passion for math and science instead of fabric and design, it's still nice to know she feels this way.

"I just wish Cassidy wasn't mad at me," I tell her.

She pats my hand again. "I know," she says. "She's worried about things changing, that's all. With her family, I mean. Remember in *Anne of Avonlea*, when Diana Barry gets engaged and Anne finds it unsettling, and wishes everything could stay the same? It's that way for Cassidy, too. You just need to be patient with her, the way she was with you a few months ago."

I try to imagine how I'd feel if my mother was going to marry

*Heather Vogel Frederick*

someone besides my dad. It's impossible. I can't. I know it must be hard for Cassidy, but still, does that give her the right to act like a jerk?

We pull into the Hawthornes' driveway and I hop out. Melville, Emma's big orange tabby cat, is sunning himself on the back steps. He stands up and stretches, then ambles over to see me. I scratch him under his chin. I like Melville. We can't have pets because my dad is too hyper about the mess. I had a Beta fish once, named Bubble, and we tried a lizard, too, back when my mom was still trying to get me interested in saving the environment.

It's not that I'm against all that stuff, it's just that I don't have my mother's passion for it. My passion is fashion. Hey, that's pretty catchy. I reach for my sketchbook. *My passion is fashion.* I jot it down. It might make a fun T-shirt logo someday.

The Sloanes' van pulls into the driveway right behind us. Mrs. Sloane gets out first. She's dressed perfectly, of course, as always. Tonight she's wearing a long tiered black skirt that ruffles out just below her knees, and a gauzy turquoise shirt cinched in at the waist with a chic black belt. There's a big silver-and-turquoise buckle on the belt, and she's accessorized with matching silver bracelets and big silver-and-turquoise earrings. She looks gorgeous. I'm going to have to sketch her later.

"Hi, Megan! Hi, Lily!" she calls.

Cassidy gets out of the car, too. She slams the door shut and doesn't say anything.

"Clementine, I wanted to ask you how plans for the vegan episode are coming," my mother says. She winks at me as she hands over a salad bowl, then gives me a little shove. This is my cue to go inside. Cassidy trails behind me, still not speaking.

"Come on in quick, girls!" whispers Mrs. Hawthorne, glancing over my shoulder. She glances out the kitchen window to make sure my mother is delaying Mrs. Sloane as we planned. "Go on into the dining room, both of you. Hurry now! They'll be heading inside any second, and we're all going to hide in there."

At least Emma and Jess are happy to see me. Jess waves her preview copy of *Flashlite* under my nose. It won't be published until August, but the editors sent us all copies of the mock-up.

"Can I get your autograph?" she asks. "Please, Miss Wong!"

I know she's teasing me, but it's fun to play along. I put the salad bowl down on the table, grab the pen, and sign the cover with a flourish. Then I pass to it Emma.

"Your turn," I tell her.

Isabelle d'Azur liked Emma's "Four Seasons of Fashion" descriptions so well she asked if *Flashlite* could use them in a sidebar about my designs. Emma got paid two hundred and fifty dollars. She says it's her "first sweet bubble of success" as a writer, just like L. M. Montgomery. Emma really admires Maud. She's even started signing her name "E. J. Hawthorne" on all of her articles for the school paper.

Her dad helped her design some business cards on his computer, and the day that she and Becca and Cassidy came to my house to interview me and take pictures, Emma handed them out to me and my parents.

"'E. J. Hawthorne, Reporter,'" my mom read aloud. "Very impressive."

Becca snorted. "It's just the stupid *Walden Woodsman*," she'd scoffed. "It's not like it's the *New York Times* or anything."

Becca gets snarky when she's jealous. I noticed she didn't have any business cards.

"Everyone has to start somewhere," my dad pointed out. "My first job was sweeping the floors at a department store every day after school."

My dad grew up in Hong Kong. Sometimes I forget that he wasn't always a computer genius. His family didn't have much money, and he started working to help support them when he was my age.

"I took that job seriously, and the owner noticed and promoted me to salesclerk. Before long, I was a department manager. I earned enough from that job to buy myself a ticket to the United States."

He tapped Emma on the head with her business card. "My point is, you're on the right track here, Ms. E. J. Hawthorne. There's nothing wrong with taking yourself seriously. Just like you girls did when you planned the fashion show."

The interview went okay. Cassidy made me pose a few times, first sketching, then at my sewing machine, and finally holding up one of my outfits.

Becca was on her best behavior, especially since my mom's office is right next to my sewing room, and she kept popping in to see how we were doing. I think she was more excited about the interview than I was. Becca asked most of the questions, while Emma wrote down my answers. It was kind of funny, because later, when each of them talked to me about how much of a pain it was to work together on the article, they both complained that they'd done most of the work. Somehow, I tend to believe Emma on this one.

"Hey, did you see Becca today?" Jess asks me, dragging me back to reality. "She was bragging to everybody about how she's your friend, and how she gives you ideas for your designs all the time. And the whole school is talking about the *Flashlite* article."

"You mean everybody's talking about the pictures of Stewart Chadwick," I say.

Becca is really upset with her brother because of what happened at the fashion show. I think maybe she was hoping she'd impress the *Flashlite* people and get asked to be a model, but instead Stewart was. Mrs. Chadwick said no at first, but then Cassidy's mother pointed out that she earned her way through college by modeling, and Mr. Chadwick, who usually doesn't say a word, spoke up and said he thought it was a great idea, and that it would give Stewart confidence. So Mrs. Chadwick changed her mind, and now Stewart's "brooding poet" face is plastered all over *Flashlite*. Becca's trying to pretend she doesn't care, but I can tell she's disappointed and jealous.

The dining room looks really nice. There are white streamers draped around the room and fluttering from the chandelier, and taped to the bookshelves are posters that Jess and Emma and I made. They have pictures of brides and grooms glued to them, and we drew big hearts with CLEMENTINE + STANLEY written inside them in glitter. The Hawthornes are the only people I know with bookshelves in their dining room. They're all bookworms, even Darcy.

There's a white tablecloth on the table, and in the middle is a tiny little wedding cake with a tiny little bride and groom on top. The bride is blond like Mrs. Sloane, but the groom has too much hair to be Stanley Kinkaid. Still, it looks really good.

The food looks really good too—platters of appetizers and turkey wraps and lots of little cookies and stuff. For once my mother brought along something edible—an ambrosia salad that has cut-up bananas and oranges and pineapple with shredded coconut and sliced almonds on top. Even though everything in it is organic, it's actually the prettiest thing on the table. Well, besides the cake.

"Here they come!" says Mrs. Delaney, darting in from the kitchen. "Places, everybody!"

Mrs. Hawthorne is right behind her. She closes the door and turns off the chandelier, putting her finger to her lips. Jess and Emma are doubled over, clutching their stomachs and trying to suppress their excited giggles. Cassidy is leaning back against the far wall with her eyes shut.

We hear the screen door slam shut, then my mom's voice, extra loud: "I guess they must be in the dining room, Clementine."

The door creaks open and Mrs. Sloane sticks her head in.

Emma flips on the light switch.

"SURPRISE!" we all shout.

Mrs. Sloane looks stunned. "For me?" she says.

Emma nods happily. "It's a wedding shower."

"A Mother-Daughter Book Club wedding shower," Jess explains.

Mrs. Sloane's eyes fill with tears. "You shouldn't have!"

"Of course we should have," says Mrs. Hawthorne briskly, handing her a napkin. "We're your friends."

"My *dearest* friends," Mrs. Sloane replies, dabbing at her eyes. "The best friends anybody could ask for."

"Kindred spirits," says my mother, giving her a hug.

"Everybody grab a plate and help yourself," says Mrs. Delaney. "Except the bride-to-be. You go sit down in the living room, Clementine, and I'll serve you yours."

"Cassidy, honey, why don't you go sit with your mom," says Mrs. Hawthorne. "I'll bring you a plate too."

Cassidy reluctantly peels herself off the wall and stumps into the living room.

"So," says my mother brightly, after we're all settled. "Have you and Stan decided where the honeymoon will be?"

*Heather Vogel Frederick*

Mrs. Sloane smiles. "He wants to surprise me."

Mrs. Delaney sighs. "How romantic!"

Our moms compare notes on their honeymoons for a while. Mr. and Mrs. Hawthorne went to England to see Jane Austen's home and all the places she mentioned in her books. No big surprise there.

The Delaneys didn't have enough money for a honeymoon trip.

"Michael was a graduate student, and I was an aspiring actress, which means I was really a waitress," Mrs. Delaney explains cheerfully. "But we managed to scrape together enough for a night at the Plaza Hotel."

"Where Eloise lived!" says Emma.

Mrs. Delaney nods. "Exactly. *Eloise* was my favorite book when I was little. I brought it along and read it to Michael, and we prowled around the floors at midnight looking for all the places in the hotel that Eloise visited. And the next day we had tea in the Palm Court, of course."

"Ooooooooo, I absolutely love the Palm Court!" says Mrs. Hawthorne, and we all laugh.

"I didn't care that all we could afford was one night," says Jess's mom. "It was just perfect."

"Jerry and I didn't have any money back then either," says my mother. "That was way before his invention, of course. We got married on the beach on Cape Cod. His uncle had a rustic little summer cottage there, and he let us use it for a week. It was heavenly."

My dad still complains about that trip—too hot, too humid, too many bugs, and the cabin smelled of mildew. I squelch a smile.

"David and I sailed from San Diego down to Baja," says Mrs. Sloane, flicking her eyes toward Cassidy, who's busy pushing a turkey wrap around her plate like a hockey stick, with a black olive for a puck. "He was such an athlete. You name it—any sport, David did it. Including sailing."

"Sounds like somebody we know," says Mrs. Hawthorne, with a nod at Cassidy.

Cassidy doesn't look up from her dinner-plate hockey game.

"Anyway, we borrowed a boat from one of his friends and off we went," Mrs. Sloane continues. "It was quite an adventure."

"I think it's time to open presents," says Jess's mom, hopping up to get them. She stacks the pile in front of Mrs. Sloane, who selects one and opens it. It's a purple leather journal from Emma. Purple is Emma's favorite color.

"I thought you might like to keep a diary of your honeymoon trip," Emma tells her.

"Why thank you, Emma—how thoughtful. I'd love to do that!"

Mrs. Delaney and Mrs. Hawthorne teamed up on a gift certificate for a day at a spa. "Some prenuptial beautification," says Mrs. Hawthorne. Seeing our puzzled looks, she adds, "Prenuptial means 'before the wedding,' girls."

Jess's present is a pair of earrings, and mine is a silk scarf.

"Gosh, Megan, you didn't need to get me another gift," Mrs. Sloane says. "You already gave me the most beautiful dress in the world."

*Heather Vogel Frederick*

She's talking about the one that Mr. Kinkaid bought at the auction. The one Cassidy hates me for. Cassidy looks up from her plate and scowls.

Finally there are just two presents left, a big one and a small one. Mrs. Sloane chooses the small one.

"A silver picture frame!" she says, opening the box. "How lovely!"

Then she turns it over. In the frame is a picture of Cassidy and her father. They're on a beach somewhere, and the wind is blowing Cassidy's hair across her face. They're both smiling. Cassidy sure looks a lot like her dad.

"Oh, honey," says Mrs. Sloane softly, her eyes welling up. "When did you take this? I've never seen it before."

"A week before Dad died," mutters Cassidy. They're the first words she's spoken all evening. "I don't ever want you to forget him."

Mrs. Sloane leans over and puts her arms around Cassidy. "If there's one thing I can promise you, it's that I will never, ever forget your father," she says fiercely. She kisses the top of Cassidy's head. "How could I? I see him every time I look at you."

Cassidy buries her face in her mother's shoulder. "Do you really have to get married again?"

Mrs. Sloane looks around at us helplessly. She sighs. "Sweetheart, just because I'm marrying Stanley doesn't mean I don't still love your dad. I always will. I promise you, everything's going to turn out fine."

"One last present," says Mrs. Delaney, passing Mrs. Sloane the big package. It's from my mother.

Mrs. Sloane tears off the wrapping paper. Her brow puckers.

"A backpack. How thoughtful, Lily," she says politely.

"Look inside," says my mother. She's bouncing in her seat like a little kid. I can't remember the last time I saw her this excited.

Mrs. Sloane unzips it and pulls out an envelope. Inside the envelope is a piece of paper. She reads it aloud: "This certificate is good for one Mother-Daughter Book Club adventure."

"We're going backpacking in New Hampshire!" cries my mother. "A mother-daughter bachelorette party! I figured you could use a little time to unwind with Mother Nature before the wedding."

"Backpacking?" says Mrs. Sloane cautiously. "Um, I've never—"

My mother waves her hand dismissively. "Don't worry, I've been a zillion times before. The White Mountains are my backyard."

This is true. My mother is always going off on weekend trips with some environmental group or another. She loves to volunteer clearing trails and stuff like that. She took me along once, but that was enough for me. I'm not a nature freak like my mother. My dad isn't either. His idea of camping is a hotel that doesn't offer room service.

"Besides," she continues, "camping is a lot like sailing, I'm sure. You'll feel right at home on the trail."

"Uh . . . ," says Mrs. Sloane.

"Won't it be fun?" gushes my mother. "I've rented a big cabin on Lonesome Lake over the Fourth of July weekend. We'll stash our menfolk there, and we can just step off the front porch and onto the trail and away we'll go!"

The room is embarrassingly quiet. Only my mother would come up

*Heather Vogel Frederick*

with such a lame idea for a shower present. I glance down at Mrs. Sloane's strappy black sandals and perfect pedicure. Somehow I can't picture the bride-to-be in hiking boots. And Emma—well, Emma's slimmed down a lot this year what with all the time she's spent at the skating rink, but she's still more comfortable with a book than a backpack. So's her mother, I'm sure. Even the Delaneys, whose farm is about as close to nature as you can get and still have indoor plumbing, don't look like the type who'd want to sleep in a tent in the woods.

And you'd think my mother would know her own daughter well enough by now to realize that I am most certainly not the type to want to sleep in a tent in the woods. Gimme a break.

Mrs. Sloane brushes Cassidy's hair out of her face. "This will be fun for you, won't it?" she says, trying to sound enthusiastic. "You used to love to go camping with Dad."

But Cassidy has clammed up again.

"I'm sure we'll all have fun," says Mrs. Delaney. "Thank you, Lily." She nudges Jess.

"Thank you, Mrs. Wong," says Jess automatically.

Mrs. Hawthorne and Emma chorus their thank-yous too.

As we're leaving, I pull my cell phone out of my purse and text Becca: S.O.S.! CALL ME!

With any luck, Becca can wangle me an invitation to her house for the Fourth of July. Then all I have to do is convince my mother to let me stay with the Chadwicks while she goes off on her lame bachelorette-party-in-the-woods.

## Jess

> *"All the silly things that were done in Avonlea that summer because the doers thereof were 'dared' to do them would fill a book by themselves."*
> —*Anne of Green Gables*

"I hate bugs!"

"Who are you and what have you done with Jessica Delaney?" says Megan, poking me in the back with a stick.

I turn around and swat it away. "Quit it." I'm hot, sweaty, seriously mosquito-bitten, and in no mood to be teased. And we haven't even been on the trail for an hour yet.

"You don't have to be so crabby," Megan replies. "Besides, I thought you were this big animal-lover. Aren't bugs animals?"

"Yeah, what happened to 'Goat Girl'?" adds Becca with a sly grin.

I start to give her the evil eye, then stop. I know she's only kidding. At least I think she is. And we all promised Mrs. Wong we'd try and be nice to the Chadwicks.

The worst part about this whole backpacking trip—well, besides the backpacking part—is that Mrs. Wong invited Becca and her mother along at the last minute. I guess she figured it would be a good idea, since Mrs. Chadwick said Becca could come back to book club when we start it up again next fall. Or maybe she just did it to make Megan happy. Megan complained about the trip for weeks after the wedding shower, but the minute Becca was invited to go with us she was all cheerful again.

I shade my eyes with my hand and look back down the trail at the cool waters of the lake below. I think the speck in the red swim trunks on the dock is Darcy. It's so unfair! The boys get to stay at the cabin with our dads, swimming and having fun, while we're stuck out here on this dusty trail.

I swat at another mosquito and take a drink from my water bottle. It must be ninety degrees out here. Mrs. Wong would have to pick the hottest weekend of the entire summer for our "bachelorette party." Some party.

Emma pauses on the trail ahead of us and turns around. Her round face is as red and sweaty as I know mine must be. "Are we there yet?" she mock-whines, then grins at me.

I manage a smile. Emma actually seems to be having fun. So far, anyway. Last year she would have been huffing and puffing and probably would have straggled way behind the rest of us. This year, though, it's a different story. She may not be a jock like Cassidy, who's been dubbed "The Trailblazer" by Mrs. Hawthorne because she stays so far out in front of all the rest of us, but Emma's in much better shape than she used to be. Even Becca has quit making snarky comments about her weight.

"What's the holdup, girls?" calls Mrs. Wong. She and the other moms are hiking behind us. To make sure nobody gets lost, they said, but I think it's to make sure nobody makes a run for it back to the lake. Which is exactly what I feel like doing right now.

"Just taking a little break!" Megan calls back to her.

"Well, get a move on! We won't get to the campsite before dark at the poky pace you're setting."

Mrs. Wong promised this would be an easy hike. "Just five miles to the campsite, then we pitch our tents and relax," she'd said.

What she forgot to tell us is that those five miles were all *uphill*.

Grumbling to myself, I turn around and start trudging forward again. An hour later, we finally stop for lunch.

"How far do you think we've come?" Becca asks, peeling off her backpack and flopping to the ground.

Cassidy pulls out a map and runs her finger along it. "Two point four miles," she replies.

"What!" squawks Megan. "We're not even halfway there yet?"

Mrs. Wong is in charge of food for this expedition, which I think maybe wasn't such a good idea once I get a look at our lunch. The peanut butter and honey sandwiches aren't so bad, although the peanut butter is thick and sticky—"I ground it

*Heather Vogel Frederick*

myself," she tells us proudly—and the bread is some kind of weird grainy stuff she probably got at Nature's Corner. That's Mrs. Wong's favorite organic grocery store. The carrot sticks are fine, and so are the apples, but instead of something normal like brownies or even a candy bar for dessert, Mrs. Wong hands out these little hockey-puck–size things that I guess are supposed to be cookies.

"What's this?" asks Cassidy, sniffing hers suspiciously. "It looks like dog poop."

"Cassidy Ann!" says her mother.

"Well, it does," Cassidy grumbles.

"It's a vegan rhubarb cookie," says Mrs. Wong, sounding defensive. "They're very good for you. The rhubarb makes them high in Vitamin C, and I used spelt flour, which has lots of protein and is also gluten-free. Plus they're sugar-free and salt-free."

"Taste-free, too, I'll bet," Emma whispers to me, and I smother a smile.

We gnaw on the cookies for a while because hiking makes you hungry and because there's nothing else to eat, and then just when we're all thinking a little nap would be nice, Mrs. Wong bounces to her feet.

"Time to move out!" she says.

"For heaven's sake, Lily," grouses Mrs. Chadwick. "You'd think we were in the army!"

Several hours and lots more whining later, we straggle into the campsite. Cassidy, who got there first, of course, has already put up her tent and collected firewood. The rest of us collapse in a heap in the shade.

Dinner is even worse than lunch, if that's possible. Mrs. Wong fishes a big plastic bag out of her backpack. It's filled with salad greens, and she opens a packet of salad dressing and pours it in, then zips the bag shut.

"Catch!" she says, throwing it to me.

I miss and it falls on the ground. "Sorry," I mumble, retrieving it.

"Now you throw it to someone else," says Mrs. Wong, so I toss it to Emma, who tosses it to Megan, who tosses it to Becca.

"Get it?" says Mrs. Wong. "We're 'tossing' the salad!"

Everybody groans.

"Mom, that is so lame!" Megan looks embarrassed.

Her mother ignores her. "Who says you can't have fun on the trail? And eat healthy too."

When we've finished our salad, she brings out this tiny portable stove and cooks up some freeze-dried thing she tells us is Ginger Sesame Pasta. It has black beans and soybeans and red bell peppers and sesame seeds and even coconut in it. It looks disgusting.

"I ordered it online," says Mrs. Wong happily. "It's vegetarian—and organic, of course."

"Of course," says Mrs. Delaney, grimly shoveling up a spoonful.

*Heather Vogel Frederick*

"It looks like somebody barfed on my plate," whispers Cassidy, this time making sure her mother doesn't hear.

"What's for dessert?" asks Mrs. Chadwick hopefully, after we manage to plow our way through the pasta.

Mrs. Wong's brow wrinkles. "Well, now, I hadn't thought about that. I think there are some rhubarb cookies left. Who'd like one?"

The response is underwhelming. Nobody raises their hand, and she looks hurt.

"Let's all thank Lily for this wonderful dinner," says Mrs. Sloane quickly. "She's put a lot of thought and effort into this hiking trip, and I couldn't have asked for a better shower present."

"I'd just like a shower," whispers Becca, and Emma and Megan and I stifle our giggles.

Mrs. Sloane goes over and gives Mrs. Wong a big hug, which restores Mrs. Wong's smile. Then Mrs. Sloane reaches into her backpack. "Now, I'm not much of a camper," she tells us, "but I've always heard that there's one thing you shouldn't go into the woods without."

"A compass?" says Mrs. Wong.

Mrs. Sloane shakes her head.

"Bug spray?" I suggest.

"Nope." She looks around to see if there are any other guesses, then pulls out a bag of marshmallows and waves it in the air.

"All right, Mom!" shouts Cassidy.

"That's funny," says Mrs. Hawthorne, "I always heard that it was something else." She plucks a box of graham crackers out of her backpack and holds it up too.

We all cheer. Mrs. Wong has kind of a funny look on her face.

"That leaves just one last camping necessity," says Mrs. Delaney with a grin. She fishes around in her backpack. "Which would be—"

"CHOCOLATE!" we all cry, as she pulls out a handful of candy bars. Even Mrs. Wong cheers this time too.

"Now you're talking," says Mrs. Chadwick. "I haven't had s'mores since . . . well, since I was a girl scout."

I try and picture Mrs. Chadwick as a girl scout. All I can imagine is Mrs. Chadwick as she looks now, only shorter, decked out in one of those old uniforms with the badge sashes. I smile to myself.

"I'll get the campfire started," says Cassidy.

A few minutes later we're all sitting around the blaze, roasting marshmallows and telling lame jokes and spooky stories. Elementary school stuff, but still fun. Even Mrs. Chadwick seems to have unbent a little, and I'm starting to think maybe backpacking isn't so bad after all. I look up at the sky. It's a clear night and in spite of the glow of the campfire I can still see the stars overhead. They're a lot brighter up here in the White Mountains than they are back home in Concord. I get up and wander off a little bit from the group, then lie back in the grass and munch on my s'more and look for constellations. I spot the easy ones first—Ursa Major and the Big Dipper, of course, and the North Star, and Orion's belt. Then I

*Heather Vogel Frederick*

branch out, challenging myself to find Cygnus, the Swan, way over in the east, and the red star Antares, which is the marker star for the constellation Scorpius.

"Time to hit the hay, everybody!" Mrs. Wong calls after a while. "We need to leave early if we're going to be back in time for the cookout."

Mr. Hawthorne is planning a big barbecue for us all tomorrow night, which is the Fourth of July. I look up at the sky again. If it stays this clear, it'll be perfect for fireworks.

Back at the campsite, I discover that Emma and Cassidy and Megan and Becca decided we should all cram into one tent for the night. We were going to each share a tent with our mothers, but they figured this would be more fun instead, and Mrs. Wong said we'd be plenty safe by ourselves. She and Mrs. Sloane are sharing a tent, and so are Mrs. Hawthorne and Mrs. Delaney.

Mrs. Chadwick gets a tent to herself because she snores.

We unroll our sleeping bags in the biggest tent, then play cards for a while by flashlight. I can hear the low murmur of voices in the other tents, where our moms are talking, and the steady buzz-saw drone from Mrs. Chadwick's tent.

"Let's play 'Truth or Dare,'" Becca suggests.

None of the rest of us except Cassidy has ever played it, so Becca explains the rules. "Whoever goes first gets to pick somebody and say 'truth or dare.' The person they pick has to choose, and if you choose 'truth,' they get to ask a question and you have to tell the truth. If you choose 'dare,' they get to dare you to do something and you have to do it."

"Are we going to get in trouble playing this?" asks Emma.

Becca gives her a disgusted look. "You are such a goody-goody!"

"I am not!"

"You are too!"

"Shut up, Becca," says Cassidy.

Becca glares at her, but she shuts up.

Cassidy turns to Emma. "Actually, it's really fun," she says. "I used to play it back in California. Watch, I'll show you. Becca, truth or dare?"

"How come you get to go first?" Becca protests.

"Do you want to play or don't you?"

Becca sighs. "Okay, okay. 'Dare.'"

Cassidy grins. She sticks a foot out of her sleeping bag and peels off her sock.

"Phew, Cassidy, put that back on!" Megan squeals, holding her nose.

Cassidy wags it around a bit to torture us, then turns to Becca. "I dare you to sneak into your mom's tent and put this sock under her nose."

"Eeeeew," I say. "That is so gross!" I can't believe Becca will accept the dare. But I'm wrong.

"Done," she says, wiggling out of her sleeping bag. She grabs her flashlight, and crawls out into the darkness.

We lie there stifling our giggles as we listen to her creep across the campsite. Very quietly, she unzips her mother's tent. Then there's a long silence except for the steady *zzzzz zzzzz zzzzz* from Mrs. Chadwick. A second later we hear *zip!*—not so quietly this time—and Becca scampers back over to our tent and dives inside.

The snoring continues for a few seconds more, then turns to a sputter as Mrs. Chadwick inhales Cassidy's dirty sock. We hear some flailing noises, and she starts to cough.

We clutch our sides and stuff our faces in our pillows to muffle our laughter as Mrs. Chadwick continues to hack for a bit. She must manage to push the sock away in her sleep somehow, because eventually we hear her lapse back into her steady buzz-saw drone.

"That was a good one, Cassidy," says Megan. "Can I have a turn?"

Megan dares Cassidy to run out into the middle of the campsite and do a crazy dance, which of course she does, and then it's Becca's turn.

"I pick Emma," she says. "Truth or Dare?"

Emma considers for a minute, then says cautiously, "Truth, I guess."

Becca looks at her and smiles her superior queen-bee smile. "Do you like my brother?"

"What kind of a question is that?" says Emma indignantly.

"You have to answer!" Becca tells her. "Those are the rules."

I can see by the expression on her face that Emma is really wishing she'd chosen "dare." She looks over at Cassidy for support. Cassidy shrugs. "She's right, Emma. Those are the rules."

"Can't I get another question instead?"

Becca shakes her head. "Nope."

"This is a really stupid game!" Emma protests.

I nod in agreement, even though I'm curious to hear what Emma has to say. Especially since she hasn't said a word to me about it. Usually Emma tells me everything.

"Don't be such a baby!" scoffs Becca. "Just answer the question. Do you like Stewart or not?"

Emma picks miserably at a thread on her sleeping bag. "Well, kinda, I guess," she admits finally.

"Ha! I knew it!" crows Becca, and begins to chant, "Emma and Stewart, sitting in a tree, k-i-s-s-i-n—"

"Stop it!" Emma says furiously.

"Why?" Becca taunts her. "It's true. You two make such a good couple. A lot better than you and Zach. My brother is the biggest geek in Concord—he's perfect for you."

Emma balls her hands into fists. "You are such a—a PYE!" she shouts.

"What is going on in here?" demands Mrs. Wong, unzipping our tent and sticking her head in. "You girls are making way too much racket!" She shines her flashlight around at us.

"Nothing," Becca mumbles.

Emma looks away.

"If you girls don't pipe down, we're going to have to separate you. We're getting up early tomorrow morning, remember?"

"Thanks for getting us into trouble, *Waldo*," whispers Becca to Emma after Megan's mother leaves.

"Shut up, *Josie*," says Cassidy.

*Heather Vogel Frederick*

I reach over in the dark toward Emma's sleeping bag to try and give her an encouraging pat. She pulls away angrily. Feeling a little guilty, I roll over. I probably should have tried to stick up for her more. Some best friend I am. It takes me a long time to go to sleep.

We're all pretty quiet at breakfast. Mrs. Wong makes oatmeal with maple sugar, which is actually not too bad, and then we get packed up to go. As she's striking her tent, Mrs. Chadwick discovers Cassidy's sock. She holds it up between her thumb and forefinger, like a small dead animal.

"Does anyone belong to this?" she asks, wrinkling her nose.

"So that's where my other sock disappeared to!" cries Cassidy, the picture of innocence. She takes it from her and looks at it in mock surprise. "I wonder how it got in your tent?"

"How, indeed?" says Mrs. Chadwick, frowning, but Becca distracts her before she can ask any more questions.

Becca and Emma still aren't speaking to each other by the time we hit the trail. The rest of us try to cover for them, hoping our moms won't notice.

"Man, I'm looking forward to that barbecue tonight," says Cassidy. "I can hear those hamburgers already, calling my name."

I'm looking forward to it too. And not just because Darcy will be there. For one thing, Emma's dad is making his special Fourth of July cake, which he makes every year. It's incredibly yummy. Much better than rhubarb cookies, and almost as good as s'mores. He bakes a carrot cake in a big rectangular pan, and he decorates the cream cheese frosting to look like an American flag, with blueberries for stars and sliced strawberries for the stripes.

For another thing, even though this trip has turned out to be a lot more fun than I thought it would, I'm looking forward to going home. After almost losing Half Moon Farm, I hardly want to be any place else these days.

"I thought we'd take a slightly different route back," Mrs. Wong tells us. She's out in front this time leading the way, instead of Cassidy. "So we can see different things."

"What, like different pinecones?" whispers Becca, and we all giggle. Well, everybody but Emma.

Becca Chadwick may be a Pye, but she can be really funny, too. I sort of get it now why Megan likes her.

After about an hour, we take a water break while Mrs. Wong consults her map. "This way," she says, and we all troop off again.

"Uh, Mrs. Wong, shouldn't we be going downhill?" asks Cassidy a few minutes later.

Mrs. Wong looks around. She frowns. "Let me look at the map again," she says, pulling it out of her backpack. She opens it up and stares at it, consults her compass, then turns it around the other way. "Aha," she said. "I see what I did. I should have turned off at this trail back here." She thrusts her finger at a bunch of squiggly green lines.

"But—" says Cassidy.

"It's not a problem," Mrs. Wong tells her, folding up the map. "There's a trail up ahead that connects to it."

*Heather Vogel Frederick*

We hike along for a while more, then turn off on another trail. The breeze is picking up, and the tall pines make a pleasant swooshing noise high overhead. It's not quite as warm as it was yesterday, which is a relief, plus the trail Mrs. Wong has chosen for us is a shady one, so the sun isn't glaring down on us like it did yesterday.

By lunchtime we're still in the woods. Mrs. Wong hands out energy bars.

"Just a quick snack to tide us over, ladies," she tells us. "We have that barbecue to look forward to, after all."

"Shouldn't we have been back by now?" Emma asks me in a low voice. I shrug.

While Mrs. Wong consults the map again, I glance over at my mom. She and Mrs. Hawthorne and Mrs. Sloane and Mrs. Chadwick are sitting on some boulders, talking and laughing. They don't seem too concerned, so I relax. Emma had me worried there for a minute.

"This way," says Mrs. Wong when we're done eating. She hoists her backpack again and sets off.

Mrs. Hawthorne starts to sing "Swinging Along the Open Road." We all join in. Even Emma and Becca, although they still won't look at each other. At least we're on flat ground now, and not going uphill anymore. We sing it straight through first, then as a round. It sounds pretty good, and it's got a good pace to hike to, as well.

An hour later, we pause for another map consultation. The singing has long since stopped, and nobody's laughing any more. Our moms are starting to look worried. Even Mrs. Wong doesn't seem as confident as she did. I shiver. The wind is really whipping through the treetops, and I fish my sweatshirt out of my backpack. It's getting cold. And cloudy, too. So much for fireworks tonight. Right now, I'm wishing I was back at Half Moon Farm, safe and snug in my room.

"Surely we must be almost there by now," says Mrs. Chadwick. "My feet are killing me!"

Mrs. Wong looks helplessly at the map. Cassidy is frowning over her shoulder, trying to make sense of the green squiggles too.

And then I finally admit to myself the truth we've all been avoiding.

We're lost.

*Heather Vogel Frederick*

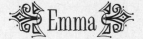# Emma

> *"I fancy it's the unexpected things that give spice to life."*
> —*Anne of the Island*

"The best thing to do when you're lost is stay put," says Cassidy.

"Nonsense," says Mrs. Chadwick. "We should find a trail that leads straight downhill. We can't be more than a few miles from the lake."

Mrs. Wong looks from one of them to the other. "Well," she says cautiously, "perhaps Calliope has a point."

Cassidy shakes her head. "Honest, Mrs. Wong. We should stay here. My dad drilled it into me. We used to go hiking all the time in the Sierras."

"She's right, Lily," says Mrs. Sloane. "David took her on a lot of backpacking trips."

"She's a child," sniffs Mrs. Chadwick. "We can't trust her judgment."

"She's thirteen," says Mrs. Sloane sharply. "And she's spent more time in the wilderness than you have, Calliope."

Mrs. Chadwick bridles at this, but before she can pick a fight my mother steps forward. "Actually, I've done a lot of reading about wilderness expeditions, and I think Cassidy's right. Staying put is the first thing they always tell you to do."

"Fine," snaps Mrs. Chadwick. "In that case half of us can stay put and half of us can go for help. I will lead the group that goes for help."

Mrs. Chadwick is used to being in charge.

But Cassidy shakes her head again. "Splitting up is the second biggest mistake people make," she says. "Stay put and stay together. That was my dad's number one rule."

"Oh, it was, was it? And what other pearls of wisdom do you have to share with us?" Mrs. Chadwick's tone is sharp. She's obviously getting fed up with being told what to do.

Cassidy holds up her hand. "STOP!"

"Stop what?" demands Mrs. Chadwick.

Cassidy ticks off her fingers. "*S* is for 'Stay calm.' *T* is for 'Think it through.' *O* is for 'Observe,' and *P* is for 'Plan and prioritize.'"

"Sounds to me like somebody knows what she's talking about," says Jess's mom.

"Hmmph," says Mrs. Chadwick.

"Okay, so we're calm," says Megan. "We've got *S* covered. So now what?"

"T is for 'Think it through,'" says Cassidy. "What time were they expecting us back, Mrs. Wong?"

Megan's mother looks at her watch. "I told Jerry mid-afternoon at the latest. It's four thirty now, so I'm sure they're a little worried."

"Worried enough to call the forest service and send out a search party?" asks Mrs. Sloane hopefully.

"Probably not quite yet, unfortunately," Mrs. Wong replies. "My guess is they'll give us a another hour or two."

"By then it will be starting to get dark, and it's going to be tough for them to find us in the dark," says Cassidy. "We'll most likely have to spend another night on the mountain."

Everybody groans.

"That means we need to make shelter, find water, and do something to attract attention, to make it easy for them to find us tomorrow morning," she continues.

"This is ridiculous," protests Mrs. Chadwick. "I still say at least some of us should try to go for help."

"Let's take a vote," says Mrs. Sloane. "All in favor of following my daughter's plan, raise your hand."

Everybody but Mrs. Chadwick raises their hand. Even Becca.

"You're outvoted, Calliope," says Mrs. Sloane.

Mrs. Chadwick grunts.

"So what was that next thing we're supposed to do, Cassidy?" I ask her.

"*O* is for observe," she says, "and I've observed that it's gonna rain soon."

We all look up at the sky. Dark clouds are gathering overhead. Thunderclouds.

"I think we should split into two teams," Cassidy suggests. "Mrs. Wong, you be in charge of setting up camp with Mrs. Chadwick and Mrs. Hawthorne and Becca and Megan. Mom, you and Mrs. Delaney see what you can find to help attract attention. Bright T-shirts we can tie to trees, stuff like that. Emma and Jess can help you."

"What about you?" I ask her.

"I'm going to go for water," she says. "There was a brook off to the side of the trail about a quarter of a mile back."

"It's probably not safe to drink," grumbles Mrs. Chadwick.

Cassidy holds up what looks like a water bottle with a pump handle and a line of plastic tubing attached to it. "Lucky I brought my dad's old water purifier along then, isn't it?"

"Maybe someone should go with you," I say.

"I will," says Cassidy's mother. She puts her arm around Cassidy. "No splitting up, remember?"

We give the two of them our water bottles and they disappear down the trail. Jess and her mother and I dig through our backpacks and come up with one pink T-shirt, one orange T-shirt, a pair of yellow-and-blue striped socks, and a red bandana.

"Do you guys have anything else that's bright?" I ask Megan and Becca.

They look through their stuff and we add a bright pink bikini (Becca's, of course) and a white baseball cap.

*Heather Vogel Frederick*

The rain starts just as Cassidy and her mother return. We all take shelter in the biggest tent, squishing together cross-legged on the floor. We huddle there, listening to the raindrops pelting down on the fabric roof.

Mrs. Sloane distributes the water bottles while Cassidy takes stock of our pile of bright items. "This will be perfect," she tells us. "We can tie them to trees along the trail in both directions in the morning."

There's a sudden loud *CRACK!* of thunder overhead and everybody jumps. Becca turns white as a sheet. She leans over to me suddenly and whispers, "If we don't make it out of here, I just want to say I'm sorry I was mean to you last night."

I nod. "It's okay," I tell her, my teeth chattering. "I shouldn't have called you a Pye."

Lightning flashes, and I squeeze my eyes tightly shut. I've never much liked thunderstorms, and I move closer to my mother. She puts her arm around me and pulls me close.

"This is all my fault," says Mrs. Wong miserably. "I should never have tried to take us a different way home."

"It could have happened to anyone," my mother says consolingly. "Besides, just think about all the great stories we'll have to tell about our adventure after we get back. Lost in the White Mountains!"

"I would have planned things much better if I had been in charge," says Mrs. Chadwick, flinching as lightning flashes overhead.

"Put a sock in it, Calliope," says Mrs. Sloane, throwing one of the yellow-and-blue striped socks at her.

Mrs. Chadwick looks shocked. Cassidy gives Megan and Jess and Becca and I a sly glance and wags her foot. That gets us thinking about last night, and we start to snicker. Pretty soon everybody's laughing, even Mrs. Chadwick. "Sorry," she says. "I guess I'm just a little nervous being out here." Thunder rolls overhead and she flinches again. "Especially in a storm."

"Let's sing," says my mother. "That always helps."

Because it's the Fourth of July we sing "It's a Grand Old Flag" and "Yankee Doodle," and then we launch into "The Battle Hymn of the Republic." Every time the thunder crashes we skip to the refrain, shouting "GLORY, GLORY HALLELUJAH!" at the top of our lungs, which of course makes us all laugh again.

"Our own private fireworks display!" hollers Mrs. Delaney as the lightning flashes overhead again.

We sing until we're hoarse and we can't think of anything else to sing. Fortunately, we don't need to. By now, the storm is slowly moving away.

Mrs. Wong checks her watch. "I'm sure they've figured out by now that we're lost."

We all grow quiet. I think about my dad and Darcy, back at the cabin. They must be really worried about us. All of our dads must be. I look over at Cassidy, and wonder who she's thinking about. I doubt it's Stanley Kinkaid. She's kind of resigned herself to the wedding, but she's still not happy about it.

Then I remember that Stewart is down at the cabin too, and I get

*Heather Vogel Frederick*

a funny fluttery feeling inside. I glance over quickly at Becca, worried that maybe she can read my thoughts and will decide to tease me again. But she's having a thumb war with Megan.

I wish Becca didn't know that I like her brother. It's worse than her knowing I want to be a poet someday. I haven't told anyone at all until now—not even Jess, and she's my best friend. I've just kind of wanted to keep my feelings to myself.

I don't know if Stewart likes me back. He's never said anything to me about it, but he always seems happy to see me. And he always sits next to me during our newspaper staff meetings. It's different with Stewart than with Zach Norton. I still get butterflies when Zach is around, but lately I've been thinking maybe it's just out of habit. I've liked him for so long—since kindergarten—but the truth is, we don't have anything in common. Unless you count the fact that we both happen to work for the school newspaper. I'm much more comfortable around Stewart. He's funny, and he makes me laugh, and he's easy to talk to and we like the same books and movies and music and stuff. Plus, I like his calm gray eyes. I can't imagine myself writing poetry about them the way I did about Zach's last year, but still, Stewart is definitely cute. I thought so even before the fashion show.

Cassidy's stomach growls.

"I guess it's getting to be about that time, isn't it?" says Mrs. Wong, starting to look unhappy again. "Unfortunately I didn't plan for two dinners on the trail."

"I'm sure we can come up with something," says Mrs. Sloane briskly.

She grabs the red bandana and spreads it out on the middle of the tent floor. "Why don't we pool our resources and see what we have left."

We all dig around in our backpacks and pockets. Mrs. Wong comes up with two energy bars and a handful of rhubarb cookies. My mother adds a box of raisins and half a packet of graham crackers. Mrs. Delaney offers up two pieces of string cheese, a pack of airplane peanuts, and an apple. Mrs. Sloane has some trail mix, Becca has a pack of gum—"Rebecca!" scolds her mother, "your braces!"—Megan has some sour-drop candies, Jess has nothing at all, and I have a couple of marshmallows that I stuck in my sweatshirt pocket last night and forgot to roast. They're stuck together and covered with lint, but I put them in the pile on the bandana anyway.

"Cassidy, how about you?"

Cassidy holds up two wrinkled packets, one of instant noodle soup and another of hot chocolate. "They're kind of old," she says. "They been in my backpack since—well, since California—but they're probably still okay."

Her mother nods and she tosses them onto the pile.

"Calliope?"

Mrs. Chadwick pulls out a bag of peanut M&Ms.

"Score!" crows Cassidy.

"Holding out on us, were you?" Mrs. Sloane teases her.

"Certainly not," Mrs. Chadwick replies stiffly.

Cassidy's mother surveys the bounty. "I'd say we have a feast in the making, ladies."

*Heather Vogel Frederick*

"Do I sense an upcoming *Cooking with Clementine* episode?" says my mother. "Dinner on the trail?"

Mrs. Sloane gives her a wry smile. "I doubt it. But let's see what we can do here."

It's still raining, so we can't build a fire. Mrs. Wong manages to get the stove going under the shelter of a big pine tree, but it runs out of fuel while she's heating up the packet of noodle soup. Meanwhile, Mrs. Sloane cuts up the apple and the cheese for an appetizer. We each get a few bites, plus a few sips of lukewarm soup, and then for dessert we split the peanut M&Ms.

"I'll save the rest of the food for tomorrow, just in case," says Mrs. Sloane.

Even though it's not that late, we're all tired. We girls decide that we want to sleep with our mothers tonight, so the Chadwicks head for one tent, the Wongs for another, and the Sloanes for another. Jess and Mrs. Delaney and mom and I say here inside the big tent, which we're sharing.

"Are you scared?" I whisper to Jess as we get settled in our sleeping bags.

"Yeah, how about you?" she whispers back.

"Uh-huh."

We're quiet for a while and then she asks me, "How come you didn't tell me about Stewart?"

"I don't know," I tell her, feeling a little uncomfortable. "I guess partly because for the longest time I didn't even realize that I liked him. And then once I did, I kind of just wanted to keep it to myself. All that stuff last year with Zach was so embarrassing."

Jess thinks this over. "I can understand that."

We're both quiet again.

"What if nobody comes for us?" I ask her, changing the subject.

"Of course they're going to come for us."

"Well, then, what if they can't find us?"

"Cassidy thinks they will."

"I wish I were home in my own bed."

"I know. Me too. I miss Sugar and Spice."

"I miss Melville."

"I miss the twins."

"Liar."

There's a pause.

"Yeah, okay," she whispers. "I don't really miss them."

We giggle.

"Girls, stop talking now," says my mother. She's using her librarian voice, so I know she means business. "You need to get your rest. We may have a long day ahead of us tomorrow."

*I hope not*, I think, as I snuggle down into my sleeping bag. I close my eyes and drift off to sleep, listening to the eerie sound of the wind high in the pine trees overhead.

Breakfast is pretty dismal. The rain stopped sometime before morning, and Cassidy managed to get a fire going, so at least we have something hot. Well, a sip of something hot—we share the mug of cocoa from the ancient packet. Mrs. Sloane pops my marshmallows in, which helps it taste better, but still, a sip is hardly enough. Also there are half a dozen raisins each, a few sections of graham cracker, and some trail mix that Mrs. Sloane beefed up with the extra peanuts from Jess's mom.

"Don't worry, girls, they'll find us today, and just think how good that BBQ is going to taste!" says Mrs. Wong, as she distributes our meager fare.

Our moms are working really hard at keeping our spirits up. Except for Mrs. Chadwick. She's crabby again. I guess she's not a morning person.

"How am I supposed to keep my energy up with this?" she grumbles.

"Now, Calliope," says my mother. "There's no point complaining. We should set a good example for the girls here."

"I still feel terrible that I got a little disoriented," says Mrs. Wong.

"A little?" snorts Mrs. Chadwick. "We're lost in the White Mountains, the most dangerous part of New England. We could be eaten by bears!"

Jess smiles at me. I smile back. It's hard to imagine any bear brave enough to try and take a bite out of Mrs. Chadwick.

"Let's focus on the positive, shall we?" says my mother, which is mom-code for *shut up already*. "It's not raining, and by now they've probably launched the search party."

Mrs. Delaney hands out baby wipes, and we all spend a little time cleaning up. I feel like I'm covered with grit. Plus, I'm alarmed to discover I could really use some deodorant.

Cassidy has us pack everything up so we'll be ready when they come to get us.

"What if we need to stay over another night?" asks Megan.

"Then we'll set up camp again."

"That's stupid."

"No it's not," explains Cassidy. "It gives us something to do, which is good for morale."

After we're done striking camp, we take the bright T-shirts and socks and tie them to branches a short ways up and down the trail. "Like Hansel and Gretel leaving breadcrumbs," says my mother.

And then we wait.

We don't have to wait long, fortunately. About an hour later, we hear whistles and shouts in the distance, and we all start yelling our heads off. A few minutes later the rescue team comes crashing through the bushes into our camp. There's a guy with a big mustache and an even bigger German Shepherd, which Jess immediately has to go over and pat, plus a forest ranger and Stanley Kinkaid. As the guy with the dog radios the other search teams to tell them that they've found us, we all cluster around Mr. Kinkaid and the forest ranger.

"We would have come for you last night, but we couldn't because of the thunderstorm," the ranger says.

"I hope you weren't too scared," says Mr. Kinkaid.

"Nah," scoffs Cassidy. "We were fine."

*Heather Vogel Frederick*

Mr. Kinkaid bends down and rummages in one of the pockets of Mrs. Sloane's backpack. The top of his head is sunburned.

"Oh, honey, you forgot your sunscreen!" cries Mrs. Sloane.

Mr. Kinkaid straightens up. "How could I think about sunscreen when my Clemmie was missing?"

Mrs. Sloane kisses the top of his head. Behind them, Cassidy pretends to stick her finger down her throat.

"How did you find us so quickly?" Mrs. Wong asks.

"Because we stayed put, right?" says Cassidy smugly.

"Well, actually," says Mr. Kinkaid, holding up a small, round, black, plastic thing, "it was this."

Cassidy frowns. "What's that?"

"It's a GPS tracking unit," replies the forest ranger. "He tucked it into your mother's backpack, as a precaution. We couldn't get a fix on you last night because of the storm. The nearest transmitter took a direct hit by lightning. But we've had you pinpointed on one of the computers at headquarters since they made the repairs this morning."

"You have?" says Mrs. Sloane.

"I'm an accountant," Mr. Kinkaid tells her. "We like to keep track of things. And you are what I treasure the most."

"Stanley!" says Mrs. Sloane. "That's so romantic!"

Cassidy looks like she's going to barf for real this time. "They would have found us without your stupid GPS tracker," she says flatly. "We didn't need your help."

Mr. Kinkaid looks a bit taken aback. "Well, I, uh—"

"Cassidy Ann! You apologize this minute!" orders her mother.

"You did all the right things, young lady," says the ranger. "Stayed put, built a fire, put up markers—somebody taught you right."

"My dad," Cassidy says proudly. The ranger glances over at Mr. Kinkaid. Cassidy glowers. "He's not my dad."

"Ah," says the ranger, looking uncomfortable. "I see. Well, we would certainly have found you eventually, but Mr. Kinkaid just saved us a little time. All's well that ends well, right?"

A little over an hour later we're back at the cabin. My dad and Mr. Delaney cook us up a huge breakfast—by now it's almost lunch—with pancakes and scrambled eggs and bacon, and we eat out on the porch, all of us talking at once as we tell everybody about our adventure. I notice that Stewart keeps looking over at me, and every time he does my tummy does a little flip-flop.

"We didn't get to do fireworks last night," says Dylan.

"Because of the storm," says Ryan.

"That's right," says Mr. Delaney. "We saved them for tonight, didn't we, boys?"

The twins nod vigorously.

"Along with the barbecue," adds my father, winking at me. "It'll be a Fifth of July feast, to celebrate your safe homecoming."

"I need a shower," Becca announces.

"No kidding," says Cassidy, holding her nose.

"How about you all go for a swim first?" suggests my mother.

By the time we get changed, the boys and our dads and Mr. Kinkaid

*Heather Vogel Frederick*

are already in the lake. I'm a little shy about being in a swimsuit in front of Stewart, but not as much as I would have been last summer. This year I don't even really need to suck in my stomach. I race Cassidy down the dock and we do cannonballs off the end. The cool water closes over my head and I just float for a while.

My brother organizes a volleyball game, and we play for hours, boys against girls, then kids against grown-ups. It turns out that mild-mannered Mr. Chadwick has a killer spike. He's also a good sailor, and we all take turns going out with him in the cabin's little sailboat.

Later, we shower and put on clean clothes and hang out on the porch in the shade, playing board games and Old Maid and talking some more about our night in the woods. Cassidy brags about her part in the rescue, and Darcy says he couldn't have done any better himself, which is saying a lot since he's working toward his Eagle Scout rank.

Mrs. Sloane, who is sitting on the porch swing holding hands with Mr. Kinkaid, keeps calling him "my hero" and "my knight in shining armor," which everyone finds hilarious because nobody looks less like a knight in shining armor than Stanley Kinkaid. He's a good sport about it, though, and cracks jokes about being "Sir Counts-a-lot" and one of the "Knights of the Bald Table."

Cassidy keeps her distance.

Mrs. Chadwick says that in spite of our "misadventure," it's been a perfect weekend.

"Don't you agree?" she says, elbowing Mr. Chadwick.

"Yes, dear," he replies.

Mr. Wong says the only thing that could possibly make it any better is room service.

The afternoon passes quickly. I beat Stewart at Scrabble—or maybe he lets me win, because you'd think somebody in ninth grade would know how to spell "abominable"—and pretty soon my dad is firing up the barbecue, and it's time for our feast. His special Fourth of July cake, which is now a Fifth of July cake, is just as good as always.

When it gets dark, Mr. Wong breaks out the fireworks. He must have spent a ton of money, because there are boxes and boxes of them. Mostly little stuff, of course, but a whole lot more than we ever get to set off at home in Concord. Only firework displays by pros are legal in Massachusetts. The twins run around on the beach with sparklers in each hand, shrieking with glee, and the rest of us set off poppers and jumping jacks and spinners and pinwheels.

After a while I wander out onto the dock by myself. I'm barefoot, and I sit down on the edge and let my feet dangle in the water. The air is cool, and the water feels warm and silky. I sit there contentedly, swishing my feet back and forth as I watch my family and friends. Our dads are starting to shoot off the bigger fireworks now, fountains and rockets and roman candles that soar out over the lake, where they burst and rain down like multicolored shooting stars.

A lanky figure detaches itself from the group and heads out onto the dock. When it gets closer I see that it's Stewart. He has a sparkler in each hand.

"Hey, Emma," he says, passing me one.

*Heather Vogel Frederick*

"Hi," I reply, suddenly feeling shy.

He lights his sparkler, and then uses it to light mine. He sits down next to me and we wave them like wands over the water, laughing. After they've burned out, we sit there quietly. Our shoulders are almost touching.

Then he reaches over and takes my hand, just like that. His is warm, and he gives mine a squeeze. I squeeze back. Even though it's dark, I can tell we're both smiling.

*Zach who?*

# CASSIDY

*"'Things are changing so fast it almost frightens me,'*
*Anne thought, a little sadly."*
—*Anne of Avonlea*

*Clop. Clop. Clop. Clop.*

The slow, steady hoofbeats in the street below echo the dread in my heart. I lean out the turret window and watch as Led and Zep pull up in front of our house. Their manes and tails have been brushed and braided, the silver on their harnesses gleams in the sun, and the carriage they're pulling behind them is decked out with ribbons and flowers and a big sign on the back that reads: JUST MARRIED.

My mother is getting married today. An hour and a half from now the wedding will be over and she won't be Clementine Sloane any more, she'll be Mrs. Stanley Kinkaid. And Stan the man will be my stepfather.

Downstairs, our house is bustling with activity. I can hear laughter floating through the window on the floor below, where Courtney and my mom are getting dressed in my mother's bedroom. My mom probably has her Avonlea dress on by now. That's what she calls it. Megan keeps saying she never meant for it to be a wedding dress, but where else would you wear a fancy getup like that? There's a clatter of pots and pans from the kitchen, where the caterers—my mom's friends and colleagues from *Cooking with Clementine*—are putting the final touches on the food for the reception, and strains of music drift up from the other side of the house, where a string quartet is setting up in the gazebo. Mom and Stanley are getting married in our backyard.

At last night's rehearsal dinner, I sat at the restaurant wondering why there's no such thing as a real-life invisibility potion. It would be so much easier if I could just make Stan the man disappear. There's nothing really wrong with him, he's just not my dad. I try to imagine him living here in this house with us, and I can't. I try to imagine having breakfast with him every morning, and watching TV with him every night, and going on vacations and bike rides and trips to the grocery store. I just can't.

The thing is, I still just really, really miss my dad.

Zep lifts his head and whinnies.

"Easy, boy," I hear Mr. Delaney tell him. Mr. Delaney is wearing a top hat and white gloves. He's going to drive us all off after the wedding.

I wish I were more excited about riding in the carriage. Courtney and I are supposed to go with my mom and Stanley as far as the train station. Then Mr. Delaney will bring us home again after they leave for their honeymoon. Mom knows about the going to the Concord Station part, but she doesn't know where she and Stanley are going yet. I do. They're taking the train to Boston, and then they're going aboard a cruise ship to Prince Edward Island. My mother's going to get her wish. She's going to Avonlea—well, Cavendish—to see Green Gables. Nobody's supposed to know, but Stanley left his briefcase open one night when he was over for dinner and I saw the brochures and couldn't help snooping. I haven't told Mom, though. Even I'm not dumb enough to do something that mean and spoil the surprise.

I can't help but wonder which voyage she'll like better—the one on that little sailboat with my dad, or this trip on a fancy ocean liner with Stan the man. But maybe Dr. Weisman told her not to compare too, just like he told me.

I glance down at the photograph on the window seat beside me. It's the silver-framed one of me and Dad that I gave Mom for her wedding shower. "So what do you think of all this?" I whisper to Dad, wishing he were here to answer me.

A couple of cars drive up and park near the waiting carriage. People are starting to arrive. I watch them get out—it's some friends of my mother's from her yoga class, and the Chadwicks, including Stewart, which will make Emma happy.

"Cassidy? Are you up there?"

It's my mother.

"Yeah," I reply.

"Are you dressed?"

*Heather Vogel Frederick*

I tug at the scratchy lace collar on my dress. "Yeah."

Trust my mother to go and pick out the frilliest, girliest bridesmaid dresses in creation. I look ridiculous. Megan says the color—pale green—goes well with my hair, but I don't care, I still feel like an idiot. Courtney, on the other hand, is wearing the exact same dress, only in a different color—hers is pale pink—and she looks like a princess. I may be sitting in a turret, but I'm just not princess material. You'd think my mother would know that by now. I'm more the dragon type.

"Hurry up, honey, you need to come down now!" she says. "People are starting to arrive, and the photographer wants to take pictures soon."

"I'll be down in a minute."

The truth is, I wish I could stay up here forever. It's so nice and quiet and far away from everything. Plus, it's breezy, what with the open windows nearly all the way around and the shade from the big elm tree. Not that it's all that hot out today, which is pretty amazing for August in Concord. It gets really sticky in the summer in New England, something it never did back in Laguna Beach.

Being up here is kind of like being in a tree house, I decide, which makes me think of last winter at Half Moon Farm. Maybe if I asked her, Mrs. Wong would lend me her handcuffs. Then I wouldn't have to go downstairs and pretend to be all happy about the wedding.

A long black limousine turns down Hubbard Street and stops in front of our house. The back doors open and Isabelle d'Azur and Wolfgang climb out. Wolfgang spots me and waves. I wave back. Cars are arriving faster now—Nana and Grampie, who are going to stay with Courtney and me while Mom's on her honeymoon; Dr. Weisman and his wife; Fred Goldberg from the Cooking Channel; the Delaneys; the Hawthornes; the Wongs; and an elderly couple that I recognize as Stan the man's parents. His dad looks just like him, only older and balder. He and Mrs. Kinkaid are pretty nice, actually, but I already have enough grandparents. I don't need any more.

I hear footsteps on the stairs and quickly shove the picture of Dad and me under a cushion.

It's Megan and Emma and Jess. They crowd into the turret, practically glowing. They're really excited about the wedding. It's easy for them to be happy. None of their mothers are getting married today.

"You look really nice, Cassidy," says Emma.

I grunt.

She's wearing a dress exactly like mine, only lavender. A lavender headband is holding her brown curls off her face. Jess and Megan are both wearing the same dress as mine too, only Jess's is pale blue, and Megan's is yellow. Bridesmaids always wear matching dresses, which I keep telling everybody is a ridiculous tradition, but of course nobody ever listens to me. Especially when it comes to fashion.

"We look like a bunch of stupid Easter eggs," I grumble.

"Stop being surly," says Emma.

"Stop using words I don't know," I reply.

"How about rude, then?" she tosses back.

*Heather Vogel Frederick*

"Or grumpy," adds Megan.

"Or cranky," says Jess.

"Okay, okay already, I get the point." I heave a sigh. "Look, I'm not in the mood for the synonym game today."

"C'mon, Cassidy, you've got to stop sulking sometime," Emma says. "Look at it this way—at least your mom chose a good guy. My mom says Stanley Kinkaid's a keeper."

"She's right," says Jess. "Just think of all the nice things he's done for you and your mom—and for us." Stanley looked over Concord's tax laws and found something called a grandfather clause, which sounds a lot like Santa Claus to me, only I know that's silly of course, and he was able to talk the town selectmen into exempting Half Moon Farm from the property tax. The Delaneys still had to pay this year, but they won't ever have to worry about losing the farm again.

"Yeah, yeah, I know," I tell her. The thing is, I'm being stubborn and I know it, but I can't help it. It's like I've gotten used to acting like this and now I'm stuck. The dragon girl is trapped in her tower.

They're right, of course. Everybody's right. Stan is a good guy. Even Dad would have liked him. I can picture the two of them hanging out, eating pizza and watching the World Series or the Super Bowl on TV, trading stats about the players. They'd have gotten along really well.

"Girls!"

It's my mother again.

"It's time for pictures!" she calls. "Everybody downstairs on the double!"

"You guys go ahead," I tell my friends. "I'll be right there."

They leave and I stare out the window a while longer. Then I hear whispering at the foot of the turret stairs. It's my mom and Stanley.

"You go talk to her!"

"Why me?"

"Please, honey? I can't get her to come down."

Stanley trudges reluctantly up the stairs, like he's coming to meet his doom. *Beware the dragon girl in the tower,* I think. *Feel my fiery breath!*

"Um, hi, Cassidy."

I hunch my shoulders and turn my back on him, staring out the window again.

"Great view from up here," he says, sitting down on the window seat beside me.

I nod.

"Wow, the Delaneys sure spiffed up that old carriage, didn't they?"

I nod again.

"It'll be fun to ride in it, won't it?"

I shrug.

Stanley clears his throat. "So, Cassidy, I thought maybe we could have a little talk here. You know, man-to-man. I mean, uh, man-to-girl."

Stanley's trying really hard. Part of me wants to cave and just be nice to him. The dragon girl part of me wants to let him squirm. I let him squirm.

*Heather Vogel Frederick*

"I know you're still not entirely on board with this whole wedding thing"—he looks at me hopefully, like maybe I've changed my mind in the last fifteen minutes—"but maybe you can cooperate anyway today. For your mother's sake."

I continue to stare out the window. I don't give him an ounce of encouragement. Wicked, wicked dragon girl!

He sighs. "Look, I know how you feel about your dad—"

I turn on him. "Do you?" I say, my anger blazing out hot as dragon's breath. "Do you really?"

"Well, I, uh—"

"Your parents are both still alive," I tell him, the words tumbling out of me. "I saw them just a couple of minutes ago. You have no idea how I feel about my dad."

Stanley sighs. "No, Cassidy, I suppose you're right," he admits. "But it's not as if I've never lost anybody I loved, and if you really try, perhaps you can imagine that I might have a tiny inkling of how you feel."

The dragon girl lifts a shoulder.

"And maybe while we're talking about feelings, we can talk a little bit about how *I* feel," he continues. I can tell he's getting worked up, because he's beginning to sound a little dragonlike himself. "Ever since I started dating your mother, you've been nothing but rude to me. I've tried to be nice to you, tried to find things we could talk about and things we could do together. The thing is, we have a lot in common, starting with sports, and there's no reason we shouldn't be friends." He sighs again, and the anger drains from his voice. "I'm not trying to be your dad, Cassidy. Your dad will always, always be your dad. Forever. That's a fact, and that's not going to change, whether I'm a part of this family or not."

I scuff my toe on the floor. I'm starting to feel really small.

"I have absolutely no intention of trying to replace your father. I thought maybe you'd realize that by now, but you keep pigheadedly clinging to this notion that I'm some horrible beast who's trying to steal your mother away. The fact is, I love your mother. I think she's the most amazing, beautiful, talented woman I've ever met. And I think you and your sister are two of the most amazing, beautiful, talented girls I've ever met. I know I'm not your dad, and I promise I'll never try to be, but maybe you could at least consider allowing me to be your friend."

By now I'm blinking back tears. I duck my head so Stanley doesn't see. "Maybe," I manage to whisper.

Stanley is quiet for a while. He nods. "Okay, then," he says. "Maybe is good. Maybe works for me. I'll take maybe. There's hope in maybe."

He reaches out and pats my shoulder. And without another word, he leaves the turret.

*Hope.*

Such a tiny word.

Such a powerful word.

I used to hope that Dad would come back, that the accident had all just been a terrible mistake. That hope kept me going for months. But I gave it up long ago.

*Heather Vogel Frederick*

I take the picture of my dad and me out from behind the cushion.

"I wish you were here," I whisper to it. "I wish you were here to tell me what to do."

Deep down in my heart, though, I already know what my father would say. *Always bring your best, Cassidy. Bring it to every game.*

Have I really brought my best to this game?

I think about my mom calling Stanley her "knight in shining armor." I don't know about the shining armor part, but maybe she's got a point. Maybe not all heroes ride white horses. Maybe some of them are disguised as short, balding accountants. Accountants with nice eyes that crinkle up around the edges when they smile. Maybe one of those accountants might even rescue a dragon girl from her tower prison.

Maybe Stanley Kinkaid is right, maybe this new life won't be so awful. Maybe I can hope a little too.

And clinging tightly to that tiny tendril of hope, I kiss the picture of my dad and set it on the windowsill, facing outward so he can watch us when we ride off in the Delaneys' carriage. I look down to the front lawn below, where Emma and Megan and Jess are standing together like colorful butterflies. They spot me. "Come on, Cassidy!" Emma calls, waving. I wave back to her. I stand up, finally ready to leave the turret and the dragon girl behind. Then I go downstairs to where my family and friends are waiting for me to step into my future.

"My future seemed to stretch out before me like a straight road. I thought I could see along it for many a milestone. Now there is a bend in it. I don't know what lies around the bend, but I'm going to believe that the best does."

—Anne of Green Gables

# Mother-Daughter Book Club Questions

Which of the girls do you think has changed the most from the first book, and how?

Have you ever read *Anne of Green Gables*? If so, did you enjoy it? If you haven't read it, did this book make you want to?

Do you have a place that you love like Half Moon Farm or Green Gables? Have you ever thought about naming places like Anne, and then Emma and Jess, did?

What are you involved in at school? Sports? The newspaper? Are the other students involved competitive with one another?

If you play a sport or are involved in another after-school activity, do you prefer being on a team, like Cassidy's hockey team, or being by yourself, like Emma's skating lessons? Why do you think that is?

Do you think Becca Chadwick has changed from the first book? In what ways is she different? How is she the same?

Were the moms right in inviting Becca and her mother to join the book club, even though Becca had been intentionally mean to some of the members in the past?

How do you think Megan felt, being torn between two groups of friends? Have you ever been in a situation like that? How did you handle it?

What do you think about the prank that Cassidy, Emma, and Jess tried to play on Becca? Was it right or wrong? What about the prank that Jess tried to play on her younger brothers? Have you ever played a prank on someone? What happened?

Should Jess's parents have told her earlier about losing Half Moon Farm? What do you think their reasons were for not telling her sooner? Have you ever been upset with people around you for keeping something from you? What do you think their reasons for doing so might have been?

Think back to the scene when Stanley took Cassidy to the Bruins game. Did you understand Cassidy's bitter feelings toward Stanley, or do you think she should have been nicer?

Have you ever been lost, like the girls on their camping trip? What did you do?

Have you ever made s'mores?

Would you ever want to model in a fashion show? Why or why not?

If you had to design an outfit for your best friend, what would it be like?

Which of the girls do you most relate to? Has this changed from the first book?

If you could get to know one of the characters better, who would it be and why?

What was your favorite part of this book, and why?

Would you change anything about the ending of this book?

## Author's Note

Exactly a century ago this year, Lucy Maud Montgomery's *Anne of Green Gables* was published. The story of the irrepressible red-haired orphan was an instant hit, and has since been read and loved by generations of girls—including me. In fact, my mother was Canadian, a native of Nova Scotia (right next door to Montgomery's beloved Prince Edward Island), so for my sisters and me, Anne was required reading.

One of the unexpected pleasures of writing *The Mother-Daughter Book Club* is the opportunity it's given me to talk with girls and their moms across the country. Invariably, many of these book clubs later write to tell me that because of my book, they were inspired to read Louisa May Alcott's *Little Women*. Nothing could delight me more than to know that I've had some small part in introducing young readers to such a classic tale—one which, like *Anne of Green Gables*, is dear to my heart. Timeless stories such as these richly deserve to have a whole new generation of readers fall in love with them, so if you haven't yet been introduced to Anne Shirley, and to Matthew and Marilla Cuthbert and Diana Barry and Mrs. Rachel Lynde and all the other inhabitants of Avonlea, I hope that reading *Much Ado About Anne* will inspire you to make their acquaintance. If you do, I can assure you that you'll definitely be in for a treat!

Behind every writer stands a huge supporting cast. Heartfelt thanks are owed to Alexandra Cooper at Simon & Schuster for embracing these books with wholehearted enthusiasm; to my fabulous agent, Barry Goldblatt, for his guidance and wisdom; and to Susan Hill Long for friendship, literary feedback, and encouragement. Many thanks, too, to the Quigley family, who once again kept me from skating onto thin ice with hockey terminology. And what would I do without my sisters Lisa and Stefanie, and my friends Patty and Jane and Sarah and Tricia, all of whom keep me laughing? Most of all, however, thanks and love are due to my husband, Steve, who is and always will be my Gilbert Blythe.

—H. V. F.
Portland, Oregon, 2008

## About the Author

Heather Vogel Frederick grew up in New England and spent her middle-school years in Concord, Massachusetts, the town where *The Mother-Daughter Book Club* stories take place. Today the award-winning author of the Patience Goodspeed books and the Spy Mice series lives in Portland, Oregon, with her husband, their two sons, the family's beloved Shetland sheepdog, and three fun-loving chickens. You can learn more about the author and her books at www.heathervogelfrederick.com.